Wilda Silva,

Secret Keeper

Wilda Silva,

Secret Keeper

Book One of the

Wilda Silva Series

A. A. Jeffery

Illustrated by Nassima Amir

Golden Bear Press

Wilda Silva, Secret Keeper is a fictional work. Characters, businesses, incidents, locations and institutions are used fictitiously and/or are the product of the author's imagination. Any resemblances in this work to real persons, businesses, events or places are entirely coincidental.

Published in the United States by Golden Bear Press

Belfair, Washington

ISBN 978-1-63649-029-8

eISBN 978-0-578-76254-8

Map by Kate Didyk

For my cheerful dad, my helpful mom,

my brother who pushed me to just keep writing,

and for my furry friend, Serena,

for never jumping the fence to run away

as I ignored her to write this book.

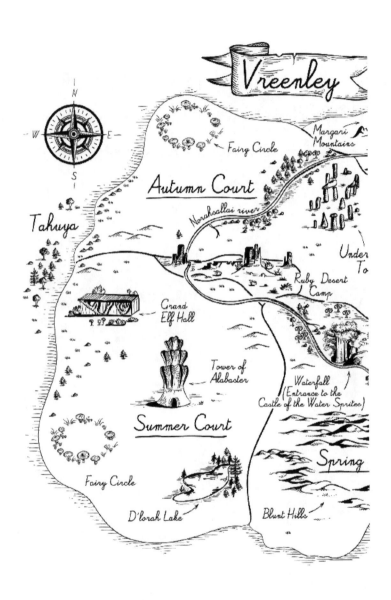

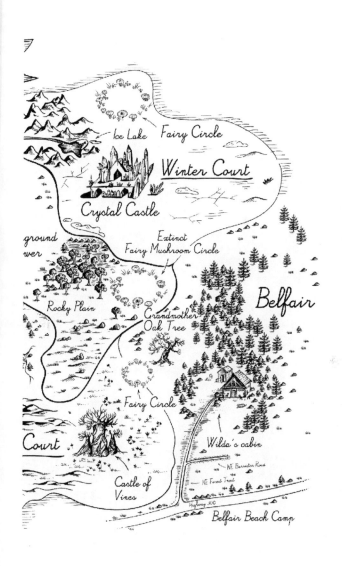

Chapter 1

Mrs. Taren's great-grandfather was a cannibal. At least that's what she told us in class. Every kid was on the edge of their seat when she walked over to the United States map under the giant smart TV in our classroom. She pointed to the border of California and Nevada with her polka dotted fingernails and flashed a big, peachy smile and asked us, "How many of you would eat your relatives to survive the winter?" Everybody screamed at the same time.

Mrs. Taren straightened her broad shoulders and tossed her head back. Her long orange hair began to slip out of the thick wooden clamp on the back of her head as she let out a belly laugh. "You never know what you're capable of doing," she said, now whispering and creeping toward the front row of desks in our sixth-grade classroom. "You don't know," she said, squinting her green eyes as she peered at us, "until you're tested by the wild." Then she smiled and stood up straight in her long, free-flowing dress and her bright indigo bolero jacket. She adjusted the edge of her wide purple glasses as she winked at me.

When I told Mrs. Taren after school that Mom and I were leaving our music charter school and moving to Washington, her smile fell. "Oh, no!" she said. "You're the best musician at this school. You're my only ginger, too! What am I going to do?" I told her that we had taken her suggestion. Last summer we'd visited the town in Washington that she'd recommended, and how Mom had talked to the realtor Mrs. Taren told her about. Mom made an offer on the place, and we would be moving into it in a few days. "I'm sad but I'm not surprised" she said. After all, it was her suggestion that I test out my resin piccolo in the woods up there and see if it was really as water-resistant as the factory claimed.

I gave her a big hug and a little drawing of us that I made, and she told me she had something for me, too. She reached into the bottom drawer of her metal teacher's desk and pulled out a polka dot box. Dots kind of are her thing. And when she opened the cardboard box it was empty.

"What is it?" I asked.

"It's your artifact box," she said. "For whatever cool things you discover up there. You never know what you might find," she said.

That was the last time I saw Mrs. Taren before we packed up our Dodge Avenger and drove for two rainy and snowy days to get to our new home.

I smiled just thinking about Mrs. Taren as I stared at the snow-covered ground outside our cabin window. I told Mom about the cannibal in Mrs. Taren's weird family history when we went out to get burgers last night but Mom didn't wanna talk about it. She said it was disgusting and I needed to stop making stuff up about adults. Mom didn't want to believe me. But Mrs. Taren didn't seem to mind telling us kids. She was proud of it. She said her family got stuck in the Sierra Mountains during a snowstorm or something like that. She even admitted how stupid it was for a group of pioneers to be out traveling with their kids in wagons in the dead of winter. Her great granddad had to eat the sick and wounded to survive. She was not shy about it at all.

"Shut up and finish eating," Mom said. "You have a high threshold for odd people."

Some people are too squeamish. It's like, if there was a slug or a spider in your peanut butter sandwich, and you bit into it, that would be something to get freaked out about, but a story about people who lived a long time ago doing what they had to do? It's just a story, right? Mrs. Taren said she always tells that to guys on a first date so they know what they're getting into. She used to tell her class everything, or at least a lot more than Mom will tell a guy she's been dating, like that she has a kid.

All the students called her Mrs. Taren but she said she was actually "single and ready to mingle." Mom said she would never get married as long as she "keeps dressing in that wacky Boho stuff." Mom thought she was "hiding under all that fabric." I blew my breath on the window and wrote "BOHO," in ode to Mrs. Taren. She was cool. I was really gonna miss her. Where else could I find a teacher who was actually part cannibal?

Certainly not here in the woods. I didn't understand why we had to leave San Francisco to come here, anyway. Okay, I sort of got why we had to leave. We were forced out of our apartment. It was too expensive and Mom didn't want to pay a landlord so much money. She said it cost a million dollars to buy a house in Noe Valley where our apartment was. I understood that we weren't rich but we weren't so poor, either. Granny gave us both cash whenever we visited her. I always got at least twenty dollars. Whenever Mom worried about money for food or something, I'd hear her get on her phone and call Granny and suggest we come see her.

I wouldn't have been surprised if Granny gave Mom the money for our new home, too, but I wasn't totally sure. I asked Granny one time during one of our visits if she'd given Mom the money to buy me this mohair sweater Mom made me wear sometimes. It itched like ants on a rainy day like today. Granny said something about, "The settlement should be enough if you all would just move out of San Francisco." Another time Granny said something about how Mom didn't really deserve the money because she "let her professor teach her how gullible" she was, whatever that meant.

Then Mom mentioned to Mrs. Taren at the school recital last year that we were "in the house poor." Mrs. Taren suggested we check things out up here because she spent some time in the area and she thought we might like it. Well, Mom loved it. So, we came up here to the rain and the trees. Belfair was meant to be a vacation spot, but now it was what we could afford. A cabin in the woods where the ground was always wet and there was nowhere to shop – that's all anyone's ever wanted, right?

I'd only been here once before. We stayed in a beach house at Sunny Shores last summer. We loaded chicken wings into cages to use as bait. We went out on the resort owner's wobbly oyster boat and sank the cages into the ocean. When Mom pulled them up they were full of crabs. We ended up roasting them on the fire pit near the beach house. Our caramel colored, white breasted Shepadoodle, Charlie, loved it. He chased all the sea hawks around and barked at them when they out flew him. It was all right, but Mom loved our vacation so much she flew back in November to meet with a real estate agent. That's how she ended up buying this cabin on the edge of town.

When Mom came back to her friend Miss Lisa's condo to pick me up after her house hunting trip, she was so happy. Her face was all bright and her eyes were like saucers. She said, "Guess what? I found the perfect cabin! We get to move to Belfair!"

Get to move. She said it just like that. I always knew when she was trying to make me do something or believe in something. I said, "You bought a house in Washington without letting me see it first?"

Then she said, "I already knew you would love it." She told Miss Lisa that she got a great deal on it.

Miss Lisa was excited, too. Seventy thousand dollars bought us a two-bedroom, one-bathroom cabin with a four-acre yard leading to nothing but more trees. And then Mom started saying something about the real estate agent being cute. That's when I realized that it didn't really matter what I thought. I was so mad at Mom that I locked myself in the bathroom at Miss Lisa's condo. Mom had to promise that I could keep Charlie before I would come out and go home with her.

So, that's how I ended up sitting on a box by the living room window of a log cabin with its snow-covered metal roof. We were surrounded by boxes, me, Mom, Charlie and the moving crew. "Damn it, Wilda, stop getting in the way," Mom fussed at me. So, I tugged Charlie by his collar to wait by the window with me.

Charlie and I watched Mom direct the movers where to put all our boxes and suitcases. Mom said I could pick my room first, probably to make it up to me for not asking me where I wanted to live. She was biting her lip when she made the offer. She either bites her lip or pours a glass of something when she's nervous.

I chose one of the rooms that overlooks the back woods. The movers had already set up my bed, and I covered it with the Rumpelstiltskin bed spread that I liked. It had an old-fashioned Brothers Grimm kind of picture on it and the princess had light brown eyes and red hair with curls, like me. But she certainly didn't have thick bangs over her eyes. That's just something I wanted. Mom said they made me look wild. "Wild Will-da," she always said. "I blame the ginger hair on your father."

I put Barbie and her two friends on the dresser. I didn't really play with them anymore but Granny gave them to me, so I liked having them around. I hadn't seen Granny since she moved to the old folks resort near Sacramento last year. I bet she was sipping frozen pineapple lemonade and knitting at the pool by now.

I never really had a dad. I didn't guess I needed one. Mom said my birth father was an old friend of hers but they couldn't be together. He sent me a birthday card every year. Mom had them because she was afraid I might lose them in all our moving stuff. Ever since I was born it had just been me and Mom, and then me, Mom and Charlie. I asked Mom why she and my dad didn't get married. She said they had "an agreement" after I was born. I didn't know what that meant and Mom wouldn't explain it. She just said, "You're too young to know that right now." It kind of bothered me that she wouldn't just tell me. I wasn't a little girl anymore. I turned eleven years old, already. That's double digits.

I put my notebook on the dresser. I liked to draw and write things down, mostly about people.

Once in a while, I drew something about nature in there, too. And I collected samples that I used to put in a drawer in our old apartment. Now I stored them in my new artifact box that Mrs. Taren gave me. I slid the box onto the shelf in my new closet. Last summer when we came here I collected an amber rock, a pine cone and an oyster shell. They didn't seem as special now, since pinecones and oyster shells were everywhere here, but the rock was unusual. I'd have to find some more rare things for this place. Mom said we'd take the ferry for a day trip to Seattle once we got settled so I could find something interesting at that old oddity shop in Pike Place Market.

The two movers finished unloading the last of our furniture into the sparse living room, a couch and an easy chair, and they stood by the living room door waiting for Mom to sign off on the paperwork to prove everything was delivered. Mom rummaged through her purse on the kitchen counter and came up with a wrinkled ten-dollar bill for them to split as a tip. When she tried to hand it to the movers the foreman waved it away. "That's okay, ma'am," he said, sounding sorry for her. "Just sign." So, Mom scribbled her name, the foreman ripped off a yellow carbon copy sheet to give to her and they skipped out of the door as the rain picked up and began to turn into snow. Mom watched them leave from the front porch.

In the movers' hurry to drive off, the moving van got stuck in the ditch on the side of our gravel driveway. I watched them try to figure out what to do from the window. First the two guys in the moving crew flattened a couple of cardboard boxes and laid them down in the mud. Of course, it was too wet for that to work. I even went back out in the sleet to the mushy driveway to tell Mom it wouldn't work but she told me to go back inside. So, I had to watch the van's wheels shred the cardboard and churn it into a gummy mess.

Then the scruffy foreman jumped out of the van all cussing and rubbing his head like it hurt under his knit cap. The movers decided to fill part of the ditch with gravel and branches from our property. Then the young crewman got behind the steering wheel and started the van back up. That's what got the van unstuck but gravel was shooting everywhere. You should have seen that foreman scram, gut first! Mom really cleared out of there, too. Before I could blink twice, she had left the driveway and come racing through the front door.

Mom saw me laughing and said, "I'm glad you had some fun at the foreman's expense because that's the only entertainment we're going to have for a while."

"Why?" I asked.

"See for yourself," she said. She pulled out her cell phone, held it in front of her face to unlock it and handed it to me. I tapped on one of my favorite apps on her phone, a game where you have to pop bubbles with a laser. The introductory graphic displayed across the screen but then it just loaded, and loaded. The swirling black circle that was supposed to show that the phone was trying to connect to something kept spinning for what seemed like an eternity. "Awe," I moaned. I handed the phone back to her. It didn't even hint at getting a signal out here in the woods. Not a single bar was displayed. I couldn't play games on it or anything until she got a new cell phone carrier.

I guessed I could start spending more time with Charlie. That wasn't really a bad thing for Charlie, but I probably sat in the living room for an hour rummaging through boxes and trying to figure out what to do for fun in this damp place without neighbors, the only sound being the unnerving echoes of hunters' rifles. The shooters resumed their target practice whenever the snow let up at the shooting range a few miles away, and the flurry seemed to have stopped.

Mom had gotten the movers to push my suitcases into my room. I hung up my clothes, found space on the built-in shelf over my bed for my favorite books, and set my canvas instrument case with my purple piccolo on the dresser. Then I helped Mom unload some of the boxes stacked in the kitchen. I put some of the dishes into the kitchen cabinets. I also put the towels and sheets in the linen closet. I finished quickly since they were already folded so Charlie and I went for a walk. Mom shouted at us to watch out for strangers but Charlie and I were more likely to run into a bear in these isolated woods than a bad guy.

Mrs. Taren warned me that it would be a lot colder here than San Francisco. She said I should pack some heavy boots because there might even be snow on the ground in late March. She was right about that.

The snow didn't faze Charlie, though. At three years old he was full of energy. He bounced all around while I trudged along, nearly lifting my knees to my chin to walk through the thickets and icy mulch, as I listened to my fuzzy boots crunch the snow. We left tracks in the snow that shimmered like white glitter. I stuck out my tongue and let snowflakes fall on it. They felt prickly and tickled my nose. The sun was white like a flashlight in the fog and the sky was almost as white as the sun. I picked up a long branch and threw it but Charlie didn't chase it. Instead, he watched it sail past him, landing against a small wooden shed at the edge of the clearing beyond our cabin. Charlie looked back at me and let out a huff. He only did that when he stopped having fun, or when he lost his nerve.

I walked past him to the shed to pick up the stick so that I could throw it back, but once I had it in my hand Charlie started to walk back to the cabin. "Done already?" I asked. Charlie turned around and sat down in the snow. I took a step back to throw the stick toward him again. As I hurled it past Charlie, my foot knocked against the shed door, opening it to a jolt of cold air against my neck. Charlie didn't run after the stick. Instead, he barked wildly. *Could it be a warning of sorts*?

I turned to look behind me. The shed door stood wide open. I stepped inside and looked around. A few tools on a shelf and a dusty floor were all I saw. I began to close the door when I suddenly sensed movement along the door jam. It was a black spider. A *big* black spider, with white specks on its back. I screamed, leaping back into the snow, and I nearly landed on my chin. I scrambled to slam the door shut. When I looked back at Charlie his dog lips had formed into curves on both ends. He was panting and smiling as he watched me slowly get up and pat the snow off of my puffy coat. "So, you're just gonna laugh at me?" I asked. It didn't discourage Charlie's fun. He sat there with that unmistakable smirk as he waited for me to give up on playing and head back to the cabin.

Before I could finish walking around the cabin to the backdoor Charlie started to bark and stomp in the direction of the shed. That's when I heard the faintest sound of something in the bushes nearby. It was almost like the sound of a baby crying. I stopped in my tracks and turned to look for it. No, it was purring. No matter where I looked, I couldn't find it. "Wee-dah." It sounded almost like a baby calling my name. I scanned the trees but I couldn't find it. What kind of animal could make that sound? *Weird*, I thought. Maybe I didn't really hear that correctly. "Come on, Charlie," I said. He rubbed his paws on the ground before bounding up the steps to go back inside the cabin.

I closed the backdoor behind us to find that Mom had managed to get logs for the fireplace but she was struggling to light them. The nearly empty glass of red wine on the fireplace mantle let me know she had at least unpacked the glasses. And of course, the wine would be found. Mom never did anything remotely stressful without a glass of something nearby.

I held Charlie's wet paws in my hands to warm them up as he leaned forward to lick my face. "It's okay here," I said. Mom smiled and her shoulders dropped as though she'd just unloaded the fear that I might dislike the place. She let out a sigh and shifted the kindling in the back of the fireplace with the fire poker. It seemed like that was all she wanted to hear. The fire picked up on cue as if it had been waiting for my approval.

"We still don't have cable or internet. Do you think you could manage for another day or two?" Mom asked.

"What if there's an emergency?" I asked.

"That's what the car is for," she said. I shrugged my shoulders and went to my room to lay down. I didn't bother to take my boots off, or my cap and heavy coat. I figured that with the house as cold as it was, why bother? I didn't think Mom would have minded if I had fallen asleep like that, either. I stared at the white paint on the uneven ceiling. It looked like faces in the paint, but I knew that could not be on purpose. They were like the side profiles of two strangers, a man and a woman. It was so interesting to see stuff like that, like art that wasn't supposed to happen.

"Wilda Rose, come out here and feed Charlie," Mom said.

Wait. "Mom," I called, still lying down, "did we pack any dog food?"

It took a while before Mom said anything so I got up and went into the kitchen. She opened up all the cabinet doors.

"Do we have any dog food?" I asked again.

She put her hands on her hips and shook her head. Then she looked at me. "I guess we don't."

I looked at Charlie. He was bouncing up and down on his hind legs and panting. "What are we supposed to do?" I asked.

"There's gotta be something in this kitchen," Mom said. She stared into the empty refrigerator. I noticed the box of Wheaty-O's on the counter.

"Can he eat cereal?" I asked.

Mom cocked her head as she looked at me. "I guess we have to go to the store," she said.

We climbed into our green two door Dodge Avenger and backed out of the gravel driveway. By the time we reached Food Town the sun was beginning to set. Mom said we needed to hurry to avoid coming back in the dark. She said she didn't know these roads. There were plenty of stunning views of the woods and the ocean as the road curved and weaved up and down the mountains, but there were no streetlights. Only reflectors on the pavement and the headlights of passing cars lit long stretches of the highway.

When we got to the grocery store we loaded our shopping cart with giant bags of dog food, milk, bread, bananas, wieners, frozen chicken nuggets, ketchup and cans of green beans. I struggled to push the cart to the checkout stand behind Mom. She was rummaging through her purse for lipstick. She turned to face me as she put the red stain on her lips. She flashed me that look when her eyes would dart to one side to tell me to get lost before shoving the lipstick back into her purse and turning around.

The cashier was a young man with dark eyes and wavy black hair, pretty much Mom's type. "Did you find everything you need?" he asked Mom.

"Well, not everything," she said, grinning at him.

"Is there anything I can help you with?" he asked.

"Maybe," she said, rubbing her fingers through her blonde hair. She looked at me as if to say: *Why are you still here?*

"I'm new in town," she said.

The cashier glanced at me. I was standing on tip toes peering over the cart. "We are new to town," she corrected herself. "There's so much to learn in a new community. What's a single girl to do?" she asked him.

"Well," he said, clearing his throat, "Welcome to Belfair."

"Why, thank you," Mom said. Now she was propping up her smiling face with both elbows on the counter and batting her blue eyes.

"You could meet a lot of helpful people at my church," he said.

"And which one is that?" Mom asked.

"St. Joseph's."

"Catholic?" Mom asked.

"Episcopal," he answered. "I'm there every Sunday. I sing in the choir."

"Do you?" Mom asked.

"Yes, ma'am," he said.

"Well, you must have a beautiful singing voice if it is anything like what I am hearing right now," she said.

The cashier took a step back. His face turned red and he chuckled to himself. He shook his head but offered no other sounds. Shortly he realized that none of the things in the shopping cart had been placed on the counter.

"Wilda, unload the basket," Mom whispered to me. "I'm Valerie," my mother said, extending her hand, "and this is my daughter, Wilda. And your name is…"

"Sam," the cashier said. "I'll take care of that for you," he said.

"Oh, I forgot to get extra milk. I always forget something," Mom said with a fake chuckle. "Wilda, honey, could you run to the dairy aisle and grab an extra carton of milk, please?"

"Fine," I said.

I started to go when Mom said, "Walk, not run." I knew not to run in the store, but I think Mom wanted to be sure that I wouldn't embarrass her in front of someone she considered a "nice man." I started to walk down the snack aisle. I looked back to see if she wanted me to hurry, but she was busy talking. Then she looked back at me and gave me that concerned look she does sometimes. Either she was afraid I would burn down the store if left on my own, or she was afraid I might come back too soon for her to exchange phone numbers the way she likes to do when she meets a "tall, dark and handsome man." So, I kept walking to the milk section, but not before grabbing a big bag of rippled potato chips along the way.

I stared at the cartons and jugs of milk. There was skim milk, two percent, and whole milk. Ah, chocolate milk, that's what I liked. But it's kinda gross in cereal. Maybe Mom wouldn't mind if I got both? I grabbed a carton of chocolate milk and a carton of plain whole milk but when I tried to hold both I dropped the bag of chips on the floor.

"Rrr." There was a purring sound in the aisle. I stopped to listen.

"Rrr." There it was again. I set the cartons on the floor, got down on my knees and looked under the milk case on the floor. "Rrr," it said again.

"Here, kitty," I said.

"Wilda," it responded. I jumped up from the floor. It sounded like the female voice I heard earlier, but only now it spoke undeniably! I looked in Mom's direction but she was still at the cash register and couldn't see or hear this.

"Wilda," it said again in a friendly and soothing tone. "I'm down here. Bring the milk and follow me."

I got down on my knees again and looked, fascinated. "I don't see you. Where?" I asked.

"I'm here," the voice said again.

"I still don't see you," I said. "Where are you?" I asked.

"Come with me, through the double doors to the exit in the stock room. Come outside," it begged.

Crawling on the floor and peering under the case, I started to feel annoyed with this thing, whatever it was. Why wouldn't she reveal herself if she wanted something. It was scary enough that this stranger was talking to me. The least she could do was show her face. At the same time, she knew my name. I was curious to know how she knew me.

"Hurry," it said.

"Where are you?" I asked louder this time. That's when I felt a tug on the hood of my overcoat. "God, Wilda. What on earth are you doing playing in the store?" It was Mom pulling me up from the floor. She hurried to stuff the cartons of milk back into the shelf as she grabbed the bag of chips off the floor. "You're too old to embarrass me like this. Come on," she said. She walked ahead of me and stuffed the bag of chips on a refrigerated shelf next to the butter.

"But Mom, I think there's a cat in here," I said.

She stopped and looked back at me with an annoyed scowl.

"Is everything okay here, ma'am?" Sam asked.

Mom whipped around to face him with her best imitation of an honest smile. "Everything's perfect," she said cheerfully. "See you Sunday?"

Sam furrowed his brows and rubbed the back of his neck. "Okay," he said after a pause.

Mom grabbed my hand and ushered me and the cart out to the parking lot. After we'd loaded everything into the car Mom said, "I know this is a big change for you, but we are not going to regress. Do you understand what that means?"

"Of course, I understand what that means," I said.

"It's when you act younger than you actually are. We are not going to start doing that now, are we?"

"I know. I was not acting younger than I am," I said.

"Well, I have to disagree based on what I saw back there," Mom said.

"I'm just being myself," I said.

"Sure," Mom said as she got into the driver's side of the car and reached over the passenger seat to open my door.

"You're regressing, too," I said as I got in.

"What's that supposed to mean?" Mom asked.

"You were acting younger than you are at the store, too."

Mom shook her head as we pulled out of the parking lot. "You are a child," she said. "You are to be seen and not heard, especially if you ruin things for me."

"Like the grocery bagger boy?" I asked.

"Like any adult I might want to talk to. Just stay out of my way," she said as she turned left out of the grocery store parking lot, contrary to the no left turn

sign, and we sped down the dark street back toward

the old cabin.

Chapter 2

It was 9:37 in the morning and we were waiting for a lady with a bobbed hairdo to print off a class schedule. We were more than an hour late for school. We had just gotten to Washington state two days prior and Mom was already at the school office, stacking my birth certificate and shot records on the fake wood counter. Who enrolls their kid in a new school on a Friday? Only my mom, that's who. She anxiously tapped her designer boots on the floor and alternated her hands on her hips. She probably couldn't wait to have the cabin to herself during the day.

Mom tucked her sandy blonde hair behind her ear and leaned slightly over the counter to check whether the secretary had finished printing everything. I looked away. Mom was showing too much cleavage again. It was a cold day but she insisted on wearing that tight red sweater with the deep V-neck she loves without a scarf or a coat. She must have thought she might catch some guy after she finished dropping me off.

Last week she said I should meet some nice girls at a church first so that when I enrolled in school I would already know somebody, but yesterday she said, "I need you in school now so I can do some things, but you better behave yourself this time." When I asked her why we took an Uber to school she said, "Don't worry about how you got here." I guess she was embarrassed about our old car with its peeling paint on the roof and a passenger door that has to be opened from the inside.

Mom seemed to worry a lot about what people thought of me. She was paranoid that I would get myself kicked out of school. I hit a boy at my old school once and it got me suspended, but I had to do it. His name was Reggie. We were playing tetherball. I'd always win so he started saying stuff like, "This is the only thing you're good at." I would say "So, what?" It made him mad that I didn't care what he thought about me so he got meaner. One day he said my mom had the school bus driver's husband come over and they were "doing it!"

I said, "How do you know if we were both at school, Einstein?" Reggie said, "Because everybody in the neighborhood knows about it. They all talk about your mom and what a skanky THOT she is." I told him it wasn't true but he kept saying it over and over, "Your mom's a skank! Your mom's a skank," in front of everybody on the playground. I didn't know how to make him stop. The only thing I could think to do was to grab the tether ball and swing it at his face.

Wham! It smacked him harder than I expected. He had blood running from his nose down to his pants. So, he did what all babies do. He ran to the office screaming and crying that I broke his nose.

I didn't break his nose but I wish I did. The principal called me into her office, demanding that I cough up why I hit him. I sat there and didn't say anything. Not one word. Why would that mean old buzzard need to talk to me? If she was going to punish me she should have just done it. But if I told her about what Reggie said then she'd be gossiping about my mom to the secretary, the lunch ladies and even worse, the PTA. The principal kept saying, "I should expel you right now. You and your mother have been nothing but trouble, and you don't even show remorse." Why should I feel bad about defending my mother's good name? Besides, Reggie got what was coming to him.

The only thing that saved me was when Mrs. Taren came into the school office on her way to her mail slot and she saw me sitting in the principal's side office. When I looked up and saw her I just started crying. She came over and knelt down beside me. She asked me what was wrong and I told her what Reggie said, that my mom was a "THOT." I must have told her several times because she kept telling me to calm down. Mrs. Taren asked the principal for a suspension instead of an expulsion. Then she called my mom from the office phone and told her to pick me up early. If it wasn't for Mrs. Taren I would have been kicked out of school. No other schools would have wanted me because I was fighting.

Mom rushed over. She was so mad she dragged me out of the building by my arm without saying anything to anybody. When we got out of the front doors she said, "How dare you embarrass me like this!" How dare I embarrass her! She said, "What could anybody possibly say that would make you go off like a wild animal?" She kept yelling "answer me" on our way to the parking lot. Of course, I didn't say anything. I knew she wouldn't like my reasons. One time a guy she was dating called her a slut in front of me. She didn't like it. I didn't know what to say that time, either, and I remembered how much it hurt her feelings when he yelled that.

But this day was an opportunity to start over at a new school in Washington. Mom excitedly snatched the printout from the lady's manicured hands and looked it over. "Can you tell her where her classes are?" Mom asked, staring at the sheet.

"There's a campus map right here on the counter," the secretary said. She slid the black and white copy over to my mom.

"Good," Mom said. She gave me the map and schedule. "Find your classes, okay, baby? I've gotta go." She smooched me on the forehead. "And be good. I don't want any phone calls. It's not like I'll be able to answer, anyway," she added.

I turned away. All the other kids in the office saw her kiss me as she slung her Gucci purse over her shoulder and made a fast trot out the door. Soon I would be able to walk in by myself. Mom wouldn't be able to put on a show over me after today, thank goodness.

I counted the numbers on the doors until I reached my class at the end of the hall. I took a deep breath and walked into a room where all the students were in groups, drawing posters about ancient civilizations. I felt their eyes shift from their drawings to me. The teacher saw me and pointed to an empty desk by the window in the front of the class. He introduced himself to me: Mr. Gumble, the world history teacher. He looked old, like probably thirty or something, and he had a small brown beard. He was dressed okay. His belt looked like one of those expensive kinds you see on a fashion model; you know, much hipper than what a typical teacher would wear. Mom would probably develop a crush on him if she ever took had the time to go to a parent/teacher conference.

"Hi. I'm Veronica Chaichana. And this is my sister, Monica," a girl said, tapping me on the shoulder before I could even open my violet vinyl backpack. "We're twins but we don't look alike," the other girl said. I turned around to look at them. It was true. They really didn't look much alike. Monica had short black hair cut into a bob, and Veronica had a long blonde streaked braid. But their faces were similar and they were the same height. It seemed more like they had gone out of their way to look different from one another. "Are you maternal twins?" I asked.

"Gosh, how did you know what maternal twins are?" Veronica asked.

"Everybody knows that," I said, but their faces twisted and they looked at each other. "Who doesn't know that?" I asked, surprised.

Monica shrugged, "Um, we had to learn that term on our own and we're like the smartest kids at this school," she said.

"What's your name?" Veronica asked.

"Wilda," I told them.

"Will-da?" Veronica asked.

I have a simple name. Was she making fun of me? "Yeah. W-I-L-D-A," I said loudly.

"Oh," Veronica said. Her nose scrunched up.

"What do you think of Veronica's hair? I did it for her in earth science class," Monica said.

"I begged her to do it," Veronica said.

"You did," Monica responded.

"Because I've been wearing a high ponytail for the past few days and now everybody's wearing it," Veronica said.

"All the girls are totally copying you. But can you blame them, though?" Monica asked.

"Not really. We're style setters," Veronica said.

"I know, right? Watch everybody have this braid by sixth period," Monica said.

"What do you think, Wilda? Don't you love it?" Veronica asked impatiently.

Veronica's hair looked sloppy. They couldn't possibly be serious. I thought I better get to the bottom of this joke soon so they didn't think I was some kind of pushover. That kind of reputation could follow a girl all year. "You're both a little full of yourselves, aren't you?" I laughed.

"For asking for your opinion on my sister's style?" Veronica asked.

"Why should I care?" I asked, shrugging it off. To my surprise their mouths dropped as a smattering of snickers revealed we'd been observed by our classmates. Just as quickly as they tapped me on the shoulder, they slinked away from me and blended into the rest of the class.

I could already feel my other classmates' stares on the back of my neck. I felt like I'd already made a mistake but all I did was be honest. Was I supposed to lie after being asked a trick question? At least, it seemed like a test. Could anybody actually be that full of themselves that they would really think that every girl in the whole school wanted to copy their hairstyle? But what if it wasn't a test and Monica just wanted to know what I thought of her sister's braid? I didn't intend to offend them. Maybe I'd just lost a chance to make new friends.

I tried to smile but my mouth felt stiff. Monica sat down across the room from me. She kept glaring at me, whispering something to the boy behind her and staring at me again. I gave her a little wave to let her know I saw her. She rolled her eyes and whispered something again to the boy behind her. I guess she was discussing why she didn't like me.

The cafeteria was drafty and dark when I finally went to lunch. Mom gave me a dollar and six quarters to buy lunch until she could get the lunch plan worked out. That only got me a frozen carton of orange juice and a white bread grilled cheese sandwich. Not the good kind of cheese like cheddar but something greasy and fluorescent that smelled like those soybeans on the side of my plate at a cheap kaiten sushi restaurant. I found an empty foldable table and sat down. I bit into the damp bread. It stuck to the roof of my mouth. I wanted to spit it out but then I wouldn't have any lunch. I decided to spit it out anyway. Just as I clutched the white paper napkin in my hand and brought it to my mouth a blonde girl in a cheerleader jumpsuit walked up to my table.

"Are you new here?" she asked.

I nodded my head.

"That's ok. You can sit with us," she said.

"No way, Nicole! Her?" asked a cheerleading girl who had been jogging to catch up to her. "She just dissed the class president and her sister. You do *not* want her to sit with us."

"Seriously?" Nicole asked.

"Yeah. She's just trouble," her friend said, dragging her friend away by the arm as they returned to their table. Everyone seemed to be staring at me now. My little gray table felt like it was part-island, part-stage. For the next thirty minutes no one else approached me, they just looked at me. I saw Monica and Veronica in front of the cash register. They were staring, their arms folded, and they were surrounded by what looked like nine or ten other kids. They were just standing there, talking and watching me. I didn't know if they meant to intimidate me. I just wanted to be respected. Maybe if I was nice this time things would be different? I smiled and waved at them.

Veronica rolled her eyes. "That's bold," she yelled from across the cafeteria. I didn't get what she meant so I shrugged my shoulders at her and kept eating.

"So, you're just going to shrug it off like that?" Veronica continued.

"What are you talking about?" I asked.

"All we did was try to be nice to you," Monica said loudly as she walked closer to my table.

"By asking me whether I could see straight?" I asked.

"What's that supposed to mean?" Veronica asked.

I had no idea what any of it meant. "You tell me," I said.

Monica's eyes got huge and she started gasping. "You think we need your opinion on whether we look good?" she asked as her sister and her friends gathered behind her.

"Apparently," I said.

Veronica patted her knees, shaking her head. "Monica was only trying to be nice to you," she told me.

"She's so weird," Monica said. "Weirdo!" she yelled. That attracted the hall monitor's attention. He came over to Monica and Veronica's group, wearing his little red striped plastic sash across his chest. He was a brown skinned boy with curly black hair pressed flat onto his head, all of five feet tall. He was just a kid himself and probably one of Veronica and Monica's friends. "What's going on?" he asked in a newly broken voice.

"Forget it, Avery," Veronica said to him. "We don't have time for her. She'll find out. This is our school."

"W-well," he stuttered at me, "I'm going to keep my eye on all of you."

"Just one eye? What's the other one going to be doing, taking a nap?" I asked. I couldn't resist saying that. After all, I didn't do anything to deserve a warning.

"Both eyes!" he yelled back. Then he blew his whistle as if to make a point. Okay. I'd just made a mess of things on my first day.

Mom had sent for a taxi to pick me up, just like she used to do sometimes when we lived in San

Francisco. I let the driver drop me off just up the road from our cabin. I walked along the soaked leaves stuck to the driveway, up to the front door of our cabin. Mom gave me my own set of keys and I used them to open the door. As soon as I opened the door Charlie ran up to me, hugged my legs and licked my hands. He always knew whenever I'd had an argument with somebody.

"How was school?" I heard Mom ask from the kitchen. She was stirring an olive on a toothpick at the bottom of a nearly empty martini glass.

"Okay," I said. I scratched Charlie on the back of his neck, walked to my room and threw my backpack on the bed.

"Did you make any friends?" She probably expected me to say no.

"Sure," I lied.

"Good," Mom said.

"Did you find a job yet?" I asked, lying down on my bed. Mom walked into my room as she tossed back the last drops of her drink.

"You don't need to worry about that," she said. "That's my business. And take your feet off the bed in those boots. We live in Washington now. It's muddy up here." She pushed my legs off the bed.

I sat up to pull my muddy boots off. "Start leaving your boots at the door. You're too old to not figure that out," she fussed. She chewed the olive off the stick and nearly swallowed it whole.

"Okay," I said.

"I mean it," she said.

"Okay," I said again as I sat up, pulled my rubber boots off and walked them to the front door. I promptly returned to my room and lay back down, staring at the ceiling while Mom sat on the edge of my bed. I hoped she wouldn't ask me any more questions about my day.

"What did you do today?" Mom asked, anyway.

I took a deep breath. "We dissected frogs." We didn't dissect frogs. She just grosses out easily.

"Oh my God, really? They should have told me you would be doing that. I didn't even get an email. I can't believe those lazy people."

"I didn't have a problem with it," I said.

"I know you didn't," Mom said. "Still, I'm the parent. I should be consulted on that type of thing."

"I guess they think I can handle it. I'm growing up," I said.

Mom shook her head.

"Different school culture here. That's what they say, right?" I said with a chuckle. "Besides," I continued, "didn't you used to dissect frogs in college?"

Mom took a deep breath. She never liked to talk about college. I figured there was no way she would continue this conversation now.

"I got a new job, actually," Mom said. Ha! I was right. She would keep going if I didn't say anything. Mom didn't realize that she couldn't stand silence. Which was really a shame because she moved us to this place in the woods.

"Turns out it was a good thing I kept that bartender license up. I'll be helping out at Mickey's Tavern."

"That place we passed on the way to school?" I asked.

"That's it, the little red barn on the way. I just happened to stop in there and I saw that they needed help, so yeah."

"Cool," I said.

"You really think so?" she asked.

"Yeah," I said.

"Thank you," Mom said, patting me on my leg. "I knew you wouldn't judge. You know what? I start next week but don't worry. I found a girl in the parking lot at your school who said she would babysit."

"What girl?" I asked.

"A high school student," Mom said. "Her name's Dana. Said she drops off other kids at your school sometimes, including this one boy. You might have met him. I think he's a crossing guard or something. An African American boy with a red sash. She babysits him sometimes. Cute kid."

"You mean the hall monitor?" I asked.

"Is that what he is?" Mom asked.

"Avery?" I asked.

"Something like that. He seems like a responsible kid," Mom said.

I closed my eyes. "Mom, that kid's a joke," I said. "Besides, I don't need a babysitter."

"I know," Mom said, "but I need one so we don't get child protective services called on us when I'm out, so you'll have a babysitter. Okay?"

I let out a sigh so heavy I felt like all the air left my body. "Don't act like that, Wilda. At least you might make a new friend," Mom said as she stood up to leave my room.

"I have friends," I said.

"No, you don't," Mom said with a wink.

"How do you know?" I asked.

"I know you, wild Wilda. You're not friendly and going around playing a flute is not gonna make you popular," she said, belching her way into the kitchen.

I didn't think playing a flute could make me any less popular than I already was. The most important girls at school, Monica and Veronica, were already calling me weird. I drew this picture of them in my journal.

Chapter 3

The stares continued the next day at school the following Monday. No one really talked to me unless a teacher told them to. The students weren't mean, but they weren't really nice. I was glad when the school day was over.

The house was quiet when I let myself in after school. I could hear light snowflakes tap against the windows. Charlie greeted me with kisses at the door. "I'm home," I yelled. Hearing no reply, I kicked my boots off at the door, walked past the kitchen counter and continued down the hallway to Mom's room.

Charlie followed behind me. I cracked Mom's bedroom door and peeked inside of her room. She was lying on top of the covers of her bed in her street clothes, her chest rising and falling softly. I was just glad I didn't have to talk to her about school again. I didn't bother to wake her up. Instead I took Charlie for a quick walk in the snow outside and then fed him his dog food. I was watching TV when the girl Mom was talking about knocked on the door and Charlie started barking. The commotion woke Mom up. She jumped out of bed and ran to the door.

"Why didn't you let her in?" Mom asked. I didn't know why so I just shrugged. I never met Dana. How would I know who she was, anyway? Mom was stumbling to get a pair of red high heeled boots onto her feet without using her hands because they were full of keys. "I can't be late on the first night," Mom said. She flopped around under a winter coat she was trying to get an arm through.

Finally, she slung open the door and rushed back to her room as the teenage stranger stepped inside. Dana was a lanky girl with silky blonde hair. She wore a lettered jacket over a black hoodie with a red skull on the front and ripped jeans over a pair of white long johns. A row of safety pins lined the seams of her pant legs. Charlie walked over to sniff her and started snarling. And Mom thinks *I'm* weird.

Mom slung a set of house keys out of her purse to Dana. Dana juggled them to keep them from falling on the floor. "Thank God you're here. Grab the dog," Mom said. She nudged Charlie out of the living room with the toe of her high heeled boot and turned around to fiddle in her purse. "Where did I put my car keys?" she asked. Then she wandered over to the couch to lift up the two throw pillows.

"Mom." I laughed. "They're in your hand!" Mom looked down into her left hand at the car keys and shook her head. Charlie trotted to Mom's room, whining.

"Thanks," Mom said. "If anybody's hungry there's chicken salad in the fridge."

"For your kid or the dog?" Dana asked.

"Whoever," Mom said. "You could help her make a sandwich. Mayo's in the side door. Okay?"

"Sure, Mrs. ...?" Dana asked.

"Robertson," Mom said. "And she's Wilda."

"Hey," Dana said.

"Lock up, would ya'?" Mom asked as she rushed past Dana out the front door.

"Sure," Dana said.

The babysitter doesn't know our names? Where did Mom get this person? I thought. Mom gave me that "be good" smirk and closed the door behind herself.

Dana looked at me. "Hi," she said.

"Hi," I said back. We were standing in the living room, me looking at this stranger in a varsity bomber jacket that was too big on her. She looked at me with a blank stare.

"Have you ever babysat before?" I asked.

"Oh," she said, sitting down on our pleather couch, "yeah. Sure." She fidgeted with her fingers and pulled her cell phone out of her pocket. "You wanna watch TV?" she asked.

"I'll just be in my room," I replied.

"Fine," she said. Then Dana leaned forward to grab the remote control from the coffee table in front of the couch. That caused her vaping pen to tumble out of the tiny front pocket of her ripped skinny jeans.

"You smoke?" I asked.

She chuckled. "No, I'm not a smoker. Only a loser smokes cigarettes these days when weed is so

..." Her smile quickly faded once the reality of her words had fallen to the floor. "But I wouldn't," she started to say.

I interrupted her. "Forget it. I'm not a snitch."

Dana smiled nervously.

"Just don't do it inside," I said. "Reefer stinks."

"I won't get you in trouble," Dana said. "I'll be sure to go outside." She nodded. "You know," she said, smiling, "we could go out there together and..."

I stared at her with eyes wide.

"I mean," she stammered, "n-n-not to do anything bad. You should feel t-totally comfortable. That's how it should be." She sank into the couch and rubbed the back of her neck.

"What grade are you in?" I asked.

"I'm a junior," she said.

"So, you're not old enough to buy it, yet," I said.

"You just said you wouldn't tell," she pleaded with me.

"I won't," I said, "But I think this means we have an understanding, now. You'll leave me alone to do whatever I feel like doing, and I won't rat you out that you're vaping marijuana. It's a win/win."

Dana rolled her eyes. "Fine," she said.

"Maybe instead of a sandwich I'll have pizza tonight," I said.

"Um," Dana said, "your mom didn't leave any pizza money so, ha-ha, no."

"Whatever," I said.

I left her on the couch. Charlie came out of my mom's room and followed me down the hallway to my room. Charlie sat down by my feet as I pulled my piccolo out of its black case in my backpack. I had signed up for music instead of a foreign language this semester because what was the point of speaking a different language when I already didn't have anybody to really talk to?

My sheet music was a little wrinkled from being in the bottom of my backpack. The song was "Stars and Stripes," a staple for marching bands. If I took it slow there would be more time to figure out which keys to play first so that I wouldn't end up practicing my mistakes. I put the two pieces of my purple piccolo together firmly, adjusting the head piece of the piccolo so that the tone hole would be slightly forward, close to the center of my lips. With my fingers ready to play the first few keys, I took a quick, deep breath.

The first note came out a little strong. It immediately signaled to Charlie to howl along, but the rest of the first line on the wrinkled sheet flowed together. Once I let out a steady stream of breath, the line took on a melodic shape and I could see colors give tint to the air with each note. My next breath felt even more familiar than the first. I slowly remembered that I wasn't bad at this. After all, it was my third year on piccolo after first learning to play the flute. I used to play both at my old school and when it was time to move, I had to turn the piccolo in. The school music teacher there, Mr. Cherry, gave me the piccolo for the price of the $50 security deposit. He said I was the only elementary student he ever had who could play a piccolo without either nearly passing out or being defeated by it in his twenty years of teaching. Still, it was really nice of him to let me keep it.

As I moved my fingertips across the metal keys, trying my best to ignore Charlie, I noticed the loud sound of the front door smacking shut. My fingers froze. *Did Dana just leave?* I slid off of my bed and walked across the cold wooden floor in my fuzzy socks to the living room. Charlie leaped to his feet to run ahead of me.

By the time I got to the living room a surprise awaited me at the door. There was someone totally different standing there. For some strange reason Charlie didn't bark. He sat transfixed by this new stranger as she wiped the snow from her black combat boots on the mat by the door. She pulled the hood of her white parka down and her thick, curly hair tumbled out. It was dark brown at the roots with dyed pink curls at the ends. She looked at me with big hazel eyes the shape of almonds. I could tell she was of mixed African descent. Her small gold nose ring shined in the antique light over the doorway, illuminating her milky brown skin. She was a beautiful girl in a sort of unusual way, tall and athletic looking in her black skinny jeans. She smiled at me with perfectly straight teeth. She looked absolutely nothing like Dana.

I froze in place, my eyes feeling cold and dry from my widened stare. Charlie jumped up to hug her leg, instantly in love with her. She smiled at him adoringly and rubbed the back of his head. To my surprise, Charlie nonchalantly sat down in the far corner of the living room.

The stranger's eyes darted down to the piccolo I had been holding so tightly that my fingers had grown numb. "She didn't say you were a musician. That's cool," she said, pulling off her red, fingerless gloves.

I was confused. *Do I run away? Where would I go in this little cabin?* I wondered. The back door was right in front of her in the kitchen. My feet were stuck. Why wouldn't they move? And why wasn't Charlie doing anything?

"You look scared," she said. "Didn't she tell you I was coming?"

"Didn't she..." I heard my voice trembling. I could barely talk now. "Dana?" I asked.

The strange teenager continued to chat as though her unannounced nighttime visit was normal. "She went out to meet up with her boyfriend in his car. I'm a friend," she said. She came over to me and knelt down. She clasped her fingerless red gloves together in her hands.

"Who... who?" I asked.

Her face changed from alert to pitying. She pulled a tuft of tight curls away from her eyes and smiled again. "I'm Reema," she said. "I'd shake your hand, but..." she said, still holding the wet gloves.

"Okay?" I asked.

"Well," she said, "I'm here now. So, let's do something fun."

I was not sure what she expected. My face must have shown my confusion because she went ahead and patted my shoulders with her cold fingers. "You're such a little innocent. I like that about you, so

68

human," Reema said. She stood up and walked over to the fire. It had died down so she blew a heavy breath on it and fanned it with her gloves. It sparked at first but then piped up a stream of smoke and came roaring back to full warmth. Reema turned to me as she sighed contently. "Wilda. That's one of those old names, isn't it?"

"I don't know," I said.

She smiled. "You're honest, too," she said. She sat on the couch, kicking off her boots into the middle of the living room floor and resting her feet in gray and white striped socks on the coffee table. "Play me something," she said. "I love wind instruments."

"Right now?" I asked. She raised her eyebrows and stared intently at me as though it were a command. I lifted the piccolo to my chin, only then realizing how pale my fingers were from holding onto it so tightly. I took a nervous breath and begin to play the "Turkish March" by Mozart, not totally sure why I was obliging this stranger's request. The song seemed to flow purely from muscle memory as I could barely think at the moment. Once I started to play a couple of notes Charlie wandered over to me, sat down and began to howl. I glanced at Reema and noticed that she was shaking her head. "No, no. Play something else."

I stopped playing. "What was it about the song that you didn't like? Or was it my playing?" I asked, trying my best not to sound offended by her interruption.

"No, it was not your playing. Just do something else. That song's so... typical." She motioned with her hands.

"Ok," I said, a little confused. The idea formed in my head of what to play and I took another deep breath. This time I started playing the song I had been practicing, "Stars and Stripes Forever," accompanied by Charlie's howls once more. Reema shook her head again and sank into the couch. "Oh, God, no. Stop! If I thought the other song was typical..."

"It's a little rude to just stop someone during a performance," I said, surprised by the strident tone in my own voice.

"Oh, is that what this is?" she asked me. "I thought we were having a conversation."

"A what?" I asked.

"You're not talking to me with your instrument. You're lecturing me on someone else's notion of military might. You're not really sharing yourself with me."

"I don't understand," I said.

"Poor kid. Hasn't anybody ever told you that music is a language?"

"Well, yeah. Of course," I said.

"Then talk to me. I'm right here."

I lowered my piccolo and looked at her. The steady look in her eyes suggested that she meant what she said, and she was waiting intently for me to respond.

"I don't know what you want me to do," I said.

"Just play whatever comes to your mind, but make them your notes, not someone else's," Reema said.

"You mean, like, write the song? Right now?" I asked her.

"What other purpose is there for sound than to send a message about right now?" she asked.

"Okay, then. What am I supposed to talk about?" I asked.

"Anything you like," she answered. "How do you feel right now? Wait, don't tell me with your words," she said, pointing at my piccolo. I really felt uneasy about having this strange person in my house ordering me to entertain her but I didn't dare challenge her. There was something intimidating about this teenager, but not malevolent. I didn't think she wanted to annoy me. Or maybe she did? I wasn't quite sure what to make of her yet. Reema looked at me from the side of her nose. It was as though she read my thoughts.

I lifted the piccolo to my lips again. What came out of them was a short, warm breath. Charlie didn't howl this time. Instead he sat and listened quietly. The notes were stilted, loud and frustrated because I rolled my tongue as I breathed into the piccolo, making the notes sound like I was growling. I played mostly sharps, and my tune had an abrupt, annoyed end. I meant to tease her with it, to show how spiteful she had made me feel. Then I lowered the piccolo, satisfied that I made my point of how much I disliked this whole lesson in how to be a demanding house guest. Reema was not offended by my playing, though. Rather she nearly fell off the edge of the couch, clapping. "That was you, the real Wilda, not those practiced scales." she said. "You're not some fussy, attention-loving maniac like Mozart. You're just a regular girl with a temper."

"Is that a good thing?" I asked.

"Impatience can be useful," she said.

"What do you mean?" I asked.

"Think about all the cool things you could be learning somewhere else ... like my hometown," Reema said. "Let me see?" she asked as she plucked my piccolo from my hands and examined it before I could give her permission. "This little thing has been good for you. May this piccolo be as loyal to you as you are to it," she said. She passed it back to me. Then she stuffed her tiny feet into her fur lined combat boots and stood up on the wet shag rug in the middle of the living room.

"How about a tour?" she suggested. Before I could decline her request, she had walked past me to my bedroom and headed straight to the top shelf of my closet.

"Wait," I said. "What are you...?"

Before I could finish my sentence Reema was already rummaging through my artifact box. "That's not it," she said as she tossed the oyster shell onto my bed. She examined a pink stone that my grandmother sent me from her trip to Arizona once. "Nice, but not it," she said before tossing it onto the bed.

"Hey!" I yelled. "You're going to lose my stuff. What are you doing?"

"Relax," she said. "I'm not gonna lose any of your precious things." She pulled the pinecone out of the box as she tossed the box onto the bed upside down. She held the pinecone up to her closed eyes, pressed it with both hands up to her nose and breathed deeply into its center. "Still fresh," she said.

"You're still collecting?" Then taking another deep breath, she looked around my room and shrugged.

"Dana should be on her way back now. Sorry about the mess," she said as she dropped the pinecone on my bed. Then walking out to the living room, she stopped to take one more looked around. "Wait, what do I see, here?" Reema asked. She walked back over to my bed, reached down, and picked up the shiny amber stone that had landed near the box on the quilt. She rubbed her thumb across the amber stone and held it against her chest.

"You can't take that. I found it!" I said.

"You … found this?" she asked, placing the stone in my hand. It fit snugly into the center of my palm. "I wouldn't dream of taking it from you," she said. "You were supposed to find it. I just wanted to know if you really were the one who did." Reema smiled brightly and turned to walk away.

"Where are you going?" I asked as she adjusted her knit scarf and opened the front door. Charlie followed her to the door and sat before her.

"I'm taking off," she said. "Your babysitter will be back soon. Just don't go anywhere, okay? And certainly, don't come looking for me."

She stepped out into the dark trees and the starlit snow. I sat by the living room window, my arm around Charlie, as we watched her descend into the frosty air. Reema stopped walking for a moment as if she could feel me watching her and turned her face toward me with a smirk across her lips. Then she took a few more steps forward and vanished into the night.

The front door opened again. This time it was Dana creeping in. She stopped when she saw me and Charlie sitting on the bench by the window near the door. "Oh," Dana said, "I thought you were in your room. I had to go out for a moment."

"For a moment?" I asked.

"Yeah, sorry," she said.

"Your friend just left," I said.

"Oh. You saw that?" She asked. "Please don't tell your mom, ok? It's not a big deal. Just don't tell your mom or she wouldn't have me back."

"Your friend seems safe, maybe a little rude though," I told her.

"What do I have to I do to keep you from blabbing to your mom?" Dana asked.

"Just let me do my thing and I'll let you do yours," I said.

She nodded. "That's fair," she said. "I'll fix you a sandwich."

"Uh, no," I said. "I think you could order a pizza."

"I thought we went over this. Your mom didn't leave any cash," she said. I looked at her, lowering my head to make my point.

"Don't you think you owe her that pizza? I mean, you didn't completely look after her kid," I said.

"Cheese or pepperoni?" Dana huffed.

"Cheese," I said. Dana slammed her purse on the kitchen counter and pulled her phone out of it. "Such a little brat," she said under her breath.

"That's where you're wrong," I said. "Brats get things that they don't deserve. I'm your boss."

Dana shook her head. She started dialing on her cell phone and waited for the pizza place to answer. That winning feeling when you've got something good to hold against someone else? Yeah, I had that against Dana. I smiled to myself. I just knew that she was going to be easy to handle.

Later that night I decided to draw Dana in my journal because, well, she kind of had this Goth vibe, and weird looking people are interesting to draw. And since Reema looked chill and also super pretty I decided to draw her, too.

*

Chapter 4

I was trying to sleep when Charlie's loud barking work me up. I assumed Charlie wanted to go outside. His warm breath tickled my nose. I opened my eyes and noticed the foggy blue light of daybreak streaming across the bedroom floor.

I blew a tuft of my red hair out of my face and watched Charlie sit down in the middle of the floor. I sat up and rubbed my eyes. It was still a little dark out and the sun always took a while to come up in winter here. The morning air, however, was usually damp and still in the morning, just like San Francisco. A chill fell upon my shoulders. I noticed that the shutters over the window beside my bed were wide open and the window was cracked, letting in the cold air. I wondered if the window was like that all night.

I slid out of bed, walked over to the window in my thick fuzzy socks and grabbed onto the top of the window ledge. I pushed down as hard as I could but it only toggled back and forth. It must have been jammed. I leaned my back against it, using my palms to press down on it with all my might until the window slid down. Charlie let out another loud bark. "Okay, you'll go out in a minute," I told him. Just then, the light across the floor shifted. I turned around to see that a long-haired cat had jumped onto the outside of the window ledge. I stepped back from the window with surprise.

The cat pawed at the window and purred at me. I imagined it wanted to be let in but Mom would have killed me if I did that. When I moved closer to the window the cat pawed at it again. Its fur was the darkest blue and shiny like the stars at midnight. When I saw the cat's sky blue eyes I suddenly felt sorry for it. It must have been cold and hungry out there. It must have needed something, maybe a little milk.

I moved closer to the window, wanting to help the beautiful, defenseless animal but I could hear Charlie behind me. He was barking loudly now. This only made the cat paw more aggressively, now jumping onto the window.

I looked back at where Charlie was. The cat would be safe so long as I kept Charlie away from it, so I walked over to the door and beckoned Charlie to come. He reluctantly followed me to the hallway. Then I walked around him back to the doorway of my room. "Wait here now and don't be noisy. Mom needs her sleep," I told Charlie. He moaned as I closed the door behind myself, leaving him in the hallway. I went back to my bedroom window and forced it up slightly. "Wilda," I seemed to hear. Was that what a cat's purr sounded like? It couldn't be.

I had to open the window further. The cat was staring at me with a mesmerizing swirl of blue, yellow and black pupils, calling me toward it. I felt the frosty air on my face as I leaned outside my window. Then I felt my whole body crawling through the window. It didn't seem like I had any control over it.

The cat jumped down from the window into the clearing by the shed. It looked back and me before it walked forward into the trees. I felt myself drawn to follow, not bothering to cover the flimsy pajamas I was wearing with a coat, and not caring that my socks were getting wet in the muddy snow. I walked through the trees, following behind the cat as the canopy of evergreens darkened the world around me. The fronds of leaves grew greener with every damp step I took, further and further into the forest. As I followed her the trees begin to sparkle around me. A golden sky emerged from their canopy and rays of pink and blue light wondrously emanated from the forest. Then the cat suddenly stopped. As if in a trance, I stopped too.

A glowing white body unexpectedly stomped from around a giant tree to face us. A black stripe ran from the top of its head to the tip of its pink nose, flanked by stripes of brown fur from the corners of its hazel eyes. The shimmering white deer stepped directly in front of us and dug its hooves repeatedly into the leaves and snow on the ground. The doe angled its head toward the feline. The cat stumbled back and hissed. Then it ran off to scale a nearby evergreen tree.

I watched the deer chase the cat that leaped into the tree. The cat curled itself onto a thick branch, but it wasn't safe there. The deer turned and pummeled the tree with its heavy back legs. The branch the cat was using for refuge began to break loose from the tree. The cat scrambled onto a nearby limb, staring at the ground below as the deer continued to violently shake the tree.

Snap! The limb came loose, hurtling the cat down to earth. The cat leaped off the branch onto its paws and magically transformed from the ground up. Its feet turned into black boots, its furry legs into human legs and its feline face into the face of a white-haired woman. She wore a black lace dress with a high jeweled collar and a proud smirk on her face. "Can't she defend herself?" the old woman asked the deer. But the deer dug into the ground again, angling its nose toward the woman.

"Fine," the woman yelled in a shrill voice. "Protect your peasant girl," she said. "Dumb human," she muttered under her breath. She turned and disappeared into the trees.

My eyes felt round and cold again. I wasn't sure if I was dreaming. I looked back at the white deer. It merely stared at me for a moment before galloping back into the forest. When the trance I was in wore off I was surprised to find myself freezing in the wintry air without so much as a robe. I ran back to the window, threw myself inside it and slammed the window shut. I tripped over my own feet to get to the door to let Charlie into the room. He ran straight past me, jumping onto the window and barking wildly. Mom came in next in her lacy night shirt. "What on earth!" Mom said. "Your socks! What have you been doing?"

I shrugged. I didn't know what to say.

"It's freaking early, Wilda. Couldn't you let me sleep in on a Saturday at least?"

"Sorry," I said.

"And why are your socks so filthy?" she asked. "Haven't I told you to wear your slippers around the house?"

"Sorry, Mom," I said.

"Jeez. Feed the dog already," she said as she closed the door. I rolled my socks off onto the floor and tossed them to the corner of the room, disgusted that I'd let myself get yelled at. Then I stared at Charlie, trying to understand what I just saw outside. He jumped down from the window and lay down on his white chest beside me as though he was trying to comfort me. Was I losing my mind?

I pulled my backpack from the closet doorknob and slung it onto my bed so I could get my pencil. I grabbed my journal from the artifact box my closet, opened it on the nightstand, flipped to a blank page, and sat down beside it at on the edge of my bed. I had to draw this strangely beautiful cat, this truly other worldly cat that sounded like it spoke my name when it purred. I started drawing with earnest, trying to remember everything about the cat, from its thick fur shimmering like crystals in the frosty air, to the bottomless black pits in its eyes. Once I finished drawing the cat I decided to draw the rare white deer that chased it away.

Just when I had finished drawing I heard a knock at the front door. Charlie perked up and sat quietly. A warm energy surrounded me. I felt like it might shed light on

whatever just happened to me. I stood up and dug through my closet for a pair of jeans and a sweater.

I threw on a red sweater over my pajama tank top and kicked my pajama bottoms across the bed. I jumped into my jeans and zipped them up as quickly as I could. Charlie and I peered from around the bedroom door. Mom was opening the front door. I couldn't see who was on the other side but I heard the voice.

"Good morning, Mrs. Robertson. A friend of mine told me you may be needing a babysitter. I do babysitting when I'm not in class. I was hoping you might take one of my fliers."

"You're in high school?" I heard Mom ask.

"No ma'am. I'm a freshman at the community college," the voice said.

"You live around here?" Mom asked.

"Close enough to walk here," the voice said. It was a familiar sounding voice, soft but smoky. "May I leave it with you?"

"Sure," Mom said. "And what is your name?"

"Reema," the voice responded.

I jutted out from behind the door. "Reema!" I exclaimed.

"You know each other?" Mom asked.

"It's a friend of Dana's," I said. Reema smiled and gave me a polite wave.

"Oh," Mom said. "Well then, why don't you come in?"

"I wish I could, but I only have a few minutes to finish canvassing the neighborhood before I have to leave for class," Reema said.

"Well, I'll be calling you if I ever need another sitter," Mom said.

"Thank you, Mrs. Robertson. Bye, Wilda," Reema said.

Mom closed the door. "Well," she said, "it looks like maybe you did make a friend here."

I stumbled past Mom to fling open the door and follow Reema outside. I was surprised to see her dressed in a stiff black wool blazer with her hair pulled back under a sparkling crocheted black cap, hiding the pink curls at the edges of her long hair. There was no sign of her ever having had a nose ring and her eyebrows appeared neatly sculpted into place. Reema stopped walking and looked at me from the edge of the driveway. "I told you, I have class now," she said.

"Do you know anything about this area? Or the woods here?" I asked. "I had something weird happen just now. Maybe I shouldn't ... I don't know."

"Don't worry about anything, especially animals. I'll see you soon," Reema said. I stood there hoping for more information but Reema didn't give me any. "Go back inside with your mother or she will worry about you, and you might never get any answers." She turned around and walked away on the dirt and gravel road leading away from our cabin. I went back inside. I wondered why she mentioned animals, but when I turned back around to ask her she was already gone. It seemed that everyone was always disappearing into the woods around here.

Mom was at the stove frying scrambled eggs. "It's already 9:15. I figured I might as well get up and get started," she said. "My shift's at six and if we're going to that oddity shop in Seattle today we should probably be on the ferry by eleven. It'll take over an hour to get there."

"Sure," I said.

"We can leave Charlie. We'll be out for only a few hours," Mom said.

"Okay," I said. I scooped out a cup of dog food from the large bag in the pantry and placed it into the dog dish by the kitchen's back door, next to a bowl of water that Mom had already filled for him. Charlie galloped over to and stuck his head into the dish.

"You know what's strange?" Mom asked. "When that visitor came to the door, Charlie didn't bark. Why do you think that is?"

I shrugged my shoulders again. I wasn't ready to tell Mom that Dana left the house last night to hang out with some boy in his slick ride and that Reema showed up in the house while Dana was still out. That was too good a piece of info to use to blackmail Dana into letting me do whatever I wanted. "I don't know," I said. "Maybe dogs can just sense good people."

"Maybe," Mom said. "Still, I'm starting to worry if Charlie might be losing his street smarts up here. It's strange."

"You think everything is strange," I said. "You probably think I'm strange."

97

"Think? I know," Mom said. She laughed as she came to the table with two plates of scrambled eggs and toast in her hands. She set my plate in front of me and sighed as she crossed her arms. "But weird people are more interesting," she said. "The world is fascinated by them."

"Then I must be pretty interesting," I said.

"Unfortunately." Mom said, laughing.

We got to the Bremerton ferry terminal early and parked on a street nearby. We were walking the three blocks downhill to the ferry terminal when Mom got a text on her phone. "Awe, man," she said. "We have to go back home."

"Why?" I asked.

"I'm being called in for work early. Someone got tied up in traffic and can't make their shift," Mom said.

"This early?" I asked.

"It's an afternoon wedding reception," Mom said.

"Just act like you didn't get the text," I said.

Mom shook her head and turned around to walk back to the car. "I'm sorry," she kept saying. "We'll go next week."

I didn't want to go home. My mind seemed to be playing tricks on me at the cabin. Charlie didn't even act normally there. My shoulders stiffened and I let out a huge sigh that Mom ignored. She got in the car and pushed my door open from the inside so I could get in, too. On the way back home, Mom kept looking over at me while driving. She pursed her lips like she does when she's nervous. "I promise you'll go next week," she said again.

When we got back to our cabin and walked inside the living room, Mom stared into space with her hands on her hips. "You know, I just realized that you need a babysitter, unless I take you with me, and I don't think they'll let an employee's kid crash a wedding reception." She looked around the room. "Where is Dana's number? Oh yeah, it's in my phone." She pulled her phone out of her purse and texted Dana, asking her to come right away while I slumped down on the couch next to Charlie. Dana's reply came almost immediately.

"Sorry. In Lewis County. All day track meet," Mom read out loud on her phone. "Damn it," she said. "You like the library, don't you, Wilda? I could drop you off there."

"All day?" I protested. Mom thought for a moment. Her eyes drifted across the room and landed on Reema's flyer on the dining room table.

"Didn't she say she had class today?" I asked.

"She didn't say all day," Mom said. She pulled out her cell phone again and dialed the number on the flyer. Immediately, Reema picked up. "Hi, you were just at my house," Mom said. "I'm Wilda's mom."

"Oh, yes, Mrs. Robertson. How may I help you," I hear the voice on the other end say, sweetly.

"Are you done with your classes for today?" Mom asked.

"Yes," the voice said.

"I have a bit of an emergency. I need a babysitter here in half an hour. Could you do it?"

"I think so but I do have a lot of reading to do today," Reema said. "Would I be able to work on my homework there?"

"Sure, sure. Wilda's a very easy child so that's not a problem at all if you need to study," Mom said.

"Okay," Reema answered. "I'll see you soon."

Mom was still racing around to get dressed in her formal black pantsuit when Reema knocked on the front door, exactly thirty minutes after their phone call. I was in my room, working on the drawing of the cat I had seen that morning when I heard her knock on the door. Mom stuffed her feet into her black leather pumps and opened the door.

"I hope I'm not late," Reema said.

"Oh, no. You're right on time," Mom told her. "Please, put your coat on the rack by the door. Make yourself at home. And thank you for coming at such short notice," she said. "What'd you say your rate was?"

"Fifteen dollars an hour, up to sixty per day. But since you only have one child, I'll waive the first hour. At most it would be forty-five today."

"Oh, thank you. You're an angel!" Mom said.

Reema giggled. "Something like that," she said.

I waited in the living room with Reema, neither one of us saying anything. Mom slid on her black overcoat and slung her red and black designer purse across her body as she kissed me on the cheek. "See you later, sweetie," she said.

"Bye," I said as she closed the door.

"Well," Reema said, pulling off her crocheted cap and twirling her pink curls around her fingers, "looks like it's just you and me now." She smiled, stretching her arms out and letting out a yawn as she slung her nearly empty black faux leather backpack onto the couch, sat down at the kitchen table and rested her foot on one of the dining room chairs. Charlie must have heard her talking. He ran out of my room, pounced on Reema and pawed at her legs. "And hello to you, Charlie," she said. She held Charlie's head in her hands and stared into Charlie's big brown eyes. Charlie sat, whimpered for a moment and lied down at Reema's feet. "That's a good buddy you've got there," Reema said. "Has he always been this accommodating to guests?"

"I guess so," I said.

"I feel like taking a walk in the woods. How about you?" Reema asked.

"That's what I wanted to talk to you about," I said. "Something weird happened to me out there. I don't know if my mind was playing tricks on me or if there's something weird about this place. Do you know anything about this property?"

"Like whether it's haunted?" Reema asked.

"Something like that, maybe," I said.

"What happened?" Reema asked.

"I must have been sleep walking," I said. "This black cat came to my window. I don't know why but I ended up following it outside and it led me to a really pretty spot in the forest. That's when the most beautiful white deer I've ever seen with big stripes on its head came out of nowhere and challenged the cat. It was wild, like some battle or something. The deer was digging its hooves into the ground, and then the cat ended up running up a tree to get away from it. Then it gets really weird. The cat fell out of the tree and... well, it can't be possible."

"Go on. What happened?" Reema asked, leaning forward in her chair.

"Well, you're going to think I'm tripping," I said.

"No, there's... No," she said.

"There's what?" I asked.

"Go on, tell me what happened. I promise I won't judge."

I took a deep breath, mustering the courage to say what I thought I saw while Reema's eyes got bigger with anticipation.

"It seemed like... I mean, it looked like it sort of... turned into a woman," I almost whispered.

"Ah-hah," Reema said. "Have you ever sleepwalked before?"

"No."

"Then how do you know that's what happened?"

"True, none of it made sense. Cats don't talk, or turn into people. I might have just been asleep."

"Yeah," Reema said, nodding her head. "That seems like the most likely thing."

I nodded in agreement.

"You're not tripping, after all," Reema added.

"It's just that…" I continued. Reema looked away from me to pet Charlie on the scruff of his neck.

"Just what?" she asked, smiling back at me.

"It's just that something weird happened before. It was like that same cat or maybe another one was purring at me in the grocery store when I first moved here. It sounded like it was calling my name," I said.

Reema laughed. "It sounds like you have an active imagination," she said. I was prepared to accept this as the answer to all the weird things I had been experiencing until Reema added, "But what if it isn't your imagination?" Seeing the look of confusion I must have had on my face made her chuckle to herself. "You're brave enough, aren't you, Wilda?"

"I guess so," I said.

"Then you wouldn't be too scared to go for a walk with me outside? I mean, if it was only a dream, right?"

"Well," I said, not sure what I wanted to do. I felt my body tense up.

"Then let's conquer your fears. Get your coat so we can go outside. Unless you're scared ..."

"I'm not scared of anything," I said, straightening my back. I walked decidedly to my bedroom closet, slid on my shiny purple parka from its hanger, put on my fuzzy yellow cap with the pompoms on either side, my warm pink scarf and pink snow boots and stood ready by the kitchen door. Reema knelt down and looked me squarely in the face, her hazel eyes swirling with light. "Ok, Wilda, come with me into the woods then."

Charlie slipped through the cracked door and ran out in front of us. Reema motioned for me to follow them outside. I felt my body moving forward, as if it had its own will, and before I knew it we were on the same path where that mysterious feline had led me before. The sound of the backdoor smacking the metal frame shook some sense into me for the moment. "Wait," I said. "Couldn't this be ...?"

"Dangerous?" Reema asked with a half-smile. Charlie turned around to face me and barked cheerfully as though he was challenging me to join them. "Take my hand," Reema said. "You'll be fine. You're with us."

I held her hand in mine. She was wearing her red half gloves again, and although her gloves were warm and fuzzy Reema's fingers were icy to the touch. The trees once again glistened in rainbow-like hues, their leaves and needles pulsating with gleaming ice and energy. The ground crunched beneath our boots as we ventured deeper into the forest behind the cabin. Then we came upon a small clearing. "Is that where she ran?" Reema asked me, pointing up into the very tree where the strange cat had sought refuge.

"Yeah," I said.

Reema's eyes narrowed as she stared at the tree. It then occurred to me that I had not yet told her all the details of what had happened that morning. "How did you know about that?" I asked.

"How do you think I know?" she asked. "It's all right. You are not losing your mind, or Charlie wouldn't be over there sniffing that tree, would he?" She smiled again, her eyes becoming larger and greener as she gripped my hand. "I know all about this place," Reema said. "Except unlike that cat, I mean you no harm."

"Why would the cat want to harm me?" I asked. "What have I done?"

"Sometimes the question is not what you have done but what you *could* do if you ever realized your power," Reema said.

For the first time I noticed an old, twisted oak tree in the distance, twirling like a candy cane. "Follow me. Pathways always give clues," Reema said.

"Pathways to where?" I asked.

"Home," Reema said cheerfully.

"We're going to your house?" I asked.

"Yes," she answered. "You'll be my guest of honor." Charlie continued to walk ahead of us, but all I could feel in that moment were the nerves in my stomach.

"How do I know I can trust you?" I asked.

Reema stopped and faced me, her head tilted. "Your gut should tell you, but what an odd thing to ask," she said.

Odd? I wondered. 'Maybe she had a point. If she was untrustworthy then she would probably lie and tell me she *was* trustworthy. But what if she was being honest? Reema didn't seem like a stranger. Mom trusted her. I thought back to how I'd already messed up any hope of friendship with Monica and Veronica, the most popular girls at school. Reema was the only person I knew here who chose to be around me and besides, Charlie liked her. Charlie would never be this friendly to a bad person. He even barked at mail carriers. Seeing Charlie bound over the leaves and snow alongside Reema put my mind somewhat at ease but I needed to be sure.

"What does your intuition tell you?" she asked as though reading my thoughts.

"I'm not sure if I have any," I answered.

"Everyone has it," Reema said. She let go of my hand and walked ahead of me.

We passed what looked like a giant apple tree that was already in full bloom even though snow still clung to its leaves. Reema walked even faster. I had to jog a little to keep up. The further we got from the cabin, the more the distance between the white sky and the snow-covered forest floor narrowed until they nearly blended together. Reema and I crouched down beneath the low evergreen branches. It looked as though we were becoming smaller and smaller as we hiked through the woods. "Where are we going?" I asked.

"To the sleeping oak," Reema said. We wound our way through the forest until we found an oak tree that was bent into the shape of a half dome. The tree's canopy was curled almost into itself.

Reema dashed across the base of its roots and tapped its trunk with her gloved knuckles. "Knock on wood," she said, smiling.

"We walked all the way out here so you could do that?" I asked.

"Good luck comes from somewhere," Reema laughed, "Come on."

I followed her under the arched tree. Suddenly a meadow surrounded by woods became clear. At the edge of the meadow stood a wide circle of purple and white mushrooms. "There's the Spring Court circle," she said. "We can use it to go to any land within the Spring Court's control. We have to enter the circle to get home, but first I need to let the tree know. Wait here."

"Let the tree know? What kind of joke are you playing?" I asked.

Reema laughed. "You'll see," she said. Then, taking off her right glove, she lifted her hand and placed her palm against the side of the tree trunk.

The tree's surrounding branches shifted back and forth mysteriously in the quiet air. The oak tree slowly unfurled itself to face us, though still bent over as though it were in anguish. Its head of leaves turned towards us, too, morphing its thick bark into the face of an old woman. "Grandmother, we apologize for disturbing you but I have very good news," Reema said.

The tree's roots rumbled in the ground, shifting dirt and powdering snow into the air as the tree let out a tired, thunderous sigh. "Who wakes me?" the tree said.

"It's Reema, your granddaughter. I have brought a human girl, Wilda, and Charlie the canine. It is the kind of help I've been looking for. I am bringing my friends to the ancestral country."

"Ah, Reema. Welcome home, my beloved. It has been quite a long time since you left searching," the tree bellowed.

"Yes, it has," Reema answered.

"You have spent many years wandering the earth. Have you found everything?" the tree asked.

"Not yet, Grandmother, but I am very close now."

"And you have brought visitors?"

"Yes," Reema answered.

"They must be important," the tree said.

"I think they could be," Reema said. "Wilda found the missing piece in the Sky King's armor. I'll have you out of that tree in no time!"

"Such good news!" the tree exclaimed in a yellow pollen-filled bellow.

"Yes, Grandmother. We will see you soon," Reema said as she looked back at me and beckoned me to follow her. Charlie was already running ahead of us when Reema ducked under the arch of the tree, her arms and legs morphing into the white arms and legs of an animal. I stood amazed as she transformed into the white deer I'd seen earlier in the forest. Charlie stood by Reema's side and barked at me from the other side of the tree. "Come on," the deer told me. "The space is open now."

"What just happened?" I asked in disbelief. The deer laughed. "Don't you want to know?" it asked, nodding its head at me. "Step into the circle to find out." As weird as it was, I had to know if what I was seeing was real. Stunned into action, I propelled myself under the tree archway, tumbling clumsily into the leaves and snow on the ground as I entered. I was amazed when the mud and snow on the ground gave way to a dry and flowery meadow filled with the scent of honeysuckle. There were no crumbling leaves on the ground. Instead there were four leaf clovers and tall, dewy green grass all around us.

I sat up on the back of my legs, staring at the wildflowers growing between the glowing greenery in front of me. My eyes wondered up toward Charlie's giant paws and the pink hooves of the white deer next to him. Charlie was now twice his normal size, more gloriously golden than ever, and he stood nearly as tall as the deer.

"Where's Reema?" I asked.

"You're looking at her," the deer said. She watched me with wide, hazel eyes that were all the more striking as they were separated by the familiar black and brown stripes down her face. She pawed the thick carpet of wildflowers as if to beckon to me to continue to follow her.

"Come on," Charlie said in a raspy voice. I stared at him, amazed.

"You can talk!" I exclaimed.

"Of course. He always could," Reema said. "The difference is that you're actually listening to him here."

"Where am I?" I asked as I looked around.

"You are on the other side of the world," Reema said.

"Australia?" I asked.

Reema laughed. "No, darling. The realm that lives beside you."

"I've really lost my mind now," I said.

A light breeze floated through the air around me as sparkling trees unfolded with spring blossoms and tufts of bright leaves. A red eagle flew overhead, its tail feathers streaming behind it like a blazing cloud. What seemed like dragonflies jutted past each other, only to reveal themselves as small, winged people that paused midflight to look at me, whisper to each other and continue on their journeys. As I turned to look around, the lilies in the ground next to me twisted to face me, unfurling their petals to laugh at my amazement. The sun shone a dark orange glow but it had a bright white center. "Don't look at that," Reema said. "The sun and the sky will trick you here."

Charlie nudged me to my feet. It wasn't difficult for him to push me around. He was taller than I was now.

"What happens if I look at them?" I asked.

"You'll lose track of time," Reema answered.

"What's wrong with that?" I asked.

"Everything," she said.

"That sounds like a good problem to have," I said.

"Not for you, it isn't. One hour here is the same as three hours in Belfair. We can't stay long," Reema answered. I shed my heavy coat and folded it in my arms over my red sweater. "You're not going to need that coat," Reema said. I took off my yellow cap and the sweater I was wearing over my tank top and set them on top of my coat by the oak tree. When I turned around to face Reema I noticed a wavy castle made of flowing branches in the distance.

"Let's go," she said. "Climb on."

"Don't you think I'm too big to ride a deer?" I asked.

"I'm no average deer," Reema scoffed. She sat down on her hind legs to allow me to sit on her back. still seemed a little weird but I took her suggestion. Her white fur was short and smooth like a real deer. Without much effort on her part she lifted me up into the air as she and Charlie walked together through the tall grass and flowery shrubs toward the castle. It

120

was interwoven from seven trees, each one a different kind of tree. All together they created a glistening, towering nest full of birds and butterflies of many colors, surrounded by numerous flying things I had never seen before. I wasn't quite sure what they were. They seemed to stop and whisper to each other.

"Where are we going?" I asked.

"To the sixth castle," Reema answered, "the Tower of Vines."

"The sixth tower. Can we see them all?" I asked.

"No living being could withstand the first tower," Reema said, laughing. "That's not how it works here! Besides, it doesn't exist in this realm."

"Where are the towers?" I asked.

"There are seven. Two are in Spring Court, and there is a single tower in each of the Summer, Autumn and Winter Courts."

I counted them in my head. "That's five," I said.

"Right," Reema said, "the first tower is in the spirit realm, and the seventh tower is what we call your world."

The closer we moved toward the tower, the more I felt the eyes of this foreign world fall upon me. When we reached the base of the tower, I could make out that the seven vining trees were wound together into a fortress. Flowers began to rain down upon us. Hands and arms of all sizes were reaching out from the branches within the trees to dangle the flowers over us before letting them float down onto our heads. "They welcome you, Wilda," Reema said.

"There are so many of them," I gasped.

"Some of my ancestors were born from these vines," Reema said.

The castle swelled open and we entered on the ground floor. As soon as Charlie and I crossed the threshold of the tower, vines grew into the opening and formed doors that sealed the tower shut. We found ourselves in a rotunda covered in colorful flowers. Across the packed dirt floor, I saw a tilted ladder of intertwined branches and leaves leading to a nest of dried vines within the tower, high in the sky. Reema climbed the ladder, still carrying me on her back, as eyes stared at us from all sides of the tower. Charlie stood at the base of the ladder on his hind legs. "You can do it, Charlie!" I yelled back at him.

"Do you think I can?" Charlie asked. He pawed at the ladder, started to climb up and then froze again.

"You got it so far," I said.

"I do, don't I?" he said back. Then, climbing again, he stumbled onto another few rungs of the ladder. "I can do it," Charlie exclaimed, and bounded up the next rungs of the ladder.

We climbed higher and higher until the air seemed to get thinner and a chill swept over me. I was still wearing my pink faux fur boots but now I had no coat or sweater over my bare arms. By the time we reached the top of the ladder two men and two women were already standing on the platform, waiting for us. They stood on either side of an empty throne made of wood and twisted vines. The outer nest revealed a wooden platform. Reema sat down on the floor of the nest, making room for Charlie to hoist himself up alongside her. I stood up and faced the four, strange-looking beings.

"You have brought the enchanted child for us to see," one of the men said. He had pointed ears and long black hair which flowed down to his waist between his furry white wings, and he wore a mohair vest with armor on his arms and legs. He had large black pupils and perfectly shaped eyebrows, and if it hadn't been for his eyes and ears he would otherwise appear to be one of the Mongolian warriors I had read about in Mr. Gumble's world history class.

"I suspect she may be, Teacher," Reema told him.

"She should be, or she shouldn't have been brought here," one of the women said. This woman had skin like lavender, deep purple butterfly wings, braided white hair in thick locks and large hazel pupils in her eyes. That's when I noticed all of their ears were pointed, their eyes were all similar looking though they were different colors, and they were all dressed in clothes that looked hundreds of years old. The males were more beautiful than any men I had ever seen. They were feminine looking with dramatic eyes, and tall and elegant without a hair out of place. A bronze man with shimmering skin, bronze dragonfly wings and golden leaves in his brown hair, and a woman with wavy blonde hair and dark skin without wings, wearing a long sea green dress stood at the side of the throne. The blonde-haired woman's ears were even longer and more pointed than the others' ears.

"What is your name, child?" she asked.

"Wilda," I said, attempting to conceal the timidity in my cracking voice.

"Wilda, the wild child," the bronze male fairy said with a deep voice that was smooth and serious. "I am Kansya Cētanā. The purple winged one is Vitmat Dalkkas. Shōniin Luu and elfin Princess Yilokwa Yipuna from the Summer Court is also with us. She is our trusted ally who will assist in the crowning of our next ruler. We have been waiting a long time for you."

"For me?" I asked. "But you don't even know me."

"We have been waiting for a child, we just didn't know who that child would be," the purple female fairy, Dalkkas said. "We are in need of a child of pure heart with the eyes to see and ears to hear. Are you the one we've been seeking all these years?"

"No, nope. Not me," I said. I looked at the empty throne they were surrounding and back to their intent eyes. "I don't know what you all are thinking but I'm not really a people person or... elf person. I think you got me mixed up with someone else."

"Perhaps you are wondering why you were brought here," the wingless one, Dalkkas said. "Did you tell her, Princess?"

I was expecting Princess Yipuna to tell me but then Reema spoke up. I wondered whether Reema was a princess, too. "No, Teacher," Reema said. "I thought I would let her hear it from my regents."

"All right," Dalkkas said.

"What is it?" I asked, nervously.

Dalkkas smiled at Cētanā. He seemed to take it as a cue to tell me about their plan.

"You have already found something of immeasurable value to us. Now we need your help to fill our vacant throne," Cētanā said. "You will be provided protection to do so but it will require you to be brave."

"How brave?" I asked.

"Well, don't you remember your last battle?" Cētanā asked.

"Battle?" I wondered. "No. There's no way. I... I don't fight," I said. Then I thought for a moment. "Well, I mean, I have fought but not like that. I... I can't do it."

"It sounds like she resists this mission," Cētanā said to Reema.

"This place is very different for her but she's young enough to adapt. She just needs a little time to get used to things," Reema said.

"If she is not our ruler then perhaps she will lead us to the one who is," Shöniin Luu said.

The fairies and elf turned to each other and formed a circle, each one resting their left hand in the palm of another one's right hand, their heads bent forward. "What are they doing?" I whispered to Reema.

"They're discussing whether to allow you to remember," she said.

"What happens if they say no?" I asked.

"Then none of this ever happened as far as you're concerned," Reema said. "You'll wake up and carry on with your life."

"What do you think, Charlie?" I asked.

"They just better not try to hurt you or I will tear them open with my sharp fangs and snap their bones," he growled. Shöniin Luu glanced briefly at Charlie with a smirk on his face. He must have heard Charlie's threat but paid it no mind.

When the fairies and the elfin princess turned around their eyes glowed like white orbs. Reema stood to hear their decision. "The girl can continue to visit our world until the Fall Equinox," the woman in the green dress, Princess Yipuna, said. "We should know her usefulness by then."

"But if she stays beyond that point she will be trapped here until the following spring. I can't risk an attack on our soldiers to escort her back to the world in winter. The Winter Court will be too powerful," Cētanā said. "If she cannot accept to our way of life, what do you suppose we do with her?"

"I would sooner return her to her world," Reema said, "maybe having forgotten all of this."

"Depending on how much she has experienced by then, she might not be able to forget. It could put us all at risk from the humans," Dallkas said. "They are greedy beings, only seeking our power to enrich themselves."

"We can determine this later," Princess Yipuna said. "Thank you for bringing the child to us first. You are the most dutiful royal ward. You have proven why this kingdom should be yours to rule when you are ready someday, keeping the crown within your family."

"But there is still more groundwork to be laid, Princess Regent," Cētanā interrupted. "We cannot make such big decisions hastily, based on one task alone."

Reema bowed to them, and they bowed back to her. Somehow Charlie's instinct informed him to bow, and the four adults bowed to him as well. Reema sat next to me and motioned with her head to climb on. Then Reema descended the ladder with me on her back while Charlie followed. "Who else might have wanted to meet me?" I asked Reema on our way back down the castle ladder.

"Any number of souls," she said. "Some good, some bad, all of them powerful."

"So, I may be in danger here?" I asked.

"There is danger everywhere," Reema answered.

"You're not scared, are you?" Charlie barked.

"Should I be?" I asked Reema.

"Don't worry. I'll protect you," she said.

"So, you're my guide," I wondered.

"Yes," Reema said, "but you know the way here. Now that my grandmother Aisosa, the old tree woman, knows you are a friend she will allow you to enter this land, as humans are incapable of entering on their own. But you must never come here without me. Promise me you won't try."

"Of course," I nodded. "That makes sense."

Once we reached the outside of the seven trees the flowers began to rain down on us again. "You will wake up tomorrow and believe this was a dream," Reema said. "I have to give you something to prove that this place is real."

"How will do you that?" I asked.

"Let me see your hand," she said. She let me off of her back and turned to face me, pulling a blue lily from among the flowers in the ground with her mouth. I plucked it from her mouth and examined it. "Have you ever held a laughing lily?" she asked.

"I didn't even know they existed," I said.

"They don't exist in your world," Reema said. "Put it behind your ear. When you wake up you'll know you must have gotten it here, where it is springtime."

"Okay," I said, placing the flower behind my ear. As soon as I placed it there the flower started giggling hysterically and blowing air in my ear. "Aaah!" I yelled.

"I forgot to tell you, they tickle a little bit." Reema laughed. "It should settle down by the time you get back home."

Chapter 5

I awoke with the sunlight streaming through a crack in the curtain. I rubbed my eyes and stretched my arms out of the quilt. Suddenly I remembered what Reema said about the laughing lily. I reached for the flower in my hair but I couldn't feel anything but my usual mess of frizzy red locks. I jolted upright, anxiously rubbing my fingers through my hair but the flower was nowhere on my head. I yanked the pillow up, pulled the sheets and blanket down and looked under the bed but I still couldn't find the blue lily anywhere.

I sat on the edge of the bed, rubbing my face with bewilderment. My eyes connected with Charlie's eyes. He was sitting patiently in the corner of the room, waiting for me to wake up. "That was a strange dream, wasn't it, Charlie?" I asked. "Can you still talk?"

He barked and stared at me. I guessed not. An overwhelming feeling came over me, pulsating through my veins, telling me to draw the castle of vines that I'd seen so that I would remember it. It seemed like the most incredible dream I'd ever had. Although I thought it couldn't possibly be real, I needed to record it, anyway.

I reached for my notebook on the nightstand, clicked the mechanical pencil next to it to move its lead down and drew the throne room of the towering vines and its smiling inhabitants as best I could. Then I put the pencil down, got up, and wandered into the kitchen to get breakfast. Mom was putting last night's groceries away when she heard me enter the room.

"Good morning, sleepy head," she said.

"Morning," I said, sitting down at the kitchen table.

"How'd you sleep?" Mom asked.

"Okay, I guess," I said.

"That's good," Mom said. "It sure looked like you had a good time yesterday. I put your flower in some water. Wouldn't want it to get messed up being slept on."

"What flower?" I asked. I had to rub my eyes and stare again at the vase on the kitchen table in front of me.

"Too tired to notice your pretty flower on the table, huh? Where did you all find a lily like that?"

I couldn't believe my eyes. I blinked several times and each time I opened my eyes, there it was in the clear glass vase on the table: a dark blue lily. 'What a coincidence,' I thought.

"We went on a walk through the woods," I said. "We must have picked it, and I ended up dreaming about it."

"Well, with flowers like that, maybe I should go too, one of these days. I haven't spent any time back there."

"You know Mom, maybe you should," I said. Mom poured me a glass of orange juice with trembling hands and set it on the table. I had seen her hands like that before. Mom would always get mad if I said anything about it so I ignored the fact as she punched thirty seconds into the timer on the microwave and pressed the start button. "I got your favorite," she said. Then after a few more seconds she opened the microwave and set a warm bear claw pastry on the table in front of me.

"Finally!" I said. "I've been waiting ages for sugar!"

"You're welcome," Mom said. She sat down to sip her coffee. "Aren't you going to eat anything?" I asked.

"No, I'm fine. Gotta protect this figure," Mom said. I noticed just behind her that there was a bottle of Patron coffee liqueur that appeared to have been opened, next to one of her vodka bottles that appeared filled halfway. I thought her coffee smelled different. I didn't say anything about it, though, even as she rummaged through the freezer for ice and dropped a few cubes into her coffee before she sat down. Mom got mad when I questioned what she drank. "Finish up so I can drop you off at St. Joseph's," she said.

I broke the pastry into pieces so that I could savor every bite while Mom watched, sipping her drink. "Finish up and get ready. And wear that pink dress in your closet with the matching leggings," she said. "And your nice shoes!" She sat back in her chair as if in slow motion.

"Okay, Mom," I said. "Are you coming, too?"

"Not today, honey. I have a lot to do," she said.

"Are you feeling all right?" I asked.

"Of course," she said. "Hurry up and get ready."

I scarfed down the rest of the pastry and left Mom at the kitchen table. I skipped to my room and put on the dress, leggings and shoes that Mom suggested without thinking much about it. I never really cared what I wore since Mom never really let me wear the kinds of things I would be into anyway. Mom only bought me clothes that were frilly and proper that other people like to see on a girl. So, I put on my ruffled outfit and proceeded to struggle with my curly red hair.

I can't really comb it unless it's a little wet. Otherwise the curls tangle too much. If I can get it into a ponytail with minimal effort, I'm happy. Mom gets mad if I take too long anyway. It didn't help matters that my curly bangs absolutely refused to lay down no matter how much gel I used on them. The last time Mom took me to a salon the stylist insisted on cutting my hair wet. When my hair dried my curls shrank and I looked like I had fallen asleep wearing a bike helmet. I wouldn't let anyone come near me with a pair of scissors since then.

After about five minutes of brushing and wetting my hair, pulling it back, slathering it with gel, wetting it and brushing it again I was able to get most of it into a ponytail holder just as I heard the front door close. That meant that Mom was on her way to heat up the car so she could scrape the ice off the back windshield. I didn't have enough time to deal with the strands of waves that accidentally framed my bangs and almost seemed to be styled on purpose. They highlighted my brown eyes, making me almost feel satisfied with my looks.

I yanked my purple coat off its hanger in the closet and threw it on, forgetting about the piccolo in its case in the inside pocket of the coat before it uncomfortably landed on my side. I gave Charlie a rub on the head as I ran to meet Mom at the car in our front yard. She had already started the car and she left the passenger door wide open for me. The car radio was playing electronic music from a Seattle high school radio station. I slid in, pulled the heavy door closed, pulled the worn seat belt over my body and let it click into place. Mom took a long sip from her thermos and set it in the cup holder. A little bit of brown liquid spilled out of the spout and dripped down the side of the thermos. It spelled like the coffee liqueur Mom was drinking earlier.

"Are you okay?" I asked Mom.

"Don't ask me that," she said. "Kid," she added.

We pulled out of the gravel driveway and made our way to the main road leading to Highway 300. There wasn't much traffic. Mom drove a lot faster than usual and my half of the car momentarily slid on the brush and ice on the side of the road. I glanced at Mom to catch her reaction but there was no expression on her face. "Mom," I said.

Her eyes stayed transfixed on the road. "I'll pick you up in about two hours, okay?" she belched.

"Okay," I answered. Just then a black truck coming from the opposite direction on the road approached our car. It appeared that we had driven onto his lane, drifting onto the wrong side of the road. "Mom!" I yelled.

"What?" she yelled angrily. Then she slammed on the brake. The sudden stop made us both jolt forward toward the dash before smacking forcefully against our seat rests.

The truck driver also stopped in the road. He rolled down his window and yelled something at Mom. I couldn't really tell what he said but Mom must have heard him because she flung open the driver side door and jumped out.

"Mom!" I yelled. She didn't seem to hear me. She walked up to the man's window and started screaming at him with so much might she bent over to say it. "You stupid loser! You can't drive, loser!"

"What are you, batty?" I heard the grizzled man yell back at her. "What's a dumb ass like you doing on the road?" Mom yelled.

"You're really asking for it," he yelled back. "How would you like to get run over today, hon?"

"I'd like to see you try," Mom said.

"Mom, stop!" I shouted, but she never looked back at me. She was pacing back and forth from the man's driver side window to the front of his truck, calling him a stupid moron while he yelled names back at her. Then she slammed his hood with her bare hands as though she forgot I was there, like it was just a private duel between her and this man. I got out of the car and walked to the front fender, rubbing the back of my head.

"Is that your kid?" the man asked, but Mom never acknowledged what he was asking.

"You stupid driver!" Mom yelled. "You're an idiot! A stupid idiot! Somebody should come take your license away, you loser! Hey, idiot! You and your stupid truck with a stupid clown driver!" she said, kicking the driver's front tire. "I used to know a user like you!"

"Do you want your kid to see her dingbat mother get flattened by this truck?" he yelled. "How about that, darlin'?"

"You can't do that because you're a coward," Mom shouted, stretching open her sweater collar to reveal her cleavage. "Look at you, hogging up the road. Bet you think you're so smart. Why don't you learn how to drive, you deadbeat?" she yelled. Then she rocked backward in her high heeled boot and spat into his window. The man responded by throwing his lit cigarette at Mom's bare collarbone. She screamed and recoiled with shock.

The man backed up his truck, steered around the corner of our car, stuck his middle finger out the window and peeled off in a cloud of tire smoke and flying slush. Mom picked up a rock from the edge of the road and threw it at the back of the truck as it drove away, hitting the edge of the flatbed.

"Mom!" I yelled again, "What's going on?"

"That asshole tried to drive us off the road. That's what's going on," Mom panted. Her eyes were wider than I'd ever seen before and for the first time that morning I could smell a whiff of tequila on her breath. "Come on, Wilda. Get in the car," she said as she started back to the driver side.

A weird feeling began to well up in me and for some reason I didn't really understand, I felt stinging tears roll down my cheeks. "No," I almost whispered. I stood still, staring at her.

"Get in!" she yelled.

I just looked at her. I couldn't move. I didn't know what to do.

"Wilda, you get in this car right now," she said from the driver seat. "I mean it, or you'll be walking to church!"

I felt my body pivot away from her, aware of the wind against my back as I walked ahead of the car.

"Get in this car, Wilda. You're going to make a scene!" she said. I just couldn't look back, though. I felt like I had to keep walking. Mom followed me in the car while two different cars passed us on the road, their passengers staring at us with looks of bewilderment.

"Fine then, walk," I heard Mom yell out of the window. When I heard the car screech to a stop, I turned my head to face her. Mom was turning the car around. She was driving away in the direction of home, leaving me on the side of the road.

So, Mom left me. *How could she?* I was so frustrated! I started sobbing uncontrollably, sitting in the snow and mud on the side of the road in my fancy pink dress. I don't know how long I had been sitting there, wiping tears away before I heard a car approach me and stop. A door swung open. I looked up. It was, of all people, the school hall monitor dressed in shiny black lace up shoes, pressed gray slacks, a plaid sweater vest and a stiff blue button up shirt with a red bow tie. I barely recognized him. His hair was slicked so closely to his head that his little curls were attempting to peel away from his angled ears. He was even more conservative looking than he was at school. Except for the colors on his vest, his outfit was almost identical to the balding driver's outfit. "Wilda?" he asked. "It's Avery."

Dana was sitting in the back seat and two middle aged African American adults, I assumed Avery's parents, were in the front of the shiny white SUV. "Are you all right?" Avery asked.

I looked at him and then down to my muddy shoes. "I don't think so," I said.

"Honey, what happened?" The woman in the front seat asked from the rolled down passenger seat window.

I stood up, afraid I had gotten Mom and myself both in trouble. "I... Well..." I thought of what to say. "I... I'm walking to church."

"All by yourself?" she asked.

I nodded.

"Where's your Mom?" Dana asked from the backseat.

I straightened up my shoulders and looked her straight in the eyes. "Asleep. She works nights," I said.

Avery spoke up. "We're all going to Bremerton Missionary Baptist Church."

"I'm observing. It's for a paper in my English class," Dana said.

"You can ride with us," the boy said.

"But we don't know which church she goes to," the man said from the driver's seat.

"It doesn't matter. I don't care," I said.

"Well then, come on, sweetie," the woman said. She seemed friendly enough in her large wool overcoat and lacy blouse. Avery motioned for me to get into the SUV. Normally I would never take a ride from a stranger but at this point I didn't think things could get any scarier. Besides, Avery wasn't really a stranger, only the biggest square at school. I didn't have many options, anyway, and for some reason I didn't feel like walking back home. Mom would be there, probably passed out, and there would be an empty bottle in the kitchen trash that I'd have to pretend not to see.

Then I remembered how dirty my clothes were. "Don't worry about that, hon. Just get in," the woman said as if reading my mind. I wiped my face and climbed into the backseat. I sat back with a feeling of relief. "Your poor mother. If she only knew you were all the way out here on Highway 3 by yourself, I can't imagine how she'd feel," she said.

I didn't have to imagine. I knew Mom wouldn't be able to believe that any of this happened. She'd deny it all, and then she would stop taking me places unless she absolutely had to. I thought about the fact that we'd arrived for my first day of school in an Uber. Had she been drinking then, too?

Dana patted me on the hand. "Did you have a babysitter yesterday?" she asked.

"Yeah," I said. "Your friend, Reema, came over."

"Reema?" she asked. "I don't have a friend by that name."

"Of course, you do. She came over that night when you were babysitting and you had to go to your boyfriend's car for a while."

"What are you talking about?" Dana asked.

The driver glanced back at us while driving. "You have a new friend named Reema?" he asked.

"No, I don't," Dana said. "She must be confused."

I decided not to say anything else about it. Dana flashed her blue eyes at me with an exasperated stare that said, *you promised*. She shook her head and looked out the window.

"What's your mother's number, honey? I'm going to call her," the woman said. "By the way, we're Avery's parents. And Dana comes with us to church sometimes. You can, too," she said.

"Sure, thanks," I responded. I told her the number and she called, but Mom didn't pick up.

"I'll try again in about an hour," she said. It was just as well. I doubted that Mom was sober enough to answer the call without getting confused, anyway.

When we got to Avery's church, a simple building with off-white siding and a small bell tower, Avery's dad parked the SUV near the parking lot exit, saying something about a Warriors basketball game he intended to get home to watch as soon as the service ended.

While I waited for Avery and his family to get out of the SUV I couldn't help but notice that Dana and I were the only people in the parking lot who were not African American. I didn't want to make a big deal out of it or anything. I must have been engrossed in looking around because Dana kind of snuck up behind me and startled me with the question, "Ever been to a Black church before?" She gave me a smirk as though she already suspected the answer was no. "It'll be fun," she said, smiling. Then she reached over and brushed a lock of my hair off of my cheek and tucked it behind my ear.

I felt her staring at the side of my head as her fingers lingered there so I turned to look at her.

"What?" I asked.

Her serious expression turned to a smile again. "Red hair is so pretty," she said.

I shrugged. I guess I wasn't in a mood to be buttered up by compliments. Besides, her response seemed almost like a rehearsed answer. I just had a feeling something else was on her mind. Maybe she pitied me. I hated it when people felt that way about me. I guess I'd rather be ignored completely than pitied.

Avery, Dana and I filed into the church behind Avery's parents. Men and women in dressy suits and designer shoes greeted each other in front of the church. The smell of spicy cologne and sweet perfumes were carried lightly on the morning breeze. The women gathered around to hug and kiss Dana and Avery's mom, while the men offered Avery and his dad handshakes. "And who's this?" I heard an older lady in a lacy, sequined hat ask Avery's mom.

"She's Wilda, one of Avery's friends from school," his mom replied.

One of Avery's friends? I looked at Avery for his reaction. He seemed unfazed as the lady reached down with her dainty white glove and shook my hand. She smiled sweetly.

Avery's mom ushered me inside of the church. A skinny woman in a vest, white sleeved shirt and on pin on her chest motioned with white gloves to a pew to take a seat. We filed into one of the wooden pews, Avery's parents leading the way. Dana ended up between me and Avery, which left me on the end of the pew where I had a good view of everything.

This church's musicians looked more like a blues band than a church group, jamming together on bass guitar, drums and keyboard below a simple wooden cross on the wall. I was surprised to see children singing in the front row of the choir stand along with the adults behind them while a giant wooden pulpit stood imposingly between the choir's lively director and the band behind her. The pulpit was flanked by formally dressed deacons in tall velvet chairs. "You know you're going to be here for a while, right?" Dana whispered into my ear with a chuckle. "The sermons are long at this church."

"How long?" I asked.

"An hour, maybe," she said, "if we're lucky." I stared back at her with what must have been enormous eyes because she laughed out loud right there in the pew. She turned out to be right about that. To be honest the sermon felt like it lasted a lifetime, mostly because I kept thinking about Mom back home, wondering if she was worried about me. Actually, I was hoping that she was pacing the living room floor at home, worried about me. How weird was it that I ended up with my babysitter and the hall monitor? During the ride to Avery's church I found out that his mom worked at the post office and his dad was a mechanic who used to be in the Navy. I thought I probably couldn't get any safer.

I looked back at Dana. She seemed to be watching Avery the whole time as she typed her notes into her cell phone, more attentive to his reactions than anything going on in the choir stand or the pulpit. The preacher mentioned something about spiritual nature and how angels were different and people were special, something like that. I wasn't really paying attention even though the band occasionally played a riff of a song in the middle of his sermon as though they were agreeing with him musically, and members of the congregation responded by saying, "Amen," or, "Preach, Pastor." I guess I just couldn't wait to see how things would get sorted out with Mom.

The sermon ended with another song by the band. The congregants got up to clap and sing along, stepping from side to side to the rhythm of the drum section. Avery clapped too and he seemed to be pretty into it. His parents were definitely enjoying the song, and his dad even tried to sing along although he wasn't really in tune. Luckily he was mostly drowned out by better singers, including an older lady who took her time singing as the band grooved to a bluesy rendition of "Oh, How I Love Jesus."

The deacons and ministers marched out of the sanctuary doors, followed by the audience, as the band continued to play. It seemed like it was time to go. "Ready?" Mrs. Johnson asked me. People were gathering near the double doors to hug each other and shake hands again. I did not really understand everything they were doing in Avery's church but I thought the music was interesting.

"Um, is it okay if I hang out and listen to the song?" I asked.

"Of course, baby," she said. "You wanna sit up front?"

"Okay," I said.

"Come on," Avery said. He ushered me to the front pew.

Dana pushed me forward. "Go ahead. I gotta do something," she said. I noticed that she was grasping the vaping pen that was poking out of her open purse. I assumed she was heading to the back of the building for a smoke.

"You're going to do that here?" I asked her.

She gave me a sly smile and looked at me with narrowing eyes. "Are you the moral police now?" she asked. She slipped away from us and slunk out of the side door with her vaping pen tucked in her palm.

I followed Avery to the front pew. The church band was improvising on a few chords from the song. That reminded me of the jazz songs my orchestra teacher used to play on his tablet back in San Francisco. Mr. Cherry always said a well-rounded musician should be able to play classical music as well as jazz. "Sight reading and improvisation," he always said. These three church musicians seemed to really take that advice to heart, inverting scales and pulling them apart, remaking the rhythm of each measure to suit their moods, all while complimenting one another.

They ended the song to applause and a few shouts of "Amen" from those members of the congregation who were still in the sanctuary. For a moment I forgot about home. I allowed myself to just enjoy the song. With musicians who played like this I was surprised that so many of the church members had already left. I supposed they were used to this type of music.

After the last note of the song I stood up and walked over to the pianist. She looked up at me from her keyboard. "Good morning," she said with a polite nod. She was an older African American lady with short, curly gray hair, dressed in a beaded pantsuit.

"Hi," I said. I almost kicked myself to make myself sound more grown up. "Good morning."

She didn't pay much attention to me as she gathered the wires from the keyboard together. I supposed I better ask her what I was wondering before she packed up all her equipment to leave.

"How did you get so good at that?" I asked.

She paused what she was doing and looked back at me. "Good at what?" she asked.

"How did you get so good at improvising music?" I asked.

She chuckled as she leaned forward on her stool. "Practice," she said. "You just have to do it. A lot."

"But how do you get good enough to start doing it?" I asked.

"Do you play?" she asked.

"Well, not piano," I said. I shrugged. "I play flute and piccolo."

"Well, that's something," she said. "How often do you practice?"

"All the time," I said. I noticed that the drummer, a teenager, was starting to take down his cymbals and the older man who played bass had already unplugged his guitar. They probably had other places to be but they seemed to be curious about our conversation.

"Well," the keyboardist said, "that's a start. I could show you if you had your flute. When you get home pick your favorite song and test out some new ways to play the melody on it."

That's when I remembered I might have that piccolo in the inside pocket of my coat. I pat it with my hands. Sure enough, it was in there.

"Actually, I have it," I said. I pulled the two pieces of the piccolo out of my coat and held them in my hands.

She laughed when she saw me standing there, eagerly hoping for a lesson.

"I can show you something but I only have a few minutes before I have to rush to a gig this afternoon." The bassist shook his head and sat down with his guitar, wondering what we were about to do. I stuffed the head join of my piccolo into the body of the piccolo and blew a couple of notes out of it to tune it. The bassist chuckled and plugged the wire back into his guitar.

"Let's see what you got," he said.

"Yeah, play something," the keyboardist said.

When I realized what I'd gotten myself into it was too late to back out. I was a little nervous but then I realized that I was a visitor at their church so I didn't really have anything to lose. I took a deep breath as I thought about what to play. Then I took a quick breath and started with a simple scale as they listened to me play.

"Okay," she said. "How about this. Can you play by ear?"

She started to play a hymn that the choir sang earlier, starting with the introductory lines from the song as she stared at my reaction. Then she started to sing along with the chorus, "Hold to his hand, God's unchanging hand. Hold to his hand, God's unchanging hand." Her voice was raspy and strong, and she rocked from side to side as she sang, "Fill your hopes on things eternal. Hold to God's unchanging hand." She nodded at me to join her as the bassist started playing a low-pitched harmony.

I nodded in agreement. I think I had the tune figured out from hearing it for a second time. I raised the piccolo to my lips, took a quick, deep breath and started to play the melody along with her. I was a little sharp when I started playing but they seemed not to mind. They instantly changed the key that they were playing in easily. The bassist nodded. "Okay," he said, encouragingly. The drummer who had been listening decided to sit back down and play along with the portion of his drum set that he had not yet taken down.

"Now listen," the keyboardist said. She sang lightly as she played each chord of the chorus simply, pausing on the notes so I could hear each part. Then she started to play each note of the chords separately. I understood what she was showing me and I started playing each chord on my piccolo. Then she started to mix up the notes, playing pieces of each chord in different combinations and with different rhythms. She played the main note of each chord a little louder than the rest of the notes to signal to me which chord it was. I was able to follow along with what she was doing as the remaining congregants started to clap and sing the chorus along with us. After a little while she said, "You got it. Now it's your turn."

My turn? I let the band repeat the chorus without me while I thought about what I would play next.

"Don't worry about the audience. Play like you're talking to angels," she said.

At the start of the chorus again I began to play, hearing the notes in my mind before my fingers touched each key. I could see the notes in the air, floating like sparks of color as soon as I played them. It was so exciting that I almost couldn't believe I was doing it. I was having so much fun that I didn't notice Avery clapping along and having a good time until the song was almost over.

The band had given me a whole chorus to myself as they played lightly, treating me like a valued member of a jazz ensemble. When I finished improvising on the chorus, I heard people cheering. The song ended dramatically and enthusiastic applause erupted across the sanctuary.

"Not bad," the keyboardist said. "I'm Mrs. Idella Gadling. What's your name, dear?"

"Wilda," I said.

She shook my hand.

"Mr. Greene," the man on bass said as he shook my hand.

"Willie Westbrooks," the boy on the drums said as he shook my hand, too.

"Nice to meet you," I said.

"Are you just visiting?" Mrs. Gadling asked.

"I guess so," I said.

"You should come back and play some time," Mrs. Gadling said. "It's a little unusual to have a piccolo on a gospel song but... I think we could make room for you on this one."

I couldn't contain my happiness in that moment. I must have had the biggest grin. The idea of me, or all people, making a band? And a gospel band, too? I couldn't believe it.

"Thank you so much," I gasped.

By then Mrs. Johnson had come to the front of the sanctuary where Avery was sitting.

"Ready?" Mrs. Johnson asked. I nodded yes and waved goodbye to the band.

"What did I miss?" she asked as she ushered us to the exit.

"Ha!" Avery said. "A lot!"

It was midafternoon when Avery's mother dropped me off at home. I got home a little bit later than she planned because she decided to let Avery and me get in line for some of the buttery pound cake that was being served in the church hall after the service. Mrs. Johnson had left Mom a message earlier that I was with her family at their Baptist church. I heard her say, "Sorry to wake you," as she left the message. I think Mom picked up the cue from there because she was sitting patiently on the porch steps when the SUV drove up. She was wearing different clothes and her hair was damp.

Mom anxiously got up and rushed over to my door as soon as the car stopped. She yanked open the passenger door and pulled me into her arms like a ragdoll. My arms flailed as I looked into her rosy face, contorted with nervousness. "I'm sorry, baby," she said, holding my face in her clammy hands. Then looking up at Avery's mother, she introduced herself. "I'm Valerie Robertson, Wilda's mother."

"Martha Johnson," Avery's mother said.

"Thank you for taking care of Wilda," Mom said.

"Sure. No problem," Mrs. Johnson said. "Has she ever just walked off before?" she asked.

"Oh... No, she's never been off on her own like that," Mom said, giving me a sharp stare to be quiet. "I'd invite you in but I'm afraid I haven't prepared for company. I've just been ..." Mom flitted her hands in the air and let out a nervous laugh before catching her breath and stuffing her hands into her jean pockets.

"You don't have to entertain. I know you've been through enough for one day," Mrs. Johnson said.

"Thank you for understanding," Mom said.

"You've got to keep a better eye on her. If you need someone to pick her up for church, you have my number. Or just hire a babysitter for the mornings when you know you'll be sleeping in."

"Of course," Mom said humbly as she ushered me into the house. She waved briefly as Mrs. Johnson drove away, then pushed me into the door. "What did you tell them?" Mom asked pointedly as soon as she closed the door behind us.

"I said you were asleep so I left on my own," I said.

"Well, I heard the voicemail message but that doesn't make sense. You were going to walk all the way to church?"

"No, you started driving me, and then we both got out of the car because you were arguing with this truck driver, and then I decided to walk the rest of the way. Don't you remember?"

"No," Mom said. She sat slowly sat down on the couch. "I just remember I woke up and had this message on my phone from Avery's mother about you being with them."

"So, you just woke up in your bed?" I asked, incredulously.

"No, I was in my car," she said. "I must have been on my way to find you but I got tired."

That didn't make any sense, but I didn't want to tell her that. It would only upset her, and whenever she's upset she drinks more so I just shrugged my shoulders. "Okay," I answered.

"Come here," Mom said. Mom took my hands in hers. She looked into my eyes and took a heavy breath. My nose twitched because I could smell the alcohol through her skin. I tried hard to keep my face still, forcing my lips into a half smile. "I know I'm not a perfect mother but I'm trying," Mom said.

I nodded.

"I'm sorry I don't remember everything that happened, but I promise I'll try to do better. Okay?"

I nodded again.

"If I ever get sick again, take my phone and call somebody."

"Okay," I said.

"But remember, we're a team, you and me. We're all we have so we have to protect each other no matter what, right?"

"Yes," I said, looking down at my muddy socks.

"I'm proud of what you said today," Mom said. "You protected our family."

I looked up at her and her face was serious. So, I was supposed to protect us both, but she could leave me on the side of the road? Why didn't she just pull over and walk with me to the nearest place to sit down and get help? Better yet, why did she have to drink this morning? Why did she have to drink at all? I felt every nerve in my body grow hot with frustration. It was like I realized that neither one of us could make things better. "Sure, Mom," I said.

I let go of her clammy hands and walked as fast as I could to my room. I pulled the two parts of my piccolo from my coat pocket and walked around in circles as I played bits of songs with improvisations, scales and whatever I could think of as perfectly as I possibly could. Charlie walked into the room, sniffed my legs in my muddy leggings and sat by my bed, so I sat down, too. He nuzzled his face onto my legs and gave me a comforting gaze. I set the piccolo down on the bed and smiled at Charlie, rubbing the back of his head. Then I got up, gathered some fresh clothes and carried them to the bathroom to take a shower.

Chapter 6

"Sooner or later somebody's going to call the cops," Mom said, pacing the living room floor. "We can't afford another close call like that. What if you'd been hit by a car?" She looked up Reema's number in her phone and worked out a plan with her. Reema ended up coming to babysit me nearly every day for the next month or so.

Whenever Reema came over we would take long walks with Charlie that I couldn't explain the next day. Our hikes always seemed to end up back at the same spot in the woods beyond the twisted oak tree and the circle of mushrooms, where the air was always warm and the flowers were always in bloom.

Reema liked to tell me stories about her family along the way that couldn't possibly be true. "My family was royal," she said. "All of them could fly." It seemed like my waking memories and my dreams blended together around her.

Reema turned into a deer again and ran with me on her back. We galloped past the vining castle and through sleepy villages where fairies made their homes beneath the southern stretch of the grassy blue rolling hills. We traveled until we reached a great lake that Reema called D'Lorah. A giant swan was waiting for us there, floating at the water's edge. He told me he was really a regent I met before named Cētanā, and that the lake was where he trained fairies like Reema for combat.

"Where do you keep that amber rock that you found?" the swan asked me with his deep voice.

"It's in my artifact box," I told him.

"Good," he said.

"But it doesn't matter because none of this is real," I told him. "Swans can't talk."

"But I'm talking to you now," he insisted.

"My daily walks with Reema are real," I said. "This part is the dream."

The next morning, as I was rolling out of bed I noticed a huge white feather on the floor by the nightstand. *How did this feather get in here?* I wondered. I assumed that Charlie must have tracked it into the cabin the last time he came in from chasing after sea hawks. I guessed the idea of a swan with giant wings ended up in my dream somehow. The feather was long and shiny so I put it in my artifact box. It seemed like my dreams were getting weirder every night.

Reema liked to hear about my weird dreams as we'd sit on the couch together, watching TV. She didn't mind listening to me practice my flute or my piccolo, either. Hanging out with Reema was the most interesting part of my day. I just wished I could also look forward to being at home with Mom.

Whenever Mom was home she was usually sleeping, and whenever she wasn't sleeping she was usually running late for work. I would try to talk to her sometimes but she was never really in the mood, telling me, "I have a lot on my mind," or, "maybe just play something." I didn't mind playing for Mom but she usually spent her time in her room by herself while I practiced. And then there was school.

I tried to sit in the back of most of my classes, except in Mr. Gumble's class where I got stuck in the front. I couldn't sit in the back of orchestra, either. The teacher liked to have me in the front. She said I was first chair. That sounds impressive but given that there were only two other piccolo players and neither of them could actually play a decent sound on a piccolo, it's just how it all worked out. I was the only one in the orchestra who could play both the plastic flute they issued us *and* the piccolo.

The weirdest thing though was how the instructor was always asking me to play the parts for other instruments too, and everybody just went along with it. They were probably too lazy to practice and get good at their own parts. The teacher had me play along with the violin section in "Blue Tango" by Leroy Anderson because the violinists were having a tough time doing the legato. Even if I got lost in the sheet music and started riffing, everybody else would just go with whatever I was doing, like they didn't know what was supposed to be played. It was like they were mesmerized by whatever I did, or something. So, yeah. Whatever.

After going to Avery's church I thought maybe we might hang out at school sometime, but no. I would see him in the hallway on my way to the band room. I would wave and smile but he'd just give me a nod of his head and a salute. He didn't even smile. One day I decided to stop by and say hello, anyway.

"Hey, Avery," I said.

"Hey," he said, looking away as he guarded the hallway.

"Are you going to the cafeteria to get lunch?" I asked.

"I go during fifth period," he said.

"But that's when everybody else is in class," I said.

"Right," he answered matter-of-factly. Then we just stood in the hallway next to each other, me wondering what to say and him looking down at his shoes and occasionally down the hall.

"Well, see you later," I said.

"Good talking with you," Avery responded. It's like he was always on duty or something. I just didn't know what was up with that kid.

Spending lunch in the band room helped me to not have to interact with any of the bullies on campus. That's why I tried to go there as much as possible, only going to the cafeteria to get lunch and come back. I would always get a salad and fruit, not because that's what I liked but because nobody was ever in line for the salad cart so I could get in and get out without running into a jerk. But this day there was a substitute teacher who locked the band room to go to lunch with the staff. I was going to have to find somewhere else to go on campus for the next awkward forty-five minutes.

I went straight to the salad bar, like always. I grabbed a carton of chocolate milk and set it in my cardboard tray. I hurriedly filled the rest of the tray with an apple, a plastic pack of ranch dressing and a clump of lettuce, an even bigger clump of shredded cheddar cheese, a few serrated carrot slices and two tomato wedges. When I turned around I almost bumped Veronica with my tray. She must have been standing behind me almost the entire time, practically breathing down my neck. "What do we have, here?" She announced to the cafeteria. "It's Wilda, the weirdo!"

I rolled my eyes at her and squeezed between her and the salad cart to get to an empty table in the corner of the cafeteria.

Veronica was standing next to two other girls, their arms folded. I pretended to ignore them as I opened my milk carton and took a sip. I watched them get in line for the pizza out of the corner of my eyes. I tried to gobble down the salad. I dropped the apple into one of the side pockets of my purple coat and tried to finish the chocolate milk before they could come back. In the middle of focusing on the upturned carton I didn't see that Veronica and her sister Monica had gathered around me with several of their friends.

"Why are you sitting here? This is our table," Veronica said.

I looked at the group of students with their trendy hair and clothes. "Look, I don't want any trouble. You can have it," I said. I stood up and picked up the tray in my hands. That's when I felt a group of hands slam me by my shoulders back down onto the hard plastic bench.

"Oh, no. Don't let us stop you from eating," Monica said. "Right, Josh?"

One boy emerged from the back of the group to take the tray out of my hands and toss it back onto the table. I recognized Josh as one of the football players at our school, a star running back with a perpetual smirk on his face. He sat in the back of Mr.

Gumble's class where he told bad jokes and pitched various objects across the room into the trashcan every fifteen minutes. "What are you going to do now, play us away with your toy flute?" Josh asked.

They all laughed. "Hey, where is it? She always has it on her," Monica said.

The obnoxious crew began to dig their hands into my coat and pants pockets. "Hey," I yelled, "Stop it!"

This only made them laugh hysterically. "Aren't you gonna finish your milk?" Veronica asked as she picked up the carton from the table and tossed it at my chest. It was mostly empty but there was just enough chocolate milk left to splash brown stains onto my white sweater. Josh reached deep into my inside coat pocket. "I got it!" he exclaimed as he pulled the canvas case with my piccolo out.

"Give it back!" I said.

Instead, Josh fumbled to open the case, dropping the two pieces of the piccolo onto the floor in the process. "Oops," he said, then grabbed the body of the piccolo by its keys, stuffed the head piece into the body piece and pitched it to another one of the boys in his gang.

"Catch, Drew," Josh said. His buddy in turn tossed it to one of the girls who was with them, who then tossed it back to Josh.

"Get ready, Nicole," Josh said to the girl who was tossing it with them as he backed up and prepared to pitch it back to her. "Ow!" Josh suddenly yelled. The other students who had been playing with my piccolo suddenly stopped laughing. They bent over and held their hands as the piccolo lay on the ground, piping out a stream of smoke.

"What happened?" Monica asked.

Josh had dropped the piccolo on the floor, and he was wincing in pain. "It's burning hot!" he said.

189

Their bullies' hands turned red and the skin in their palms had bubbles of blistered skin. "Oh my God!" Nicole exclaimed.

"What the hell?" Joshua said. "What did you do to it?"

I shook my head. I had no idea what he was talking about.

"You tricked us! You booby trapped that thing to hurt us!" Drew yelled.

"How was I supposed to know that you would try to take it from me?" I asked, straightening my clothes.

The commotion got the attention of the hall monitor, Avery. He marched over to us with his back stiff with righteousness and a serious expression on his face. "What's going on over here?"

"Wilda burned us with her piccolo. She must have microwaved it," Josh said.

"How do you microwave metal?" Monica asked.

"I don't know. Ask her," Josh said.

"Oh my gosh! You sound like a complete idiot," Veronica said.

"Well, how else did she do it?" Josh asked.

Veronica shook her head. "You never heard of an oven, Einstein?" she asked.

"Is this it?" Avery asked. He knelt down and picked up the piccolo. He paused to look at it, then juggled it in his hands. "This thing is ice cold. You kids are full of drama," he said, handing it back to me. I examined it. The piccolo felt cold to me, too. I shrugged at Avery before putting it back into its case and stuffing the case into my pocket.

"I need my hands to catch the football. You're gonna just let her get away with that?" Josh protested.

"As far as I'm concerned she was just minding her business until you guys came over and started pestering her," Avery said.

"Whatever," Josh moaned. He was a full foot taller than Avery. He thought nothing of it when he reached out his long arms to shove Avery backwards. Josh quickly learned that he'd made a mistake. Without warning Avery wound both of Josh's arms behind him and had him bent forward with his cheek on the table like a criminal about to be placed in the back of a police car.

"Hey bruh, what's that all about?" Josh whined.

"I can haul you to the office right now for your suspension or you and your crew can get out of here. Take your pick," Avery said. Josh was too busy whimpering to answer so Avery tightened his grip. I think everybody was stunned to see Avery out-muscle the school jock this way.

"Actually, I was just leaving," I said. I gathered the carton and tray and walked them over to the trashcan. When Avery saw me put my tray on top of the trashcan he let Josh loose from his grip.

"Come on," Josh said, and the gang of bullies slunk out of the cafeteria.

"Thanks," I told Avery. He simply nodded back at me before continuing on his beat.

I spent the remainder of the lunch period on a cold concrete bench just outside the office window. I knew Veronica's crew would have to be pretty bold to confront me there where all the staff could see their antics. I pulled the piccolo out of its case and examined it. The springs were intact and none of the keys appeared bent. Then I put it up to my lips and blew into it, pressing down two of the keys. It let out a clear tone, strong and mellow. There seemed to be nothing wrong with my piccolo. In fact, it seemed to be easier to play than ever. The keys, which would sometimes stick, were now loose to the touch.

I lifted the piccolo again to my lips and let out a breath as I played. This time the melody that emerged was smooth and professional sounding. I could feel myself being watched so I paused and looked behind me at the people in the office window. They were staring back at me, transfixed. Weird. I turned back around to notice a black cat across the street. It had the same midnight colored fur that I'd seen before, and it was staring back at me. The cat unmistakably winked at me with one of its slanted green eyes and then slinked between the bushes of a house, away from view of the sidewalk. *Was my mind playing tricks on me?* I thought it must have been my imagination. I cautiously walked back inside the building, hoping I wouldn't be getting any more trouble from Veronica and her crew for the rest of the day.

When I finished the long walk home from the bus stop at Belfair Beach Camp and let myself into our cabin I found Mom stumbling around her bedroom, looking for her keys while simultaneous trying to stick her feet into a pair of red pumps. "Hi, Mom," I said to let her know I was home.

She turned to look at me as I passed through the hallway, hunched over by the side of the bed. "I can't find my keys and it's time to go," she said. As she bent down in the middle of the living room looking under the couch, her cell phone rang. She flipped her purse strap down from her shoulder and rummaged through the bottom of the purse to find her phone.

"Hello?" she answered it. "Her counselor …? From who? Mr. Gumble's class?"

Oh, no! The school was calling my mom! My stomach sank as I plopped down on the couch. I swallowed dryly as I tried to remember if I had turned in my homework in his class over the past week. I nervously sat on my hands on the couch. Mom straightened up her back and plopped her hand on her hip.

"Wilda, what's this about burning people? Did you do that?" Mom asked incredulously as she held dropped the phone to her side.

All I could do was stare at my knees as I scratched my head, wondering how I was going to explain this. I didn't even know how it happened. Mom gave me a serious stare that lasted a long time before she lifted the phone back to her ear.

"Why shouldn't I be angry?" Mom asked, turning away from me. She sounded surprised. "You want to talk to her? Sure." Mom held the phone out to my face. "It's Mrs. Taren on video call," she said.

"Mrs. Taren!" I exclaimed.

"So, her counselor called you to ask what kind of issues she had in your class," Mom said. She gave me a disgusted look as she walked with the phone to her room to continue getting ready for work. Although I couldn't make out what Mrs. Taren was saying I could still hear Mom on the phone. "They were thinking about a suspension?" Mom asked. "I was hoping we could start fresh. I didn't know new schools could request students' records from their old schools... Ah, thank you for not making a big deal out of that in her file. I don't know how to thank you... Go easy, huh? I'll try. Here, Wilda." Mom came out of her room and handed me the phone.

"Well, hello to you," Mrs. Taren answered sweetly. "I just wanted to check up on you since I got a call from your new school saying that things might not be what you expected up there. Can you tell me about it?"

"I miss you," I said.

"I miss you, too, and I'm a bit worried about you. I heard you had a problem with some students today. I told her counselor that it's just not like you to plan to hurt anybody. What really happened?" she asked.

"Oh," I said, taking a deep breath, "I don't know. You wouldn't think it could really happen."

"You can tell me," she said. "I've already asked your Mom not to get angry, whatever happened."

"It's just...," I started. "Mom, can I talk to Mrs. Taren outside?"

"You're gonna have to make it quick," Mom said. "I need my phone and I'm gonna be late for work." Mom rushed back to her room so I crept outside with her phone and sat down on the chipped porch steps.

"Uh," I wondered.

"Yes?" Mrs. Taren asked, softly.

"I didn't do anything to the piccolo. It just for some reason got really hot. No one would believe me."

"Well, there had to be a reason for that," Mrs. Taren said.

"I can't think of anything," I said. "But these kids have been picking on me and I haven't done anything to them. I don't really like it here. I only met one friend, maybe two if you can count my babysitter."

"What are they like?" she said.

"Well, Avery is the hall monitor at school. He never gets in trouble. And my babysitter is okay. She tells me some unbelievable stories about her family but she's cool."

"What's her name?" Mrs. Taren asked.

"Reema," I said.

"Reema," Mrs. Taren said. "Sounds like someone I've heard a lot about."

"For real?" I asked.

"For real," she said. "If you had to pick an animal that she reminds you of, what would you pick? A deer, maybe?"

"A white deer with stripes on down her nose!" I said. "You know Reema?"

"She's a very important person," Mrs. Taren said. "I would be so lucky if I knew her personally but I've only seen her once."

"I told my mom about your cannibal relative. She doesn't believe me," I said.

"There are a lot of things adults have trouble believing. And of course if you don't believe in something, then you can't see it."

"Really?" I asked, reaching for Charlie as he squeezed through the open front door to sit beside me. Mrs. Taren smiled and adjusted the clunky glass necklace around her neck with its sparkling medallion, a four leaf clover encased in resin. "You know, my great-grandfather was a boy when he and his fellow pioneers got stuck in the mountains during a snow storm. Most of the other pioneers didn't survive, but he was very, very lucky because when the adults started fighting his parents ordered him to run away into the woods. He was even younger than you. There was no way he could have survived on his own out there. He used to tell the story that a magical helper came along and found him in the woods." Mrs. Taren chuckled. "He grew up with his helper and even got married to a woman from their village. And when he got older and he decided to rejoin the society he left behind, he came out of the woods with his wife and that was that." She laughed. "But he always knew that his family would have to pay that generosity forward someday. If a child can survive something like that, a child can survive anything."

"You think so?" I asked.

"Absolutely! Reema's from your town. Maybe she can be your guide, just like my great-grandfather had his guide," Mrs. Taren said. "I bet you still have your artifact box."

"I do," I said. "I still use put things in it."

"If you ever wonder whether something is real, go through the box. Look at the things you found. Touch them. Smell them. Do they ever change or are they always the same?"

"Wilda!" Mom interrupted us. "I still can't find my keys. Do you remember where I might have put them?"

"Did you check the car?" I asked.

Mom froze in the doorway for a moment. "Right," she said. She stalked out of the house for the car, yanking the phone from its perch on my knees.

"Bye, Mrs. Taren! Thank you!" I yelled.

The driver's door was left open and the key was still in the ignition. "Reema's on her way," Mom told me. "I'm sorry, Mrs. Taren, but I have to go to work," she said into the phone. "Thanks for lecturing Wilda. I swear that child is going to drive me bonkers."

"You're welcome," Mrs. Taren said. Mom hung up the phone. She started up the engine and began to pull backwards out of the driveway. She suddenly stopped, turned off the ignition and opened the driver side window. "I forgot..."

"Your purse?" I asked. I went inside the cabin, walked back out with the black designer purse in my hand and carried it to the driver side window.

"Thank you, honey," Mom said. She leaned out the car door window to take the purse and then leaned back again to kiss me on the cheek. A floating breeze lofted a hint of beer between us. I leaned away.

"Oh, come on," Mom said. I reluctantly leaned forward and accepted the wet kiss on my cheek. Mom wiped it off for me with her thumb.

"See you later, Mom," I said. She peeled out of the gravel driveway and sped away down the street.

I thought about what Mrs. Taren said and rushed to my room. Charlie followed me as I pulled the artifact box down from the closet shelf and sat with it on my bed. I tossed the lid to the side and pulled the long white feather out of the box. I held it up in the afternoon light.

"What do you think, Charlie? Is it real?" I asked. I held the feather to my nose and took in a deep breath before holding it in front of Charlie's nose. He sniffed it several times, sat back on his hind legs and grinned with his tongue out. "It smells sweet, doesn't it?" I asked.

Charlie barked, contently. I set the feather back into the box and shook it around, listening as the rest of the contents rattled back and forth in the box. I picked out the amber rock that was in the box and clutched it in my hand, shaking my fist up and down to feel for its weight. Then I dropped it back into the box and pulled out the sketch book I had been drawing in. I flipped through the pages, looking at the deer, the cat and the four fairy regents. I shook my head. *If all of it was real, then what was really going on? What kind of favor did Mrs. Taren's family owe to Reema's family, and why did Reema need my help?* I wondered about that as I put the lid back onto the box.

"Well, I know I'm not dreaming right now," I said. I left the box on my bed, walked back to the front porch and sat down to wait for Reema. After a few minutes I saw Reema walking toward me from a distance.

"I didn't hear you drive up," I said. "Where's your car anyway? I don't think I've ever seen it."

"I don't need one," she said. She opened the front door for herself and hung her white parka on the coat rack.

Charlie bounded into the living room and wrapped himself around Reema's legs but I wasn't interested in cozying up to her just yet.

"You know, Reema, I have a few questions about this."

"Sure," she said as she sat down on the couch. She continued to pet Charlie as she looked at me. "It's only natural," she said.

I cornered her on the couch and stood directly in front of her with my arms folded. "Who are you?" I asked.

"What do you mean?" She laughed. "I'm Reema."

"Reema who?" I asked.

"Just Reema," she said matter-of-factly.

"You don't have a last name?" I asked.

She tilted her head and uttered a wispy name that sounded completely unintelligible. Her voice actually split into two tones when she said it. "I doubt you could pronounce it," she said. I tried to hide how amazed I was to hear how her last name sounded as she stared at me.

"We'll return to that," I said, not wanting to get side tracked. "What were you looking for in my room that time?"

"You're probably not ready to understand."

"Try me," I said.

Reema looked away and took a deep breath. "I guess now is as good a time as any to remind you."

"Now is the only time to tell me, or I'll have to ask you to leave," I said.

"You would do that after all we have been through together?" she asked incredulously. She stood up and wandered into my room again.

"Hey, where are you going? I doubt you're even Dana's friend. She says she's never even heard of you. For all I know, you could be a... a kidnapper, or a drug dealer, or... even a ghost."

Reema laughed. "A ghost? Do I look like one?"

"I don't know. Maybe," I said.

"Do you really think your old teacher would send you to a bad person?"

"So, it's true," I said.

Reema smiled. "Come, sit down. I'll tell you all about it." She sat down next to my artifact box and motioned for me to sit near her at the foot of my bed.

"I'll stand. Thank you," I said.

"Fine," Reema said with a shrug. She took a brief sigh and stared at the floor. "This cabin was given to my parents by my father's mom and dad as a wedding gift. I'm looking after it."

"Why do you still care? Someone sold it," I said, "to us."

"It's not that simple," Reema said. Her eyes darted up toward me, green and gleaming with an overwhelming light. I tried not to show my discomfort as I looked away. "Haven't you wondered what's in that shed out back?" she continued.

"I looked when we first moved here. There's just some old junk in there," I said.

"You really have no idea?" Reema asked.

"About what?" I asked.

Reema stood up, her tall frame looming powerfully over me. I fought the urge to shrink a little, uncrossing my arms and pushing my shoulders back.

"Funny," Reema said, smirking. "I'd have thought an inquisitive girl like you would have explored every inch of this place by now. I guess it was hidden well." She rested her open hands at her sides. "Wilda, your mind isn't playing tricks on you," she continued. "I am able to change my shape because, well... I'm not entirely human."

"What are you, then? A spirit? Or a ... a demon?" I asked, trying to ignore the crack in my voice.

"A demon? No, not me," Reema said. She reached for my hand and held it. Her fingers were as cold as the snow that clung to the ferns outside. Stunned, I nearly dropped it. "Sorry," Reema apologized. "I forget sometimes how cold my hands can be to a human." She let go of my hand and swept her curly hair behind her ear before getting up again. She walked back to the kitchen and sat down at the table. "You believe in magic, don't you?" she asked.

I nodded. "You mean like a magician at a birthday party?" I asked.

"Not that. Those are just tricks. I mean, the power of the ether," she said.

"I don't know," I said.

"Well," she said, "You will. My people are pretty good at using it. If you're wise you can train it, or gain its consent."

"Its consent?" I asked. "You mean energy is alive?"

"Everything is alive," Reema said, "For us it's awake. Things pretend to be asleep to you humans because if you knew all this you would become more destructive than you already are."

"Why do you assume that?" I asked.

"Well, you take rocks like uranium, and instead of making a cure for something you turn it into a bomb."

"Okay, you have a point but what makes your people any better?"

"Our memory is longer, maybe because our lives are longer," Reema said. She crossed her legs and sat back in the chair. "We're careful," she said. "There is spiritual power in the ancient armor of the fairy Sky King, transforming whoever wears it into a warrior with the power to bend time in the right hands. But in the wrong hands it can destroy … on an unimaginable scale. That's why my people must guard it."

"How did you end up guarding something like that? Did the government ask you?"

"Not the kind of government you answer to, Wilda," Reema chuckled. "I'm a Fay. So were my mother and her parents. We have our own government. I've been taking you to meet them, and I've struggled to get you to believe your memories of that."

212

"So, all that was real? You really are a fairy?" I asked. I sat down at the kitchen table and this time I really observed her.

"Some call us that, yes," Reema said. I noticed a twinkle in her long eyes when she said it.

"I thought that was all a dream," I said. Reema smiled with a steady gaze.

"I was afraid you might continue to tell yourself that so your world would keep making sense. I had my reservations at first. We tend to not invite older children because they are so hard to convince. I left so many clues for you."

"The blue laughing lily," I wondered out loud.

"I hoped you would remember why you had it," she said. "But these questions are great. I'll take them."

"Then what was that place?" I asked. "I want to know all about those four people we met."

"The regents?" Reema asked.

"Yeah," I said.

"They're allies. Our union stretches all over the world in solidarity with the royal Spring and Summer Courts," she said proudly. "Fays and elves come from Ireland, Benin and the Philippines, and places as far north as Norway and as far south as Australia. Each fairy tribe has guarded our armor for a thousand years, fighting with their magical weapons to keep it out of the wrong hands. My grandparents brought it here from their Dahomey fairy territory in Africa at the Spring Court's request."

"And you trust them with it?" I asked.

"Why wouldn't I? Spring Court fairies are golden ones," she said. "We believe in doing good, but the Unseelie Fay ... they just want to conquer the human world, so they can destroy the humans before the humans get the chance to accidentally destroy the world for everyone else."

"If the Unseelies are such bad fairies, you must be at war with them," I said.

Reema got up and stood in the front doorway, her hand on the doorknob. I stood behind her as though I was being drawn to the door, too. "We will always fight on behalf of a weaker species of beings. We have no interest in overpowering your people to take over your world," she said, turning the doorknob and allowing the door to swing open. "It is only right that the majority of humans be left alone to their fate. Besides, our weapons are for our protection, not to conquer anybody." Reema took my hands into her cold fingers as she led me onto the porch. "The armor chooses its rightful owner, and the last owner was my grandfather."

"So, your mother's parents are Fay. Is your dad a Fay, too?"

Reema breathed a long breath and shook her head as she led me down the stairs. The door seemed to shut on its own. "They say he sold us out," she said. "He was indeed a human. But I don't think all humans are bad. You seem all right."

"Why did he do that, if you don't mind me asking," I said as we walked around to the back side of the cabin.

"All I know is that he left when my mother was pregnant with me, after he stole the armor for some Unseelies. They couldn't use it so they destroyed it, and the ruins were scattered all over this property. I've been searching for the pieces and putting them back together. No one ever saw my father again, and I've never met him. I guess they paid him well."

"I've never met my dad either. I never even heard his voice," I said, "but Mom gives me the birthday cards he writes to me every year."

Reema stopped walking so I stopped, too. "You think your father really writes them?" she asked, her forehead wrinkling.

"Who else would write them?" I asked, confused.

Reema ignored the question and continued walking as the brush got thicker off the trodden path. "The Unseelies and their Fomorian monster allies launched a surprise attack on my grandfather, the king. He died in battle. They knew he wasn't armed." She stopped walking again and stared at the shed in the distance as she spoke solemnly. "I try not to hate my father," she said. She tried to put on a smile when she looked at me. "When my mother died from the grief, I had no one left, but the Regent Cētanā found me and rescued me. He's raised me since I was a baby."

"What about your grandmother?" I asked.

"She was transformed into the tree you met. It is a punishment for allowing my dad to get access to the armor. But the regents protected me. They made sure I was raised in the royal tower."

"I'm sorry that happened to you. That really stinks," I said.

"Why? The regents took good care of me," Reema said. "I had two close friends growing up whom I loved very much, a warrior boy from the desert who left the tower when we were young, and the pixie, Zyzzyva. She's like a sister to me."

"Do you have any brothers or sisters?" I asked.

"No," she said. "Where I come from, children are rare. Precious, even," she said, patting me on my head. Then she stared at me with a longing, wistful look in her eyes. I had never seen Mom look at me that way. I looked down at the ground and shrugged my shoulders.

"You're so lucky to have a best friend," I said.

Reema looked away with an earnestness in her eyes. "She can't help me with this," she gasped. "Since it was my father who lost the armor, I have to make it right. But your teacher did a good thing sending you here to help me."

"Why me?" I asked.

"I've been needing a little help for a while, someone who could see what I couldn't when I look at this place. Of course, it helps to be a musician. You see with your heart, through sound," she said. I peered back at her and noticed that her eyes had become tender. I looked away again as I fiddled with my fingernails as Reema continued to say, "You must have enchanted this forest when you found that last piece of armor while playing your piccolo here last summer. That missing piece drew me back to this place, to you."

"A piece of armor," I wondered. "You mean that amber rock? The one you went through my things for?"

"Come, grab your coat. I'll show you what I'm talking about."

I went to my room to put on my winter gear and met Reema at the backdoor.

"Are you sure you need all that?" Reema asked. "It's warming up now."

"I'm from California," I said.

Reema chuckled to herself and beckoned me to follow her through the trees to the shed. I never thought much of that small, dilapidated structure. Its wooden frame had long worn from its clapboard siding and its rusty tin roof swayed inward under the weight of the snow. "Is it in there?" I asked. "I'm surprised some drifter hasn't stolen it."

"Humans can't see what they don't believe in," Reema said as she pulled open the rotting shed door.

The shed was musty and damp inside. Drops of water dangled in the cobwebs that clung to the tin ceiling. I peered nervously into the corners of the shed for spiders. Reema stepped in front of me and pulled a hammer from among the clutter of fabric scraps, old metal boxes and sandpaper on the wooden shelf along the wall. That's when we both saw them: A stash of full and half empty liquor bottles, a couple of dozen of them at least, lined up along the back wall.

"It's a good thing you hadn't discovered this yet. There's a small fortune in here," Reema said.

"A fortune?" I asked. "I thought we were poor."

"Watch this," Reema said. She knelt down and banged the hammer on the dusty ground. The perimeter of a secret compartment bounced up, kicking up dust as it revealed itself. Reema wrapped her long fingers under the front edges of the compartment. She pulled up what appeared to be a secret door and revealed the stony pieces of an armored vest with winged edges jutting from its shoulders. The stone feathers were curled back like a once-living bird. "You are looking at my best efforts to put the armor back together. I've been scouring all of Mason County over the past ten years searching for that last missing piece, until you showed up with it."

"What is it?" I asked.

"The heart," Reema said. "And there is only one thing to do now."

"What?" I asked.

Reema stood up and turned to face me. "Put it on, of course," she said.

"Who, me?" I asked.

Reema ignored me, pulling the armor out of the dirt floor and placing it around over my head. "The last piece," she said. She pulled the amber stone out of her pocket.

"You had it all along?" I asked. "I thought you'd put that back."

"I did, and I just got it again from your room. Pay attention, Wilda."

Placing the amber stone in the center of the armor, she bowed down before me and pressed it with one palm on top of the other. She said a prayer of sorts in a language I couldn't understand that included sounds that I couldn't imagine a human being able to make.

Reema stood up and backed away to the door of the shed. Her face was intent, searching for something, when her eyes widened. "The heart glows!" she exclaimed. "Could you be..." but as Reema continued to watch, her eyes and shoulders lowered. "The light is out," she said, disappointed. "Rest assured, Wilda. This armor does not belong to you."

Reema walked back to me and slid the heavy stone vest from my shoulders. She held it out and thought for a moment before she placed it around herself. She closed her eyes and held her breath for a moment before looking down at the amber stone heart. It was as dull as ever.

"I didn't think so," she said. "I don't even want to be queen." She smiled at me as she removed the armor and laid it back into the hollowed floor.

"But your grandmother?" I asked. "Maybe she can wear it."

"That is impossible. She is a Fay but not of the royal line," Reema said.

"Now what?" I asked.

"The search for the rightful owner of the armor continues," she said. "Keep this on you at all times." She held up the amber stone heart piece of the armor. She grabbed a piece of cloth from the shelf and tore a piece from it. Then she threaded the cloth through a slot in the top of the stone and wrapped it around my wrist like a bracelet. "Do everything with it. Don't let it out of your sight."

"If it's so important, why are you giving it to me?" I asked.

"It wants to belong to you. That's why it allowed you to find it. Maybe because you're a human. Fomorians dare not enter the human realm."

"That's a good thing. It would be a terrible thing if monsters went prowling about," I said.

As soon as I said that Charlie started barking from the cabin. I felt my heart skip a beat as I clutched the stone against my wrist. "We've been watched," Reema said. She hurriedly closed the trap door of the floor and smoothed dirt over it. As we emerged from the shed, a branch fell from a tree nearby. Reema turned first to the direction of the noise.

"That cat!" I yelled.

Reema took a step back before tossing her hand behind us. She had scattered shiny dust from her hand along the threshold of the shed. "Go to your room, Wilda," she said.

Before I could even begin to run to the back door of the cabin a woman suddenly appeared in my path, looking down at me. It was the white-haired woman I'd seen before, the one who transformed from the cat to what I imagined was the kind of evil Unseelie fay Reema warned me about.

"Leave the girl alone," Reema yelled.

The Unseelie paid no attention to Reema's demand. "Well, well," she said, smiling at me, "what have you been up to?"

"Don't answer," Reema warned me. The Unseelie's gaze bolted to Reema with a glare. I took the opportunity to run past the Unseelie into the cabin as she stood there, laughing at me. Once I was inside the cabin I hurriedly locked the deadbolt on the kitchen back door. I peered through the closed shutters of the kitchen window as Charlie paced in circles around the floor. I could see the Unseelie walk toward Reema while Reema stood her ground with her arms out to her sides and her palms open. "You have a lot of nerve coming around here," I heard Reema say.

"What's in the shed?" the Unseelie asked.

"Don't you have better things to do than to scare children?" Reema yelled.

"Children are only scared when they have something to hide," the Unseelie said nonchalantly. "I should know. I've been watching you, Princess."

"I never thought I would see you again. You died in battle even before Grandfather died, but here you are," Reema said.

"It turns out your king isn't the only one who could be brought back. They say cats have nine lives. So, what have you got, there?"

"These things do not concern you," Reema said.

"What things?" the Unseelie asked. "Let me in on your project. I can help you."

"Nothing has changed, Gwaelwyn. I still don't trust you," Reema said.

"I am not interested in fighting you," the Unseelie said.

"But you are a huntress from the Winter Court. A hunter's job is to kill," Reema said. I was shocked when I heard her say that.

"I'm not inflexible. I might stop if we can get something that we can use. So, let's negotiate," the Unseelie said.

"I told you before. The answer is no," Reema said, firmly.

"Fine," the Unseelie said flippantly as she took a few steps to her side. Then quickly she turned and raised her arms into the air, pulling a long staff from her back and slicing it through the air. It produced thick black smoke that poured out of the side of the staff and curved in midair toward Reema, like the shadow of a cobra. Before it could reach her, Reema had already positioned her palms as a shield. She pushed against the black shadow with sparks emanating from her fingerless gloves, forcing the black cobra to curve back against the Unseelie. The old fairy stumbled backward and the shadow sank back into her staff.

"Is that all you got?" Reema scoffed.

The Unseelie straightened her shoulders and tossed back her head. "It would be easier to work together," she said. Then pulling her staff back across her body, she slid her left palm beneath it and let out what appeared to be another snake, spinning like an orb of red light. Unfazed, Reema chopped it in half with her hand. The top of the orb shot up to one of the trees, cutting a large branch that fell directly in front of the Unseelie.

The Unseelie backed up again as she huffed and folded her arms. "Why don't you join us? Be a leader and bring your people out of their stubbornness!" she shouted.

Reema shook her head. "We've got nothing in common," Reema said.

"Your king is dead. All your hope is lost," the Unseelie said.

"You're lying," Reema answered. "We can both sense that the king has been reborn and he is here, in this place, in this county! You wouldn't be here in these woods if you didn't believe that!"

"Is it the girl?" the old Unseelie fairy asked.

"Don't you trust your magic? You've read the same signs I've read," Reema said.

"I will find him before you do. He will join me and when he does your people will beg for our mercy. But they will not receive it. Unless you join us the fires of our vengeance will consume you, too!" the Unseelie said. Just as quickly as she appeared, she morphed back into a black cat and ran off into the woods.

Reema noticed me peering through the shutters over the kitchen window. She walked calmly to the back door. I hurriedly let her in and locked the door.

Reema leaned her back against it. "I appreciate your vigilance but locks won't stop her," she said as she walked over to the couch and sat down. "She is one of the Unseelies' most notorious assassins, ruthless and corrupt. She has been murdering the Winter Court's enemies for decades."

"So, we're not safe here?" I asked.

Reema looked at me with a pitiful look in her eyes. "You're not safe from her, anywhere. She's probably going pretend to be your friend. Whatever you do, be careful who you trust, ok?"

"No way am I trusting a dark fairy from the woods," I said.

"She can change her shape, so beware," Reema said.

I nodded in agreement.

"We'll figure this thing out," Reema said, "but if you dare to go back into the deep woods, make sure you're with me."

"Of course," I said.

Reema stood up and clasped her palms together above her head. Then lowering them to her sides, she spread the glittering dust from her fingers across the entrance to the hallway. "Just in case," she said. "If you ever don't feel safe and I'm not here, go to your room. Use your piccolo to signal for help." Then she picked up the remote control from the living room table and turned on the TV. "How about some pizza?" she asked.

"How can you eat at a time like this?" I asked.

Reema sighed. "You get used to it," she said.

She got up and went into the kitchen, leaving me to the mindless show on the TV and my worried thoughts. I watched her rummage through the cabinets, pulling out half a loaf of bread and a can of tomato soup. She opened the refrigerator, glanced over the bottles of ale on the first shelf and stared into the nearly empty second and third shelves for a moment.

"We don't really have anything, just milk, cereal and maybe something to make a salad or a sandwich," I said. "Mom doesn't cook so much, and I don't know how."

"That's all right," Reema said. "I'm sure I can make a hot meal out of something in here."

I turned around and tried to refocus my thoughts on the remote control, flipping aimlessly through the few channels our satellite by the road could pick up. I couldn't really pay attention to anything. I kept thinking about that Unseelie fairy who could turn herself into a black cat, who'd taken an interest in me. I tried to wrap my head around the existence of monsters and powerful Spring Court fairies, including the one who was now in my kitchen, and Mom not really being around to tell. Who would believe me, anyway? Were the kids at school normal kids? Was I?

"You're a good musician, Wilda," Reema said from the kitchen as she chopped tomatoes on the counter. "I hope you continue to play your flute as you get older."

"You think so?" I asked. "I want to get good, like really, really good. Like Ian Anderson from Jethro Tull. If I get famous everything will get better."

"You know, even the greatest people aren't perfect," Reema asked. "It just happens that you *are* pretty great at the flute. That's nice, but you're great whenever you do your best."

"I just wish Mom would notice how much better I've gotten," I said.

"I'm sure she does. She might not show it because she has a lot on her mind," Reema answered. "New home, new job. This is all very new to you too, I'm sure," Reema said. When I turned to look at her she was stirring something in our only mixing bowl with a wooden spoon. The sight of her doing something normal was reassuring. "But I suppose your destiny has brought you here, and I am supposed to protect you. Of course, I will... with my life if necessary. But I doubt it would ever come to that. Trust me, we'll be ok," Reema said. "Do you trust me?"

Charlie wandered to the edge of the kitchen, sat up straight and let out an enthusiastic bark. "I know you do, Charlie," Reema said.

"I guess," I answered.

Reema nodded to herself.

"So, you're like my fairy grandmother," I said.

"You mean to say 'godmother,' right?" Reema asked incredulously.

"Yeah, that," I said.

Reema shook her head. "I'm not *that* old," she said. I laughed. Then, Reema laughed too. "I'm more like your fairy god-sister," she said. I laid my head on the couch and exhaled a little stress.

"Dinner's ready. Go ahead and wash up," Reema said.

I went to the bathroom to wash my hands. When I returned Reema was setting a plate with a slice of cheese pizza on the table. I was surprised by her effort as I walked to the kitchen table. "Wait," I said. "How did you do that with what we had in our kitchen?"

Reema shrugged. "Magic?" she suggested.

"Hmm," I wondered out loud. I sat down at the table, smelling the slice of pizza apprehensively. Reema looked away, trying not to be offended by my skepticism regarding her cooking skills. "Would you like a knife and fork?" she asked.

"No, thank you," I said. I held the slice in both hands, turning it to get a good look at it, even checking the bottom for burnt crust. "Not bad," I said. "I'm impressed."

"Wait 'til you taste it," she said as she sat down to a slice of her own Margherita pizza.

"When it cools down a little I will," I said.

"Oh, is it too hot?" Reema asked. She blinked nonchalantly and sat for a moment. "Okay, now try it," she said.

"Here goes," I said. I took a bite of the slice of cheese pizza. The savory red sauce blended perfectly with the fresh melted mozzarella cheese over a hardy wheat crust. The basil smelled sweet as the vapor from the warm crust wafted up to my nose. It was the best slice of pizza I'd had since leaving San Francisco.

"What do you think?" she asked, anxiously.

Someone who would take the time to cook for me like this must at least care whether I was happy, I thought. "All right, Reema," I said, "I trust you."

Reema smiled as she bit into her slice of pizza. In spite of wanting to eat more I set the warm crust down on my plate for a moment. I stared down at my plate, wondering whether I should tell her my secret.

"What's wrong?" she asked.

"Reema," I said, wondering how to say it. Reema stopped eating and stared, concerned. I didn't know how to say it respectfully. "Mom drinks too much," I blurted out. I tapped my foot on the floor to keep the tears from spilling out of my eyes.

To my surprise, Reema answered, "I know."

When she said that my tears rushed down my cheeks as though a flood had been let loose. I buried my face in my wet hands. "How do you know?" I asked.

"The bottles in the shed," Reema said.

I guess saying the secret out loud made it more real because I found myself sobbing at the table. "She always drinks, when she's home, when she drives... all the time," I said.

Reema bent down next to me and hugged me. She held me there and let me cry all over her cool clothes. "You're not alone. I got your back," she said. "So, don't worry about anything. Just call on me, okay?" Reema kissed me on the top of my red hair and rubbed my shoulder.

"Okay," I said. I started to smile.

"Good," she said.

I stared down at the pizza on my plate. "I'm hungry," I said. I guess my rumbling stomach returned my thoughts to food.

"Go ahead," Reema said. We both laughed and Reema sat back down to eat her pizza. Then I was able to relax because I didn't have to carry the secret on my own.

Chapter 7

As soon as I woke up the next morning I
immediately reached for my wrist. It was a little sore
from me sleeping on that rock in the makeshift
bracelet all night. It had to be all real. There was no
way to deny it now, not with proof of the ancient fairy
armor right there, tied to my own body. I thought
about that scary fairy as I rubbed the stone against my
wrist. *Reema would protect me from her.* "What did I
get myself into?" I whispered into the cool air.

I stared at the funny shapes in the ceiling for a moment. The morning light sifted into my room through the spaces in the shutters. When Mom's old CD alarm clock went off in her room, I remembered it was a school day and I'd have to see those same annoying kids again. Mom's alarm clock started playing the last track on an album by Lily Allen, one of Mom's old favorites. After the song finished, I rolled out of bed and let Charlie out of my room. He ran into the living room while I walked down the hall to the bathroom to wash my face and brush my teeth.

Mom's door was open so when I finished up in the bathroom I went to her room. Her bed seemed to be already made. I assumed she was already in the kitchen preparing toast or cereal so I opened the lid of her alarm clock and popped the Lily Allen CD out. Then I helped myself to the CD rack in Mom's room, next to her dresser, tucking the disc back into its case and sticking it between Green Day and Still Corners, next to Howling Wolf. I was hopeful after hanging out with Reema the night before so I skipped past my classical favorites, popped in a different CD and set it to play "How I Roll" by Savant, a song about hanging out with friends. I barely had any friends here except maybe two, and I guessed a couple was better than none.

I wandered into the kitchen to see what was for breakfast. From the corner of my eye I noticed my mom spread out in the living room chair with the TV displaying a morning show. She looked like she must have been in that same position since coming home late last night. Her legs were twisted in opposing directions, straining the seams of her tight black miniskirt. Her high heeled boots were still on her feet and her purse strap was wrapped around her elbow.

I walked over to her, not bothering to tiptoe since music was blaring anyway. I tapped her on her cheek. "Mom?" I called. There was no response. I panicked, backing away with my hands on my head.

After a few seconds, to my relief, I heard Mom hiccup. I called her again. "Mom, wake up!" She turned a little and let out a rum-filled belch but she didn't open her eyes. I nudged her sequined white tank top against her shoulder and watched her body rock back and forth like a limp doll. Then she squirmed, curled her arms into her chest and turned to her other side.

"Mom!" I yelled.

She squirmed again but didn't wake up.

"Get up! I have to go to school!" I demanded. Mom started to lift her hand as if she was trying to swat me away, but she could only muster enough energy to slap my face with the back of her fingers before her hand fell flat upon her bare leg.

I shook my head, went to the hall linen closet, pulled out a blanket and came back to the living room. I laid the blanket across my mom and looked at her. I was so mad at her. I didn't even know why I still got her a blanket. Looking at her curled up in the chair

246

made me feel like she didn't deserve it. And here I was, helping her let me down. I guess I felt more disappointed in myself than anyone else. I struggled to refocus on what I should do but my face was hot and my head thick with anger, sadness and worry.

I searched through Mom's purse and found her phone. I'd seen her put the phone next to her face to open it so I did it too, facing the phone toward her face so that it would recognize her and unlock. It worked. I searched the directory on her phone and the number for Dana was the first one I saw so I called it. The phone only rang twice before Dana picked up.

"Mrs. Robertson?" she said on the other end.

"Hi, Dana. My mom's not feeling well. I guess I need a ride, or I could skip today."

"Don't worry," Dana said. "I'll swing by with Avery to pick up you."

"Thanks, Dana," I said. Then I stuffed the phone back into Mom's purse and zipped it back up. She didn't notice at all. When I turned around and leaned against the counter I saw Charlie sitting in the hallway, staring at me.

I let Charlie out the back door for a few minutes while I poured some dry dog food into his bowl and set it by the kitchen door. When I let him back in he ran right past his food and into the living room. Charlie sat by Mom and licked her hand. She still didn't budge.

"Forget it, Charlie," I said. "It's just like the time we couldn't drive to Grandma's for Christmas because Mom was too tired." Charlie ignored me and leaned his body against her leg.

While waiting for Dana I decided to go back to the kitchen to see if there was anything Mom usually did that I would need to do now. Dirty dishes from the bar where Mom worked filled the kitchen sink, covering up the decomposing onions in the garbage disposal. I ran some cold water in the sink and turned on the garbage disposal for a few seconds, moving away as the rancid water splashed off the dishes and out of the dirty sink. I found the dish liquid on the counter and squirted it over the dishes. I looked around the sink but I couldn't find any gloves so I smeared the liquid soap on the plates with my bare hands and rinsed them in the warm water. It was a good thing I'd never really been squeamish. Reaching around to one of the kitchen drawers, I found a dish towel to dry the plates and glasses in the sink before shoving them in the empty spaces in the cabinets.

I looked in the refrigerator, found an apple and one last stick of string cheese and stuffed them in my violet backpack. "Take care of Mom, Charlie. If she does anything dangerous, run up the road and bark for help," I said. He perked up his head for a moment before lying back down near Mom's foot. I think he understood but he seemed disappointed, too. Then I got dressed in a plain long sleeve gray shirt and jeans, put on my puffy coat, threw on a headband and my backpack and said bye to Charlie as I locked the front door behind me with my key. I leaned against one of the side pillars of the front porch as I wondered how Dana would be able to pull into our driveway. Our car was parked diagonally and partially in the weeds along the side of the driveway.

I watched as Dana maneuvered her car around ours to arrive at the front of our cabin, just able to avoid the snow and weeds along the other side of the driveway. Avery was sitting in the passenger seat. I slowly walked down the steps and across the snowy gravel driveway, feeling a little embarrassed about the situation, let alone the fact that Dana's car was newer than my Mom's and she was just a teenager. I opened the back door of her shiny blue Porsche SUV and climbed onto a blanket with the faces of a Korean boy band emblazoned on it. The whole car smelled like cotton candy incense.

"Hey, Dana. Hey, Avery," I said.

"Hey," Avery said back.

"Thanks for picking me up," I said.

"No problem," Dana said. She pulled out of the driveway and started up the street.

"I'm glad you called instead of deciding to walk this time. You know how careless drivers can get out here," Avery said.

"Yeah, just call," Dana said. The pair of fuzzy pink dice hanging from the rearview mirror led me to notice her pitying blue eyes staring back at me. "Is everything all right?" she asked.

"Sure," I chirped. "Mom's fine. Let's go."

"They treat the highway like an Autobahn," Avery continued, oblivious to the issue affecting my mother that I was trying hard to hide.

"An auto what?" I asked.

"Autobahn. It's like a road where everybody drives like it's NASCAR."

"Oh," I said.

"It's really called Bundesautobahn," he said.

"Wait. What?" I asked.

"Is he nerding you out yet?" Dana asked.

"It comes from a German term meaning federal auto track, but people say Autobahn for short because..."

"Yeah, yeah. Thanks, Avery," Dana said shaking her head.

"I'm just explaining it to her," he said.

"Why is it called something in German?" I asked.

"Because..." Avery started to say.

"Because he's a know-it-all." Dana cut him off.

"No," Avery insisted, "Because that's the name of the federally controlled freeway system in Germany where drivers often exceed over 130 kilometers per hour in some areas. That's 81 miles per hour in imperial units."

"Imperial units?" I asked.

"See, Wilda? This is what I deal with every other morning," Dana said.

"Well, you're paid to put up with it so shut up and drive," Avery said.

"Sorry. I didn't mean to throw off your game," Dana said. "What impresses a lady more than your infinite knowledge of the metric system?" She tossed her head back with laughter.

"Just try to graduate, Dana," Avery said.

"I get it," I said. "Cool."

"That was cool?" Dana asked, laughing.

"Stop, seriously," Avery chided her.

I shook my head and tried to play it cool, smoothing my bangs under my yellow knit cap.

"Hey Wilda," Avery called.

"Yeah," I answered.

"I've been wanting to ask you this. What did you do to your piccolo the other day?"

"Oh," I said. "Are people still talking about that?"

"Well, yeah," he said. "Did you put some kind of chemical on it? Or did you heat it up on a furnace before you stuck it in your pocket?"

"Um," I said. I wasn't sure what to say. I hadn't done anything to it. Avery continued. "And how did you know those kids were going to try to take it? Did you dare them to?"

"No," I protested.

"So, you just happen to have a burning instrument in your coat at all times?"

"That doesn't make sense. Wouldn't I burn myself?"

"That's what I was wondering. Unless you had some kind of special casing for it to protect yourself."

"Well, you saw them just grab it and start messing with it. They could have been acting for all I know. Maybe they were trying to get me suspended or something."

"But I saw their hands. They were beet red," Avery protested.

"Maybe they used red beets from the salad bar in the cafeteria," I said.

"Or maybe it was magic," Dana said with a smile. Her eyes grew big for effect as she looked at me through the rearview mirror. "Do you practice the occult, Wilda? Are you a good witch or a bad one?" she asked.

"Neither," I said.

"Maybe you should be. It sounds like you might be a natural. Imagine making a piccolo heat up merely from the strength of your anger, your desire to get revenge." Dana chuckled to herself. "We should play around with that some time."

"Mom and Dad say witchcraft is against the faith," Avery said.

"Your parents are against everything," Dana replied. "No dancing."

"No *inappropriate* dancing," Avery said.

"No *smoking*," Dana whined.

"Smoking's bad for you," Avery said.

"No herb."

"What do you mean by herb?" Avery asked.

Dana gasped. "You know what that bendis auto bundo thingy is but you don't know what herb stands for?"

"You mean marijuana?" Avery asked.

"Duh!" Dana answered. "And no drinking."

"Underage drinking is against the law," Avery said.

"As far as I'm concerned," I interrupted, "adults shouldn't be allowed to drink either. I hate it."

"That's a strong opinion. Why do you hate alcohol so much?" Dana asked.

"I don't want to talk about it," I said staring out the window. I could tell Dana was looking at me again from the rearview mirror. I hoped she wouldn't press me on it.

"Fine," she finally said. She pulled the car into the middle school parking lot and stopped in a space near the school entrance. Avery grabbed his backpack, opened his car door and jumped out. He started to open my door for me when Dana stopped him. "Why don't you go ahead? I have something I need to work out with Wilda.

"Ok," Avery said. "See you later."

I took a deep breath and clutched my backpack against my chest, not sure if she was about to ask for money for the ride. I didn't have any on me. "You know, I can pick both of you up after school today. Your houses are both on the way to mine."

"Ok," I said, still looking out the window.

"So, should I wait for you after school?"

"Sure," I said.

"Ok," Dana said.

"Thanks, Dana," I said, looking at her blue eyes in the rearview mirror.

"You're welcome," she said. I slung my backpack over my shoulder and flung open the car door and got out as Dana cleared her throat. "Wait," she said. "Is everything ok with you and your mom?" she asked.

"Yeah. Why?" I asked.

"Well, it's just that you seemed a little different this morning. Like you were upset about something… Maybe something that we said."

"Just drop it," I said. "It's ok."

"Are you sure?" Dana asked. When she looked at me the black pupils of her eyes were sharp and probing. It felt as though I was staring into a blue abyss. "I don't want to see you sad," she said. I twisted my mouth as I felt a tear roll down my cheek. I don't know why I suddenly found myself crying as the school bell sounded in the distance, seemingly on cue. It was something about the way she said that word, 'sad.'

"Don't cry," she said. "You can talk to me. We have an understanding, you and I. Remember?" she said, pointing at my chest and then back at herself.

But the only thing I could bring myself to say was, "I'm going to need a tardy slip. I'm late."

"Lucky me. I don't have class until third period," Dana joked. I tried to muster a smile. "We'll talk later," she said. She peeled my hand off of my backpack and held it with her cold fingers for a moment. "I'm here for you," she said. "And I mean that," she added. I nodded. Dana smiled and reached for my other hand, shaking them together. As she looked down at my hands, preparing to let them go, her head tilted to the side. Her eyes narrowed. She rubbed her thumb across the amber stone tied to my wrist. "What's this?" she asked. "It doesn't look like a charm."

"It's not," I said. "Just something we put together."

"Who helped you put it together?" Dana asked.

"Reema," I said.

Dana's eyes perked up as she looked me in my eyes. "Why are you wearing this?" Dana asked.

"I don't know. Safe keeping, I guess," I said.

"Safe keeping? From what?" Dana asked. "What is it?"

I squirmed unintentionally. I pulled my hands away from Dana, wiped my tears and clutched my backpack over my shoulders. I was afraid I had said too much, looking toward the school building for a way to escape Dana's questions. I wasn't sure how much of Reema's story I could tell. Dana seemed to notice my apprehension and mercifully changed the subject. "It's ok," she said. "Go ahead. I'll see you later."

I nervously walked toward the building. Turning back, I waved at Dana. She was still sitting there with her driver's door open, and she smiled and waved back. Dana watched me enter the school as she started the car engine.

Once I was inside the main building I went straight to the attendance office. To my surprise it was packed with kids and adults. I stopped in the doorway. "Let's get our party started, now!" I heard a voice say. "I skipped breakfast for this!" It was Monica and Veronica. I almost didn't recognize them in their wild birthday makeover looks. Monica's hair was parted in sideways ponytail hair extensions coated in silver and pink hair wax. She wore glittery silver eye shadow and a glittery pink t-shirt with the word, "Womanish" in cursive letters. Veronica wore her hair down, streaked with orange hair wax and coated in gold glitter that matched her oversized hoop earrings. Long cat eye liner was drawn on her eyes, and her baseball t-shirt read "Better than you." The twins wore matching skater skirts that barely reached the middle of their thighs, knee length lace socks, and I assumed based on their additional height, platform shoes.

"It's our day, April 5th," Monica said. "We're getting it started right!"

"So, who's ready to party?" Veronica said.

"All day," Monica replied.

A crowd of students were gathered around them to sing happy birthday while the twins stood at the counter staring at two separate pink birthday cakes. One of the cakes had milk chocolate shavings and the other had white chocolate shavings, and both cakes had sparkling lit candles in the shapes of the number twelve. As Veronica looked around the room at her mother and her admirers, her eyes landed on me standing in the doorway. "Hey Mom, look! There's that loser I told you about," Veronica said. "Is there a way to make her go away?" she whined.

"We only have a few seconds to have lit candles before the secretaries make us put them out," her mother said. "Be nice and make a wish."

"And don't blow the frosting off," Monica told her.

The twins took a deep breath at the same time, and Monica blew out her candle easily. But as their friends were applauding Monica, Veronica's head suddenly jerked back as though her orange hair had gotten pulled behind her. The white-haired Unseelie I had seen dueling against Reema earlier suddenly appeared, standing behind Veronica. A wad of Veronica's hair was in her fist. I looked around to see if anyone else could see her but everyone's attention was on Veronica. It seemed like I was the only one who was witnessing this uninvited guest behind Veronica.

The Unseelie shot a mischievous smile at me and motioned with her finger over her lips to be quiet. Then her fistful of Veronica's hair jerked forward as the woman mysteriously disappeared. It appeared as though an invisible hand still clutched Veronica's head by her hair. Suddenly Veronica's whole face smashed into the top of her birthday cake with such force that her forehead drove the candle through the cake to the bottom of the plate. When Veronica lifted her head, her face was full of pink and white frosting with bits of yellow cake clinging to her hoop earrings.

Monica looked on in horror. "Oh my God, Vi, what did you do?" she asked.

"I don't know what happened!" Veronica yelled. "Did you push me?"

"No! Why would I do something like that?" Monica asked.

"Somebody obviously pushed my head into the cake, Moni!" Veronica cried. "Why would you do this to me?"

"I didn't do anything to you!" Monica shouted.

"Nobody did anything to you," the main office secretary said. "We all saw what happened. You head butted the cake on your own."

"Veronica, why on earth would you pull this stunt? It took me two days to make that cake," Veronica's mother said.

267

268

A familiar female voice piped up from the astonished crowd. "Probably for attention," it said. Veronica scanned the crowd for the person who said that. I casually took a step back from the doorway to make sure that no one could blame me for it.

Even I searched for the student who was bold enough to make such a statement. Then, out of the corner of my eyes I caught a glimpse of the movement of a black tail. My eyes settled on the black cat again, this time slinking across the windowsill. The cat jumped out of the window before anyone else noticed it.

"She thinks she's *batter* than you!" one of the girls yelled, to snickers.

"Were you trying to kiss it, Vi?" Another girl laughed.

"Yeah," a boy said, "she's a cake banger!"

The kids around them roared with laughter. I slinked away from the doorway as tried to stop the corners of my lips from growing into a smirk. Someone powerful wanted to teach the ringleader a lesson. I had to admit it felt kind of good. I was a little grateful for the Unseelie's mischief even though I did feel sorry enough for Veronica to not laugh. Meanwhile Veronica was bent over in shock.

"Honey, are you sick?" Veronica's mother fussed. I turned to go as Monica and her mother scrambled to find an extra chair so Veronica could sit down.

"I don't know what happened," I heard Veronica sob as I walked down the hall to Mr. Gumble's class.

"You're tardy," Mr. Gumble grumbled as I walked in. He was standing near the front of the class while all the students had their laptops open on their desks.

"There was a commotion in the attendance office. Sorry I couldn't get a tardy slip," I said as I sat down in my seat at the front of the class and pulled my laptop out of my backpack. Mr. Gumble sighed and continued with his media presentation about Sargon the Great as if nothing had happened. I was grateful that Mr. Gumble chose not to stop everything and give me a detention slip. He was a low drama teacher. Instead of telling the principal right after the problem with the bullies in the cafeteria he had my counselor go through my file and call one of my old teachers. I guess he wanted to find out whether I was the type of kid who would do that before jumping to conclusions. Of all the teachers at this school, Mr. Gumble was the nicest one. He was the kind of guy I wished my mom would talk to.

Mr. Gumble had been lecturing for a few minutes when everybody's head turned to see who was at the door. It was Veronica, her face completely clean of makeup, wearing a plain white gym shirt. Her

271

sister, Monica, walked behind her. They slowly entered the room and sat at their desks. Veronica held her head down, careful not to look at anyone.

As Mr. Gumble began again with his lecture I felt a piece of paper shoved against my back. I turned my head. The student behind me handed me a folded piece of paper in his left hand. I dropped my hand to take the note, unfolded it in my lap, and read what it said. "Sorry I called you weird," was written in rounded letters. I turned to see who sent me the note. The boy behind me shook his head no. That's when I saw Veronica watching me over his shoulder. She nodded her head at me. I didn't know how to feel about it so I gave her an acknowledging nod of my chin, stuffing the note in my pocket. Was she serious?

"Wilda," Mr. Gumble called. His stern voice jolted my attention back to the lecture. "What protective animals were depicted outside of Sargon the Second's palace in ancient Assyria?"

"Uh, a lion?" I asked, scrolling through the screen on my laptop.

"Close," Mr. Gumble said. "Everybody, ask somebody," he said. "Turn and talk."

As I turned around to the boy behind me, Veronica leaned forward and said, "They were like bulls or lions with human heads and... wings, I think?"

"I think I remember seeing something like that online. Thanks," I said. Veronica nodded again.

When the chatter died down, we turned to face the teacher. "Did you get a possible answer?" Mr. Gumble asked me.

"They were like winged bulls with people's heads," I said.

"That's it," Mr. Gumble said. "Can you imagine seeing something like that outside of our school? What impression do you think that would make?"

"It would tell our rivals to back up 'cause we got the best team. Ha, ha," Josh said from the back of the class. He slapped hands with one of the boys sitting next to him.

"I think you're right. That's probably the impression it made on any visitors coming to ancient Assyria," Mr. Gumble said.

"Say, Mr. G," Josh asked, "why did they go around making statues of human heads on animal bodies to make that point? Seems kinda weird."

"Good question," Mr. Gumble said. "It seems fanciful to us but it's what they believed in. It was part of their faith."

"Yeah, but..." Monica asked, "Was it like one day somebody said, 'Let's all believe in a part human, part lion that flies around'? I mean, there's no such thing as a... what would you call it? A liger?"

"It's called a lamassu," Mr. Gumble said. "And it is a bit fanciful. But when you think about it, it's really not much different from what some people believe in today." Mr. Gumble walked in front of his desk and sat on its edge. "Ancient people carved their ideals into stone using symbols to convey liberty and strength. They dreamed of having wings to escape the corruption of daily life, the body of a bull to stand up against threats to the community, the head of a wise man to make good decisions and such. So, they put all these things in their statues. These are ideals we all value today, but instead of putting wings on statues of animals we put fins on cars. Instead of building stone bulls we build tanks. You get the idea," he said.

"So, they didn't actually have half men, half animals walking around?" Josh asked. The class erupted in laughter, but Mr. Gumble answered seriously. "You mean chimeras? What if I told you that when a society truly believes in something, that thing is real to them?"

Right at that moment the bell rang. "Please read the rest of chapter seven tonight. The new section starts tomorrow," Mr. Gumble said as students streamed out of class, still laughing with Josh. As I sat stuffing my laptop back into my backpack Veronica slowly crept up to me. I looked up to see her dangling over me with her backpack over her shoulder. She sat down in the seat behind me. Her face was pensive. She fiddled with the loose strands of hair on her pale forehead, fresh from having her makeup scrubbed off after the cake incident. I sat up cautiously, not quite sure if she was about to go through what I suspected she came to do.

"Wilda, I wanted to say this to you," Veronica said. Her sister Monica lingered in the doorway for a moment before deciding to sit back down. Veronica rubbed her forehead, saying, "I think I know now what it feels like, you know, to be..." She looked down at her gym shirt.

"To be what?" I asked. I wanted her to say it all to me.

"Well," she said, "like when people accuse of you being something that you're not."

"You mean weird?" I asked.

Veronica sighed and looked away. "Yeah, weird," she said. "I'm sorry. I hope we can be friends and if not friends then just... not enemies."

"Well, Veronica," I sighed, "I appreciate that because I was a little rude to you when we met. I guess I was scared."

"Scared of what?" Veronica asked, confused.

"Scared you wouldn't like me. You and your sister... you have lots of friends. You have clothes. You have makeup. You have each other. You have everything! I guess in a way I guaranteed you wouldn't like me so I wouldn't be disappointed."

"But you didn't even give us a chance," Monica said.

"Yeah, that's actually not okay," Veronica added.

I shrugged. "I don't always make friends, but I'm not your enemy," I said. "And if you really want to change things you can tell your friends to be nice to me. Or not even nice, just decent," I said.

"Sure, done," Veronica said.

"So, it's a deal?" I asked.

"It's a deal," she said. She stood up and stuck out her hand. I stood up too and we shook hands. "We're gonna get lunch," she said as she slung her backpack over her shoulder. "You can come if you want."

"Actually, I'm heading to the band room, but thanks," I said.

"All right. Well, see you around," Veronica said. As I watched them walk out of the classroom, I breathed a sigh of relief that the twins' petty war with me seemed to be over. Mr. Gumble nodded approvingly at me as I left the room.

I came out of the main building and walked to the parking lot after school. Dana was already there, standing by the open driver side door of her SUV and talking on her cell phone. When she saw me, she finished up her call and stuffed her phone into her front jeans pocket. Avery was already in the car, pulling off his hall monitor sash. Dana smiled at me as I hopped into the back seat. She got in and closed the door. "I was just letting your mom know that I'll be bringing you home," Dana said.

"Cool. Thanks," I said.

"So, what's going on?" she asked as she pulled out of the parking lot.

"Oh, same old stuff," I said.

"A girl got her head smashed in her birthday cake!" Avery said. "Nobody knows who did it but a lot of kids think she did it herself for attention."

"Who was it?" Dana asked.

"You know the twins? Monica and Veronica?"

"The popular ones?" Dana asked.

"Yeah. It was Veronica," Avery exclaimed.

"No way!" Dana said. "Wilda, did you see it?" she asked.

"Yeah, I saw it," I said.

"What happened?" Dana asked with wide eyes staring at me through the rearview mirror. I just shrugged.

"It was weird. I don't really know," I said, looking out the window.

"They say she reared back and head-banged it! Seriously," Avery said.

"That sounds hilarious," Dana said. "I hear she's a bully. Serves her right, don't you think?"

"I don't know," I said. "I kind of feel sorry for her."

"Sorry for her? Why?" Dana asked.

"Well, she did apologize to me for not really being nice."

"That's all it takes for you?" Dana asked.

"Well, yeah," I said.

"But what about her sister? Isn't she a brat, too?" Dana asked, angrily.

"What about Monica?" I asked.

"Did she apologize?"

"No," I said.

"Then it's not over yet," Dana said. "She should learn her lesson, too. You're too nice, Wilda." She looked at me through the rearview mirror again. "Your selflessness can trap you."

We pulled into the gravel driveway at my cabin. I threw my backpack over my shoulder and hopped out of the car. "I have to talk to your mom for a sec. Does she work tonight?" Dana asked.

"No, not on Mondays," I said. Dana turned off the ignition and motioned with her head for Avery to get out of the car with her. He shrugged and stepped out of the car, leaving his backpack in the front seat. They followed me up the steps into the living room.

"Mrs. Robertson?" Dana called. Charlie heard her voice and came from around the corner of the hallway, barking wildly. He ran toward Dana, jumping on top of her and snarling, his white fangs flashing against her stomach. Dana stumbled backward in shock.

"Charlie, no!" Mom yelled, hurrying to set her splashing wine glass down on the kitchen counter. Mom stumbled into the living room and grabbed Charlie by his abdomen.

"Down, Charlie," I said. It was as though he didn't hear us.

"Charlie, no!" Mom yelled again.

I helped Mom pull Charlie off of Dana as Avery tried to stand between Charlie and Dana. Charlie managed to tear a slash across the bottom of her black hooded t-shirt before Mom and I could get him off of her. We pushed Charlie into the bathroom and closed him up inside. All the while he kept barking, wildly. "I've never seen him act like that," I said.

"I'm so sorry," Mom apologized to Dana over Charlie's growls.

"It's okay," Dana said.

"It's just not like him to do that, especially with somebody he knows," Mom said.

"Dogs are like that sometimes. I'm fine," Dana said, waving her hand in the air as if to wave it off.

"But your shirt," Mom said.

"It's second hand. It didn't cost me anything. You don't have to worry about it."

"You sure you're okay?" Avery asked Dana. She chose to ignore him entirely as she took a seat on the couch.

"Wilda, could Dana borrow one of your gym shirts?" Mom asked.

"Sure," I said. "Middle drawer. Help yourself to whatever fits I guess."

Dana got up and walked to the hallway but once she reached the seam of the hallway floor, she froze mid-step. "Oh," she gasped as she turned around.

"Is everything OK?" Mom asked.

"Yes," Dana said quickly. "I was just thinking, I actually don't need it. I'm a bit cold and my sweatshirt will be better. Thank you." Dana hurried back to the couch and sat down, rubbing her hands together. "I don't mind taking Wilda to school. We could work something out to help cover gas," Dana said. "Maybe… $20 a week?" she asked.

"Would you take $10?" Mom asked as she took a sip from her wine glass and sat down with it on the couch. Charlie continued to bark so loudly from the bathroom that Mom had to almost yell to continue the conversation.

"Well, okay," Dana said, tugging on the hem of her shirt. "$10 a week is fine. Do you work tomorrow? If so, I could babysit. I just have to drop Avery off, or not."

"I can't stay here every night. I have stuff to do," Avery protested.

"Well, I don't know how well you and Charlie would get along," Mom said over Charlie's howls.

"It probably just startled him that you had a visitor. I'm sure it'll be fine," Dana said.

"I don't know," Mom said. "Maybe it's better if you just pick her up and drop her off. Besides, I already have Reema babysitting after school."

"Her?" Dana asked, her eyes growing large as she shook her head and sighed loudly.

Dana's reaction got Mom's attention. She looked away from the bathroom door where Charlie continued to create a racket. "I've been meaning to ask you," Mom said, "You said on the phone that I shouldn't use Reema. Why not?"

This was the first I'd heard of their conversation about Reema. I stared at Dana, confused. Either Dana didn't notice or didn't care how I might feel about it.

"Well, it's just ... How well do you really know her? She literally came out of nowhere." Dana said. "But it's your call," she added.

"You literally came from nowhere before your parents got you." Avery chuckled. "Sheriffs found Dana in the woods when she was little. She couldn't even talk."

"Avery!" Dana whispered forcefully.

"What?" he asked. "Everybody knows the story except them because they're new in town."

"What story?" I asked.

Dana rolled her eyes and shook her head. "About how... when I was little" she said with exasperation, "and a patrolman spotted me in the woods from the highway. I had no memory of who I was or how I got there. I was pretty young. So, they checked the missing person reports and they couldn't find a match, and I ended up in foster care. It was a really long time ago." Dana twisted her lips and looked down. "My past does not define me," she said.

Mom looked over her drink at Dana with a concerned smile. "Of course, it doesn't, honey," she said. "I'm sorry for prying."

"Being adopted or in foster care is not the end of the world, Dana. I'm adopted," Avery said.

"I know," Dana said.

"She just gets tired of telling her story," Avery said.

"Over and over to every new person in town," Dana said.

"Sorry I made you tell it again," Avery said.

Dana threw up her hands and shrugged.

"You poor girl," Mom said.

"Don't worry about me. I love my foster parents. I'm actually very lucky to have them," Dana said. "Blessed," she added, looking at Avery. "You just can't trust everybody."

"Is there something about Reema I should know?" Mom asked.

Dana glanced at me with a tilt of her head as if to remind me not to talk. "Well, as you can see, I take good care of my clients' kids. As for other babysitters? I don't know."

Dana stood up and walked around the living room, admiring the bare wooden walls and ignoring Charlie's renewed protest from the bathroom. "You're really fortunate," she said, changing the subject. "I always loved the idea of a cabin in the woods. I'd love to see the rest of your property someday."

"Well, if you're not in a hurry maybe Wilda can give you a tour of our yard while I let Charlie out," Mom said.

"We're in no hurry at all," Dana said.

"Wilda, won't you take them out back?" Mom asked.

"For a tour?" I asked.

"It's really lovely here," Dana interjected. "We don't have a yard this big at my foster parents' house."

"Please, Wilda," Mom said. "I could use some peace and quiet for a while. All this barking is giving me a headache."

"Okay, I guess," I said.

Dana followed me to the front door. Avery began to get up, too. "Stay here, Avery," Dana said.

"Why?" he protested. Dana gave him a wide-eyed stare.

"Run along, all of you," Mom waved at us as she took a sip from her wine glass.

"Okay, Mrs. Robertson," Dana said, grabbing my hand and ushering me out of the door. "We'll be right back." She gripped my hand tight in her gloved hand as she led me into the woods behind our cabin. Avery followed close behind us.

"Oh, look at that!" Dana said, pointing to the old shed with its peeling white paint behind the cabin.

"What's so interesting about a shed?" Avery asked.

Dana ignored him. "Do you ever use it?" she asked.

"Why would *she* use it?" Avery asked.

"Shut up, Avery," Dana spouted angrily.

She let go of my hand and ran across the muddy patches of snow to open the door. It flung open, letting out a fierce wind filled with dust so thick it pushed Dana down to the ground. She lay there for a moment, stunned by the powerful gust of dirt now covering her face and clothes.

"Dana, are you all right?" Avery asked, running toward her. He knelt down at her shoulders, unzipped his black puffy jacket and rubbed her face with the bottom of his flannel shirt.

"Oh, stop it!" she shouted.

Dana sat up, wiping the dirt from her mouth with her jacket sleeve.

"You go in there," Dana said, pushing Avery's back forward. He stumbled into the shed, tripping over his feet and falling face down onto the secret door in the floor with a thud. "Ow," he moaned.

Dana stood up and dusted herself off. "How about we play a game, Wilda?" she suggested.

"I don't think so," I said, "I think you just broke Avery's nose."

I walked past Dana and into the shed to check on Avery, grasping him by his arm to encourage him to leave.

"You two should search that whole thing," Dana continued. "There's got to be something interesting in that shed. Show me what you find."

"I don't think my mom wants us in there," I said.

"What do you see in there, Avery?" Dana asked anyway.

Avery fumbled through the rags on the back shelf of the shed, accidentally knocking the hammer from the shelf onto the dirt floor. "Whoa," he said, "there's a ton of alcohol in here!"

"Yeah, I know. My Mom's a bartender," I said.

Avery suddenly jumped back as a black object crawled around one of the bottles. "Oh, man! I almost got bit by something! Wouldn't be surprised if there was an old rifle hidden in here, too."

"We really shouldn't be messing with guns," I said, surprised by the authority in my own voice.

"Oh, come on, Wilda. You know there's no gun in there. I bet there's moonshine, though," Dana said.

"Moonshine?" I asked. "What's that?"

Dana chuckled at me. "Back in the old days of prohibition when alcohol was illegal, the fishermen sailed down from Canada with alcohol in their fishing ships, and then hid their money, guns and liquor under the floorboards of sheds like this. Don't you want to see?" Dana gave me a wink.

"I don't have to see," I said, shrugging.

Dana smirked. "Take that hammer, Avery," she said. "See if there's anything down there."

"All right. This tour is over!" I yelled.

"But we're only getting started, Wilda," Dana said.

"Are you sure this is safe?" Avery asked, holding the hammer.

"It's not," I said. "You're not keeping us safe, Dana. You're a bad babysitter!"

"Serious, Wilda, stop being a baby," Dana whined. "Hammer around there, Avery. See if there's a secret door in the floor."

Avery got down on his knees, found the hammer and started using it to find the seam of the trap door in the ground so I ran grabbed hold of the hammer. "What are you doing?" he asked incredulously, tugging the hammer away from me. In the midst of our tug of war my makeshift bracelet came loose. The amber stone slid from its tie and landed to the floor.

"See what you did?" I yelled.

"Sorry about that," Avery said, picking it up off the ground.

"What are you doing?" a familiar voice rang out from the woods. Our heads all turned at the same time. It was Reema plodding over the snow and underbrush as she walked towards us. I hurried to the doorway of the shed, leaving Avery on the ground behind me.

"Just a little game," Dana said with a sheepish chuckle.

"What kind of game?" Reema asked seriously. She stood directly in front of Dana, staring her down. Dana stepped back, rubbing her hands together anxiously as Reema stood closer to her. "What kind of game?" Reema repeated in a menacing tone.

"Nothing," Dana said innocently.

"It's dangerous to encourage children to go snooping around a shed not knowing what they'll find," Reema said.

"What kind of danger?" Dana asked, curiously.

"Mrs. Robertson should know about this," Reema replied.

Dana shook her head. "We were just leaving, right, Avery?" Dana said over Reema's shoulder. "Avery?" Dana called again.

Avery didn't answer. He was rustling with something in the dark. His silence drew Reema's attention, and I noticed her eyes to widen with astonishment. A crack within the secret door in the floor was glowing with brilliant amber light. Reema faced the shed with bated breath. I took a closer look at the shining light for myself. Avery couldn't believe his eyes either. "Whoa," he said staring down at the dusty vest he had placed over his shoulders.

"What is it?" Dana turned to ask.

"Wow. This is cool!" Avery said. "Too bad it's got a hole in it."

"Take that off," Reema demanded. "Wilda, go close the door!"

"Hey, that stone is about the right size. That'll fix it," Avery said, placing the amber stone into the center of the armor upon his chest.

"Fix what? What is it?" Dana asked.

"Now, Wilda!" Reema yelled. I hurried back into the shed.

"What?" I asked.

Reema didn't wait for me to figure out what she was talking about. She reached down, grabbed two handfuls of snow and slung one of them into Dana's face. It landed in her eyes.

"Oh," Dana vowed, "you're gonna get it."

But before Dana could do anything Reema slung the other handful of snow into the trees above us. Several icicles suddenly came crashing down from the trees in front of Dana. She leaped back from the falling ice with catlike agility, landing on her back.

"Hey," she yelled, temporarily blinded by the dirt and snow. "What are you, nuts?"

I turned from her cries outside the shed to watch the armor Avery had put on transform from dull brown to polished amber stone in the shapes of feathery scales. Suddenly amber wings emanated from Avery's back, threatening to push through the gaps of wood siding to the outside of the shed. His wings grew upwards toward the sky. Avery himself seemed to grow in stature, a full foot taller than he had been before. "What's going on?" Avery yelled in a panic. Then Reema burst into the shed, slamming the door behind her.

"Say stop, before she tries to come in," Reema said, frantically.

"What?" Avery asked.

"Say it now," she pleaded.

"Stop!" Avery said.

Soon after that moment Reema pushed the shed door open. A clump of wet snow falling from the evergreen trees was halted as it fell halfway to the ground. Likewise the wind which buckled the bottom of Dana's jacket was also suspended, as though Reema, Avery and I were inside of a snow globe, still breathing, still moving and seeing everything while the world around us stayed still.

Avery looked around in a panic. "What just happened?" he asked. "What happened?"

Reema whispered to herself, almost in a daze. "I found you," she said, triumphantly. Then she yelled with excitement, "I finally found you!"

She grabbed Avery by the hand and pulled him out of the shed. "For a moment time has stopped," she said, "but don't worry. Only you have the power to change it back," she said.

"He stopped time?" I asked, incredulously.

"I don't understand," Avery said, nearly shaking.

"It's okay," Reema said, smiling. "I promise."

Avery looked back at me, his forehead creased with worry. I nodded with encouragement. "You can trust her. It's weird but she's cool," I said.

"See if you can remember," Reema said, rubbing her hands in anticipation.

"Remember what?" Avery asked.

"Who you are," Reema cheerfully said. She reached out and held his hands in hers. "Close your eyes. Empty your mind and just let the thoughts come."

Avery closed his eyes and moved his head as though he were seeing something even though his eyes remained closed. "I've been here before," Avery declared, backing away from Reema. "I keep having this dream that I was a warrior a long time ago, and I was trapped by my enemies. I see it now. I thought it was just a dream!"

"Why didn't your armor save you?" Reema whispered.

"Because a man I trusted, my son-in-law, stole it from me. He was not one of our people. He was... human."

"What happened to you?" Reema asked.

Avery's eyes widened and his breath quickened. I watched his hands ball into fists.

"I... I...," Avery gasped breathlessly, "I died?" He stared down at his arms and hands, then back at Reema for answers. "But I am alive."

"Yes, you are, now."

"And I lived before," Avery said.

"Yes. You were the Sky King. When you died, so did the power to stop time with your armor. But your armor still has magic. It helped us find you," Reema said. "Do you know who I am?" Reema asked.

"You can't be," Avery said. "You look like my daughter in some ways, but she would be much older than you, unless... Are you... my granddaughter?"

"Yes, I am, Grandfather," Reema exclaimed. She jumped into Avery's arms and hugged him. "I've wanted to find you my entire life!" Reema lifted her tear streaked face toward Avery's gaze. Avery stared into her hazel eyes, and his own eyes began to widen as he held her face into her palms. "I am a grandfather?" he asked.

Reema nodded and the two shared a long embrace before finally noticing me. "And Wilda brought us together. Unbelievable," Avery said. They smiled as they looked at me.

"If you could have anything in the world happen, or anything at all, what would it be?" Reema asked me. In that moment I had so many thoughts racing through my mind that I couldn't stand still. I felt my heart pounding in my throat. Was this a wish? Were they really offering me anything I wanted? What should I ask for?

"Ah, you are not sure," Reema said. "Take some time to figure it out."

"Just protect my mom," I blurted out. "I'm worried about her."

Reema nodded. "Okay," she said.

"My kingdom," Avery remembered, "what has become of it?"

"It is under the control of the regents on my behalf," Reema said.

"Regents? Shouldn't my daughter be in charge?"

Reema shrugged and sheepishly looked over at me. I knew why she didn't answer. She was hiding the truth from Avery about his daughter's fate. Maybe she would tell him when the time was right.

"Shall I go back now?" Avery asked. "I have no plan."

"I'll hide the armor again until you are ready to reclaim it. But in the meantime, don't tell anyone else about this," Reema said.

"What if it's found?" Avery asked. "Tie the stone back on Wilda's wrist. That way no one will notice that anything unusual has happened."

"Are you sure no one will find the armor?" I asked.

"Even if they do it won't work," Reema said. "You will hold the key, Wilda."

Avery slid off the armor and let it drop into the hole in the shed floor. The air began to pick up again as if in slow motion. Time was thawing. Reema hurriedly fastened the stone back to my wrist and knotted the ragged edges together. As Avery took his position at the shed, time regained its course.

Dana rubbed her eyes to see Avery standing in the doorway, his chin in his hand and a triumphant look on his face. Dana grabbed a clump of icy snow in her gloved hand, pressed it tightly into her palm and pitched it back toward us. Reema ducked away from the snowball as it hit the shed with a loud crash, exploding on impact.

"How'd you learn to throw like that?" I asked as though a snow fight was the wildest thing to happen in that moment, trying my best to sound convincingly naive. Dana ignored me as she grabbed another clump of snow. This time Reema let Dana hit her with it, only slightly ducking out of the way as it hit her shoulder and spread an icy mist everywhere. "Come on, Avery," Dana said.

Avery trudged through the mud and snow back to Dana. "I guess it wasn't the best idea to go in there, but it was still kind of cool," he laughed nervously.

"Dumb human," Dana said under her breath.

As soon as she said it Reema's head whipped back around. She stared at Dana with wide eyes, then back at me. Reema nudged my back to say something.

"See you later, Dana. Bye, Avery," I said.

Avery waved back as they rounded the corner of the cabin. Reema and I watched them in silence until after we heard the car engine sound, the tires turn and the car squeal down the highway.

"I don't think her real name is Dana," Reema said plainly.

"How do you know?" I asked.

"She reminds me of someone else. There are just certain things a person can't hide."

"What is her real name?" I asked.

"I dare not say who I think she might be," Reema answered. "Unseelies can always hear their true names no matter where you are when you say it." Reema turned to me with a serious look on her face. "We have to find a way to separate them without raising her suspicion. Ask him to come over."

"A date with your grandpa? No way!" I said.

"I didn't mean it like that," Reema said. "Maybe a study session."

"I got a better idea," I said. "How about if you help me throw a party with other kids my age, and him. That way nobody who's watching will be able to figure out which kid is probably the fairy king."

"But how would you get them to come?"

"All I have to do is get the twins to come. And then say we're all having a party at my place and Mom won't be there."

"But your mom would never approve of that."

I tilted my head and gave her a look with a smirk. "Honestly, she'll be relieved that I have any friends at all and I'm not just weird, and you'll going to be the one to clean up," I said.

"Sounds like you'll be needing my help a lot," Reema said, folding her arms. "How do I know this is not just some ploy to become popular at school?"

I gave Reema a blank stare and shrugged my shoulders. "You don't," I said, "but come on Reema, please? I'm helping you." I grabbed her by her forearms and pouted as best as I could. "I never ask you for anything," I said.

Reema slapped her forehead and shook her head. "All right, I guess I'm throwing a party," she said.

"Yes!" I celebrated with an air punch.

"But don't tell Dana or anyone her age." Reema said. "We don't want her finding out and crashing it. Don't trust her under any circumstances. Got that?"

"I won't tell her anything," I said.

"I mean it. I won't be able to take you back to the fairy realm if you break our trust."

"I promise," I said.

Reema pulled a cell phone out of her jacket and handed it to me. "Here," she said.

"Wait. You're giving me a brand-new smart phone? This thing costs, like, a thousand dollars," I said.

"We need to be able to keep in touch," Reema said as she started walking back towards the cabin. I followed behind her, trying not to drop my new cell phone in my excitement.

"Thank you, Reema!" I exclaimed, hurriedly putting it in my coat pocket before she changed her mind.

"You're thanking me?" Reema asked.

"Well, yeah," I said.

Reema's brows furrowed. Her piercing hazel eyes narrowed as she stared at me, shaking her head.

"What's wrong with that?" I asked.

"My people don't even have a word for that," she said as she started walking again toward the cabin.

"What?" I said. "Why?"

"Because gratitude is shown by what you do, not by what you say. What does 'thank you' even mean?" Reema asked.

"Well," I said, following behind her, "I think it means someone is grateful for what you gave them."

"Show me your gratitude by using that phone responsibly," Reema demanded.

"Oh," I said, surprised by her suddenly changing mood.

"There's so much you don't know!" Reema exclaimed.

"Okay," I said.

Reema shook her head, took a deep breath and looked away as we walked together on the frigid ground. "I have patience with you because you are a child," she said. "Don't act silly with the phone just because you have one now."

312

"Oh, no. I'll be totally responsible, and respectful," I stammered.

"Let your mom know I'm loaning it to you," she said. "Tell her you need to have your own phone in the house when your mother is away."

"Okay," I said, bouncing with joy.

"No talking to strangers. There's a lot of weirdos out there... adult weirdos."

"Tell me about it," I said, trying to sound serious.

"I can monitor your social media on there so if you talk to adult strangers, I'll have to take the phone away. And don't use it in class," Reema said.

"What kid doesn't use a cell phone in a boring class?" I asked.

Reema smirked. "A kid who gets their phone taken away by a teacher, which means a kid that I can't depend on anymore," she said.

"Oh," I said. "Got it."

Reema stopped walking for a moment. She looked at me with intensity in her eyes. "There's a war going on and we're in it. Do you understand?" she asked.

"I said I got it," I said.

"What happened to being respectful?" Reema asked.

"Yes, ma'am. I know not to cross you. After all, you shoot lasers out of your hands," I laughed, hoping to calm her sour mood with a little humor.

Reema rolled her eyes. "Save the sarcasm for the humans," she said. "Speaking of humans, you better get back to your Mom. I'll be going, now."

We started to walk again when a thought hit me. I turned back around to see that Reema had already transformed herself into her white deer alter ego. I thought I'd ask anyway. "There's only one problem with the party idea. We really can't afford much food," I said.

"Don't you remember the pizza? I made it work, right?" Reema asked.

"Point taken," I said.

"And it was good, wasn't it?" Reema asked, smiling.

"It was okay," I said.

"Just okay? Really?" she asked, incredulously.

"Just kidding. It was honestly the best pizza I've ever had in my life," I said.

Reema laughed. "I knew it," she said before trotting back into the woods.

When I got back inside, I was surprised to see Mom standing by the kitchen window with a full glass of red wine in her hand. I froze.

"Who was that you were talking to?" she slurred.

"Oh," I said. Charlie wandered over to me. I knelt down and rubbed him behind his ears, giving him all of my attention as though nothing out of the ordinary had happened. What better time to ask for a party than when Mom was loosened up and I needed to change the subject anyway? "Can I have a few classmates come by to study on Friday night?"

"Yeah, whatever," she said, trying to get back to original conversation. *Success!* "But we need to talk about what I just saw."

"What?" I asked.

"You heard me," Mom said. "You were pretty close to a wild animal. It looked like a deer or something, but it was white like a sheep. It was beautiful, a snow-white deer. But at first it looked like you were talking to a person in the distance and then an animal. You're not letting your imagination put you in danger, are you?"

"How is that possible?" I asked.

"At first it looked like Reema so I thought, what's she doing out there? Were you talking to Reema before getting close to a wild animal?"

I didn't want to say this but I didn't know what else I could do. If I explained any of this to Mom, first she wouldn't believe me. Then she'd have my head examined. And that would be in addition to some kind of punishment. So, I relied on my emergency fallback talking point.

"Mom, you know you've had a lot to drink today," I said.

"Don't tell me what I've been doing," she charged. "I'm a grown woman."

"It's just that sometimes you don't see things clearly when you're drinking."

"You know what?" Mom said, setting her glass down. She walked toward me with a labored gait. "You can go to your room. That's what you can do. I know what I saw," she said.

Instinctively Charlie got up and trotted to the hallway where he waited for me. I wasted no time rushing to my room after Charlie. "For your information I see things better when I *have* had a drink. I don't have a drinking problem!" Mom yelled from the hallway as I closed my bedroom door behind me and Charlie.

Chapter 8

"What kind of stuff do you keep in that shed, anyway?" Dana asked. I didn't want to deal with Dana anymore, but Mom insisted on having her drive me to school so that she could sleep in. So, here we were, pulling into the crowded school parking lot. Dana asked me that same question for what seemed like the third time that morning.

"Ask Avery," I said.

"I did. He says it's full of alcohol," Dana replied.

"I'm not sneaking it out for you," Avery said. He turned around and looked at me, rolled his eyes and shook his head as though Dana was a pesky inconvenience to him. He acted like he thought she was a troublemaker whose rebelliousness could blow his cover.

"Why does it matter so much to you?" I asked her.

"It doesn't," Dana lied. "Who said anything about stealing alcohol, anyway?"

"Isn't that what you're getting at?" Avery asked. He tapped his fingertips along the door handle and stared out the window as though he couldn't wait to get out of Dana's Porsche. I got the impression that Avery getting annoyed with her nosy questioning.

"I seriously don't need your help to score a drink," Dana said, shaking her head emphatically. Avery shook his head again and kept looking out the window.

I decided to play along with the idea that the only valuable thing in the shed was alcohol. "Well, I bet my mom measures what's left in every bottle. You're not getting me in trouble," I said.

"Relax," she whined.

The SUV came to a stop. Dana parked by the entrance as usual. Avery was quick to jump out of the passenger side. "See you," Avery said, slinging his backpack over his shoulder and sprinting into the building.

I started to slide out of the SUV when Dana leaned into the backseat and slung her arm across the door handle, blocking me from getting out of the SUV. "You know you can tell me anything, right? We're friends," she said.

"I know," I answered quickly. "See you, Dana." She sat up with her arms folded, watching me get out of the SUV and walk into the building. I tried not to look back. I could feel her gaze upon my back.

I had to be so careful not to arouse Dana's suspicion that I was on to her, even though I suspected that I was failing miserably. If she really was what Reema said she was, an Unseelie sent by dark forces within the fairy world to pretend to be a normal person so that she could spy on us humans, she probably could sense that I suspected her. No wonder she wanted to discourage my mother from having Reema around. And of all the small towns she could end up living in, she had to land in Avery's town. Perhaps she was already onto him, too.

My school day didn't start until second period and I had a few extra minutes before class started. I could have talked to Veronica later, since we had second period together, but I needed her undivided attention to convince her to attend my party. I found Veronica in the administration office. She was a teacher's assistant there for first period, and her job usually consisted of stapling papers, placing coupons from local businesses into the teachers' boxes and decorating her fingernails on a slow morning. She was gluing a pink plastic bow onto her pinky to match her other hand when she looked up and saw me across the stacks of color copy paper on the counter.

"Hey," I said.

"Hey," she shyly answered with a kick of one of her fresh, white high-top sneakers. "What's up?"

"I'm throwing a party this Friday. Wanna come?" I asked.

"Thanks for inviting me. I have to see what Monica wants to do. We've actually been to a lot of parties, usually at the bowling alley, the pizza parlor or the drive-in. We've also been to a few different parties at the state park and the lakes around here, so... she might want to do something else. We'll see."

"Well, it's not at any of those places," I said.

"Oh, yeah? Where's it going to be? Tacoma?" Veronica asked, perching herself at the edge of her seat.

"No, better," I said. "My house."

"Oh, a party with you and your mom." Veronica sighed and leaned back into her chair.

"Well, she probably won't be able to make it. She works nights," I said.

"Just you?" she asked.

"And whoever else you think should come as long as they don't get into the bar," I answered.

"That doesn't sound like any party I've ever been to," she said.

"I mean, not everybody is mature enough to handle it," I said. She thought for a moment.

"I'm mature," she said.

"So, are you in?" I asked. "Unless you can't handle that kind of responsibility."

She thought for a moment. "Of course, I can! I'll be there," she said, perched on her seat again.

"Cool," I answered.

"You should let me help you plan it. I can put together the guest list. I'll get it poppin'," Veronica said.

"Sure, okay, as long as Avery's on the list," I said.

"Oh," Veronica said, her chin in her hand. "Why him? He doesn't strike me as your type."

I shrugged, giving her a blank expression. "Okay, then. We'll get your crush there," she said.

"He's not my crush," I answered.

"Right," Veronica answered, stretching the word as long as she could while flashing a giant smile.

"I'm thinking maybe a dozen kids would be a good size party," I said.

"Don't worry. Leave it to me and people will be talking about this party for the next hundred years," Veronica said.

I walked out of the office casually, playing it as cool as possible, trying not to appear eager to get the most popular kid at school to come to a party where she would have to supply all the other guests. I was walking down the hallway to class when I noticed Avery by the water fountain. He was just standing there with his arms folded over his monitor sash, waiting for me to walk down the hall. "Hey," I said, giving him a slight wave. Avery took it as an opportunity to stop me, grasping me by my arm with his hand wrapped firmly over the tied stone on my wrist and tugging me towards the lockers. That's when I noticed the dark circles around his eyes.

"Whoa. Are you okay?" I asked.

"I haven't been able to sleep for days," Avery whispered. "It's like I'm remembering things from somebody else's life, but it's my own."

"That's weird," I said. I tried to slip out of his grasp but it was surprisingly strong, much stronger than I imagined it could be before he'd tried on that armor in the shed.

"Why do I have all these new memories?" he asked.

"Your guess is as good as mine," I said, still squirming.

"I need to know what you two did to me back there," Avery demanded.

"I didn't do anything. It was all Reema."

"What is she, really?"

"You already know that. You just have to trust what you know is real. And let go of me. Your grip is really strong," I said.

"Oh, sorry! I didn't realize…" Avery said. He dropped my arm and looked down at the floor.

"You always wanted to be in charge, keeping everybody in line," I said, rubbing my wrist.

"Yeah?" he asked, holding his chin.

"Turns out you're a protector for real. I guess it's who you've always been," I said.

"But time stopped. How did I stop it?" he asked.

"Look, I'm having a little get together at my house after school on Friday, just me and a few friends. We could play Dungeons and Dragons, maybe. Come if you want to find out," I said, taking out the cell phone Reema had given me. "Let me know?" I asked.

He took his phone out of his pocket and we touched their screens together to share directions to my house before I put my phone back into my coat pocket. I backed away from the lockers to head to class. "I really hope you come," I said, "I mean, if you can handle the answers."

He stood there watching me helplessly as I walked away. I have to admit I felt a little sorry for him. Avery used to annoy me but now I understood him to be something he could not fully understand. He must have been scared to accept what he really was. To be honest, it astounded me how I ended up involved in all this. Still, it felt pretty cool to hold the key to something truly important.

I pulled the cell phone Reema gave me out of my coat pocket and looked in the contacts. Her face and name popped up immediately. I sent her the text, "Party's on. 2EZ. Avery prolly in."

Immediately Reema texted back a thumbs up emoji and the words, "K. Follow plan."

When Friday afternoon arrived the first hint of spring came, too. The local TV forecasters had predicted that temperatures would be "closer to normal." Just as they said, the last of the snow near the coast had melted away. We finally had a sunny day in Belfair.

Reema came right on time as usual, greeting us while Mom hurried to gather her purse and rush out the door. Reema was good at reassuring Mom, saying, "Yes, Ms. Robertson," "Don't worry, Ms. Robertson," and "We'll be all right but I have your number just in case, Ms. Robertson." Mom sped down the street to her job without any sense that a wild middle school dance party was about to happen in her house.

Reema smiled at me with widened eyes. "Well, Wilda, shall we get started?" she asked.

"Let's go," I said.

"If there's anything you don't want them messing with, put it in your dresser," she said.

I ran past Charlie to my room, pulled my flute and my piccolo cases out of my backpack on the bed and stuffed them in my dresser. I could imagine someone experimenting with the piccolo to see if it would burn them. I also remembered my laptop, unplugged it from the nightstand and stuffed it in the dresser along with my artifact box. Then I came back out to the hallway. "Ready," I said.

Reema stretched out her palms and absorbed flickers of light out of the ether. She emitted a sparkling dust from the edges of her fingertips. She then strolled through our cabin, touching the drawers in my room, my mother's closed bedroom door, and the bathroom medicine cabinet as Charlie trotted back to the living room to get out of her way. When I tried to open my mother's bedroom door, it wouldn't budge. Neither would the drawers in my bedroom.

"Does your mother hide any weapons or anything else you might know of?" she asked.

"I don't think so," I said.

I followed her back into the kitchen and living room. To my surprise the living room was decorated with colorful lights streaming down the walls. The kitchen counters were already covered in stacked boxes of pizza, a giant bowl of shrimp cocktail and huge pans of boneless buffalo chicken wings, enough to feed a hundred people.

"Whoa," I said, "This is the good stuff."

"What did you expect?" Reema asked.

"Junk food?" I asked.

Reema chuckled. "You don't need my help to serve potato chips. But there's that, too," she said.

The kitchen table was filled with platters of chocolate peanut butter cup cookies, lemon cupcakes and blackberry cobbler. When I opened the refrigerator, it was filled with bottles of exotic juices, foreign sodas and mineral water. The freezer was packed with vanilla and toffee ice cream. Our usual plates and bowls, shined to perfection, were set neatly on the counter nearby. Charlie was calmly chewing on a giant turkey bone by the door. I assumed Reema must have given it to him. I didn't get much of a chance to think about that before I noticed that next to Charlie was a short female, about Reema's age, with spiked platinum hair cut very short. She was leaning against the wall wearing a light blue dress full of eyelets and long white, thick heeled boots. Her wide golden wings jutted from her back.

"Who ...?" I asked.

"This is my friend, Zyzzyva," Reema said. "You didn't expect me to make all of this by myself, did you?"

"Uh," I wondered out loud.

"We've been friends since childhood. Did I tell you about her?" Reema asked, smiling.

Zyzzyva unfolded her arms and walked over to me. "Everybody's buzzing about you back home. It's nice to finally meet you," she said quickly.

"Nice to meet you," I said, surprised.

"You look positively flummoxed!" Zyzzyva exclaimed. "I don't know why. You've seen pixies before."

"I have?" I asked.

"Yeah, back at the castle. Don't you remember?" Zyzzyva sulked. She was shorter than I was but her fast talking nature and charismatic demeanor made up for her small size.

"I guess I convinced myself that I dreamed that, too," I answered in my defense.

"Look at me," she said, "Honey, I *am* a dream. You know it's all real now, don't you?"

"I do now ..." I said.

"Good," Zyzzyva said with a decisive nod. Then she pivoted to Reema. "Now, tell me where you want me to post up."

"On the couch, maybe?" Reema suggested. Zyzzyva flitted to the couch and dropped herself down on it.

"Wait," I said, "doesn't your friend stand out as a ..."

"A magical?" Zyzzyva finished my sentence. She clicked her fingers and she was surrounded by a ball of sparkling dust. "Don't worry, I'm little. I blend in," she said. And she did blend in, transforming her clothes into a frilly white sweater and tight denim jeans tucked into the same white boots. Her face looked young, too with childlike, wide blue eyes. She shimmied to tuck her wings into her sweater, between her shoulder blades. Zyzzyva clicked her fingers again to make a cell phone appear in her hand.

"I suppose you have a wand, too," I said.

Zyzzyva laughed. "Wands are for amateurs," she scoffed as she lay down on the couch and scrolled through her cell phone.

"What are you looking at?" I asked.

"Human stuff. You are quite an entertaining species," she said before turning her attention back to her cell phone.

Reema beckoned me to take a look at the bottles of alcohol in one of the kitchen cabinets. "I took it upon myself to change over all your Mom's liquor for tonight," Reema continued. "It won't have any alcohol content just in case they get into it, but they probably won't know the difference. Kids."

"Could you do that every night?" I asked her.

"Why?" Zyzzyva asked from the living room, looking up from her cell phone.

I suddenly remembered my promise to my mother to keep her drinking a secret. "No reason," I answered. "Wow. This is so cool, Reema."

"I told you I'd take care of the food," she said. "Oh, and I had the cell phone reception jammed out here. Just for a few hours. We can't have anybody livestreaming about this or the sheriff may shut it down. I'll be outside watching when the guests start arriving. Just makes sure you get Avery to go with you to the shed."

"Got it," I said.

Reema left from the backdoor in the kitchen to wait outside as the first couple of kids emerged from the road and started walking down the driveway. It was Josh and a boy I didn't know too well, but I'd seen him hang out with Josh. *So, Veronica went and invited that bully!* I breathed a heavy sigh. As Josh and his friend walked closer to the house along the gravel driveway, I spotted Monica and Veronica behind them, stumbling to keep up in their kitten heel shoes. They all got out of a commuter van up the street.

Josh leaped up the steps in two strides and bounded through the door. "All right!" he shouted. He looked around and spotted Zyzzyva on the couch. She sat up and glanced at him for a moment before looking back down at her phone, shaking her head to herself. "Hey," Josh said to her. She looked at him again and gave him a lackluster wave before returning her attention to her phone.

"I thought this was gonna be lame, but there's like a butt-load of food!" Josh said. He threw himself onto the couch. His buddy also jumped on the couch next to Zyzzyva. She frowned and set a throw pillow between them. "This is Drew," Josh said.

"Hungry, man. What'cha got to smack?" Drew said to introduce himself.

"There's plenty of food. Help yourself," I said politely.

"Nah, I'm gonna let one of them girls serve me," Drew said.

"Yeah, that's their job," Josh added.

Zyzzyva looked up from her phone and stared with disgust at the two boys. "Has anyone ever thrown you through a ceiling before?" she asked in a sweet tone that disguised the seriousness of her question.

"That must be a joke," Josh said.

Zyzzyva smiled at him from ear to ear. "Is it?" she asked, smiling.

"Please don't break anything," I said. "I still live here."

Charlie ran from my room barking and stood in front of the two boys. They jumped up onto the couch with their shoes on the cushions.

"I think that's an order." I laughed.

"Does he bite?" Drew asked.

"Well, he does have teeth," I said, watching them squirm.

Just then, Monica and Veronica entered through the living room door. "Hey, girl," they said, running to take turns hugging me and giving me air kisses over my cheeks.

"Oh, wow. You've done such a good job," Monica said. "And it was a good idea to tell people we were meeting to study. My mom assumed it was legit nerd stuff and dropped us off up the hill."

"Let's get this party started!" Veronica exclaimed.

The twins looked over the living room and noticed Zyzzyva sitting on the couch. They waved at her at the same time and introduced themselves to her. "You can call me Zizzi," Zyzzyva said.

"I don't think we've met before. How do you know everybody?" Veronica asked.

I wandered back to the living room, trying to think of an excuse for her being there. "She's my..." I started to say.

"Cousin," Zyzzyva said. "Just passing through. I thought I'd visit for the day."

"Cool," Monica said. "Where are you visiting from?"

"Oh, from out of town," Zyzzyva said.

A stream of cars pulled up alongside the road, letting kids out along the driveway before pulling off. Reema was standing as a deer on the other side of the road where everyone could see her. I was surprised none of their parents bothered to venture down the hill to check out my "study session" for themselves. It was as though they had been hypnotized into thinking everything was fine. I guessed that was Reema's doing.

The kids steadily proceeded to trek down the driveway and into the living room and kitchen. A few of them glanced at me to speak but most of them went straight for the food on the counter and helped themselves to the drinks in the refrigerator without even bothering to say hello. Then Josh put the TV on a music station and cranked the volume as high as it could go, making the walls in the living room rattle. The house was abuzz with laughter as plates of food traveled back and forth from one room to another.

Some of the kids hopped up onto the living room furniture, jumping around while everyone else shouted into each other's ears, piled their plates with food and danced shyly below them. A seemingly never-ending parade of trendy looking kids proceeded to walk up the driveway. I found Veronica dancing on top of an end table in the living room. I tapped her on her bare leg. She bent down, tucking her blonde streaked hair behind her ear. "How many people did you invite?" I asked.

"What?" she yelled back.

"I said, how many people did you invite?"

"I don't know, fifty? Sixty?" Veronica said.

"So basically, you invited the whole school?" I asked, crossing my arms in disgust.

"What?" she yelled.

I waved her away and turned to check on Charlie. He was lying down in a corner in my closet, chewing on a hamburger that someone had either given him or left on the floor. My room was filled with kids lounging and dropping crumbs on my bed. "Are you okay, buddy?" I asked Charlie. He looked up at me for a moment and then continued to gnaw the meat on the sticky closet floor. "Don't feed my dog!" I yelled to anybody who would listen.

A crashing sound interrupted Charlie's meal and his ears perked up. I looked in the same direction as Charlie and noticed a girl kicking a broken glass toward the wall with her leather shoe. "Sorry," she said, sheepishly.

"I'll get it," I said. I walked into the kitchen to get the broom and dustpan. I came back to my room with them, scooped up the broken glass and carried it to the kitchen trashcan where I dumped it with a loud clang. By the time I entered the living room again the floor was already filled with empty soda bottles, forks, dirty napkins and plates of half-eaten food that had been piled high. Two boys were running laps against each other to see who could run the fastest from the bathroom to the fireplace. As they jumped over the furniture, I noticed an enormous grease stain on the back of the couch. "Oh, no! How am I supposed to get that stain out? Mom will kill me when she finds this!" I shouted.

I started back toward the kitchen to get a wet dish towel when I noticed the front door open again. This time it was somebody I actually wanted to see, Avery. He walked through the front door and nudged his way through the thick crowd of kids. "What the..." I heard him say. Halfway through the living room he caught my eyes and gave me a confused stare. I smiled back at him from across the room, relieved that he came. All of this was merely an excuse to get him back to my house, anyway.

"I found the juice!" Monica shouted. I turned and saw her standing in the middle of the hallway entrance holding two large bottles of unopened strawberry vodka over her head.

"Aw, yeah! Who's ready to turn up?" Joshua shouted.

"I'm ready to get turnt!" Veronica pushed her way through the crowd to Avery and grabbed him by both arms, pulling him to the hallway. She motioned for everyone around her to get close and waved the bottles of vodka in the air as she shouted, "Truth or dare!"

"Yeah!" the kids around her yelled.

"Wait," I yelled back. "You're not supposed to get into that."

"Oh my God, Wilda. Calm down. People are actually starting to like you," Veronica sneered. Monica came running into the hallway with her arms full of red plastic cups. I wasn't even aware we had them.

"I'll go first," Joshua shouted. He grabbed the bottle and took a long swig from it. "Woo! I just did that! Wilda's the best!" He handed it off to his buddy.

Drew took a drink and shook his head. "Tastes a little different from my dad's. Must be better," he said.

The open bottle got passed around. When the bottle ended up in front of Avery, he shook his head and waved it away.

"Yay, we're being so bad right now! Come on, Wilda!" Veronica said.

"Wilda! Wilda! Wilda!" the kids shouted.

"I gotta check on my dog," I answered.

"Aw, come one," several of them complained. I made my way back to my room, anyway. Avery followed me through the crush of kids in the living room. I had hoped the party would be a good way to get Avery to come back while making friends, but I didn't stop to think about whether I would be having any fun. I actually ended up spending more time worrying about getting in trouble than enjoying the party, and that was starting to really bother me.

"I need everybody out of my room," I said when I entered my bedroom.

"Yeah," said Monica. She was behind me, carrying empty cups which she unloaded on my bed. "Everybody out unless you're playing!"

Monica and Veronica pushed me and Avery down to the floor by my bed as several other kids streamed into the room, grabbing cups from the bed for Veronica to fill them up.

"Hey," Drew shouted, "I'm trying to livestream this on my phone but it's not working. Your cell coverage sucks out here."

"Thank God. You'd have us shut down," Veronica said. "Put that away!"

Joshua followed behind Veronica and Drew, popping Drew on the back of his head. "Yeah, man," he said.

"Ow," Drew moaned, rubbing his fingers through his brown hair.

"This is how you play," Veronica said, excitedly. "Somebody asks a question, you answer it honestly. If you can't, you take a drink."

"And if you don't drink you have to do some other dare," Monica said.

"This is stupid," I said.

Monica threw her hands in the air. I rolled my eyes with disgust, ready to get up and walk out of my own party when I noticed Reema as a white deer staring through my bedroom window. As if noticing my hesitation to trust her, she took a step toward the window and nodded her head.

"I'll go first," Veronica said. "Have you ever taken money out of your mom's purse?"

"Hah, no," Josh said. "That's messed up. Wilda probably has, though."

"No," I protested, "I don't even have a reason to do that."

"Right?" Monica agreed. "Wilda wouldn't do something like that. Her mom doesn't have enough money to steal. Right, Wilda?"

"Why are you saying that?" I asked.

"Well, I mean, you live here," Monica said.

Veronica interrupted her. "She is throwing this kick ass party, though," she said.

Josh nodded. "That's true," he said, "but my boy Drew hasn't said anything."

"What am I supposed to say?" Drew asked.

"Here. Take a puff," Josh said, pulling an e-cigarette out of his jeans pocket. Immediately someone appeared, standing in the doorway. It was Zyzzyva suddenly stalking towards our circle. She plucked the e-cigarette out of Josh's hand and stood over him with it.

"Hey, what are you doing?" Josh asked.

"This isn't cool," Zyzzyva said. "Who here wants to see all the spit coming out of Josh's mouth?" Everyone stared at her, then at Joshua, and back at her.

"Exactly," she said. Then she dropped the e-cigarette on the hard floor in front of her and stomped the thick heel of her white boot on top of it, cracking it open.

"You're just gonna break my stuff?" Joshua exclaimed as he started to stand up to confront Zyzzyva.

She didn't bother to look at him. Instead she just laughed and pushed him down by his shoulder as she sat down in the circle next to him. "Relax," she said, "you know you swiped it from that gas station across the street from the taco place."

"How do you know that?" Josh asked.

Zyzzyva looked at him with a mesmerizing smile. "I don't like liars," she said.

"Okay, then. Drink!" Veronica demanded, haphazardly pouring the vodka Reema had secretly removed the alcohol from into Drew's red plastic cup. Drew took a long gulp from the cup.

"All right," Drew said, wiping his mouth with his flannel sleeve. "It's my turn. Who here has ever kissed somebody else at our school?"

"Me," Monica said, raising her hand high into the air, "last year, summer Bible camp. Bobby Wong."

"Everybody knows that," Veronica said, exasperated.

"We were just friends. I only wanted to know what it was like."

"How special," Josh sneered.

"How about … Wilda? You ever kissed somebody?" Monica giggled.

I looked around and with the exception of Avery, everybody seemed to be snickering. "What's so funny?" I asked.

"Well, it's just that I can't imagine you kissing someone. You don't seem like the type," Veronica said.

"I think we have to fix her hair, first," Monica said. "Give her a total makeover."

"Seriously, those bangs gotta go," Josh said.

"Well, have you?" Drew asked.

I looked back at the window for Reema but she was gone. I could feel my face growing hot. "You know what?" I announced. I stood up and grabbed Avery's hand. "Dare! Avery, let's just go," I declared.

"Go Wilda! Go after what you want, girl," Monica said as Josh pulled out his cell phone to record us. I looked at Avery with an expression that must have suggested how awkward I felt but he shrugged his shoulders and said, "She's making me go." I held onto Avery's hand and led him through the crowded hallway.

"Look, I don't want to kiss you or anything," I said.

"What?" he yelled over the music.

"I said…" Before I finished my statement, I thought of a better idea. "Let's go to the shed, now," I said.

"Good idea," he answered. I led him through the crowd toward the back door.

"Hey," Veronica said, following behind us, "Where are you two lovebirds going?"

"Don't worry about it," Avery said.

"What? OMG, are you guys about to kiss right now?" Veronica asked, but Avery shook his head and ignored her as we made our way outside. A few of the kids from our Truth or Dare circle followed us outside, and a couple of them had their cell phones out and were discussing how they could get a signal.

Somehow Charlie nuzzled his way through the packed cabin and followed us outside. Avery's hand in mine felt awkward and I stumbled trying to keep up with his charge to the shed. Charlie caught up to us, barking and nipping at Avery's heels. "Down, boy," I said. "It's okay." Avery paid Charlie no mind as he flung open the shed door and ushered me inside, slamming the door in front of Charlie.

Before I could get my bearings within the dusty shed, Avery spun me around. Our eyes met and for a moment I feared that the Avery I knew from school might go through with the twins' stupid dare as he leaned toward me. Then he said with a commanding tone of voice, "Do what we came for."

I felt the nerves in my body freeze as I stood there in the dark. I held my breath, unsure of what would happen next, hopeful that Reema would show up in time to stop anything romantic from happening. Avery was nice, a little square maybe, but I didn't feel any special feelings for him. He was two people, after all. I had never felt like kissing somebody before and the part of him I didn't know honestly creeped me out.

"Wait!" I found myself saying with such clarity that my own voice in the dark space surprised me.

"What's wrong?" Avery asked.

"Reema told me to bring you here so you could start your quest. I don't want to do anything romantic with you."

"What? No! You're a child," Avery huffed as he rolled his eyes. I don't know why my cheeks started to burn hot but something about the way Avery answered so fast caught me off guard.

"*Actually*, we're the same age," I reminded him, trying not to sound offended.

"Not really. I'm *actually* a king who's, like, a hundred years older than you," he replied.

"In your head," I said.

"Isn't that what matters?" Avery asked.

"Whatever, Avery. Just remember what a dork you are with your hair all slicked back as if a cow just licked your big fat head for salt. You and your teacher's pet sash."

"Just give me the stone, please," he said.

I pushed my bruised feelings aside and untied the fabric dressing around my wrist, tugging it apart. The amber stone fell into Avery's palm. I stepped back in the darkness, rubbing my bare wrist when a tall figure emerged from the darkness in the back of the cabin. It was Reema, holding the armored vest with outstretched arms.

"How long have you been in here?" I asked Reema.

"Long enough to know you two don't get along," she mumbled under her breath.

Avery slid into the armored vest effortlessly as he placed the final stone in its place. It shone with amber light again, permeating every opening between the shed's wooden slats.

Avery stretched out his arms, pleased with the transformation before his eyes. "Still, she's proven herself to be responsible enough," Avery told Reema. Then he turned to look at me, his face seeming to grow more powerful by the second. "It wasn't a fluke after all. I could learn to get used to this," he said.

"I told them you were coming. They are expecting you," Reema said.

"I can't wait," Avery said.

Reema smiled. "Well done, Wilda. You have earned your place among us in our land, if you so choose," she said.

"I guess I should be going back now, to finally learn my past," Avery said.

"And to prepare to take over as king. Just be sure to stick to the path in our Spring Court's territory," Reema turned and told Avery, smiling.

"I will," Avery said. The amber light grew brighter until it was nearly blinding as the liquor bottles on the dirt floor rattled, and then Avery turned, took a deep breath and walked right through the back wall of the shed. He disappeared completely, the amber light folding in on itself and disappearing with him.

The shed door crept open to reveal Charlie still barking and pacing back and forth, warding off Monica and Veronica and a few of their nosy partying friends who'd come to eavesdrop. I drifted outside of the shed. "What happened in there?" Veronica asked with her arms folded. "Did you guys kiss?"

"Yeah, and did you hang a disco ball in there?" I heard Josh ask.

The absurdity of his question broke my pensive gaze upon the ground. "Yeah, Josh. That's what it was. A disco ball. In a shed," I said sarcastically.

"I didn't hear any disco music," Josh persisted to say.

"This boy is your friend?" I asked Veronica.

Just then, Reema emerged from behind the shed as the white deer. The small crowd of revelers stared in amazement, watching her slink into the woods beyond the clearing. Their confused stares all flowed back to me. I shrugged my shoulders and headed back towards the cabin.

"Where's Avery?" Monica asked.

"I don't know," I said.

"But he was with you," she replied.

I shrugged again. "He had to go home," I said.

"So, you guys went into a shed together, you guys obviously set something on fire, he disappears from the party of the century for some weird reason, and we're all supposed to believe that nothing went on in there?"

"Yeah," I said.

"Must have lit a cigar or something in there and took off," Josh guessed. "I have to admit, I didn't think he had it in him, always trying to be all good and stuff."

"This is one wacky party," Veronica said.

"But is it a fun party?" I asked.

"Yeah, I gotta hand it to you. You know how to throw one freakin' awesome party," Veronica said.

Everyone there seemed to agree, getting back to the same playful vibe as before. "Yeah! Woo-hoo!" Josh yelled at the top of his lungs. I shook my head. Josh was really starting to get to me and being able to score touchdowns didn't make him any more charming.

As I started to walk back to the cabin Veronica met up with me and held onto my elbow. "You can tell me," she whispered. "What kind of kiss was it? Did you get all bubbly in your stomach?"

"Bubbly?" I asked. "Is that what it feels like to be kissed?"

"You mean, you didn't?" Veronica asked. "I thought you liked him."

"I don't like any boy at this school," I said. Veronica nodded as we continued to walk.

"Well, there's other girls like you at school. I don't judge," Veronica said.

"Everybody thinks you kissed him anyway. They're probably already talking about it," Monica said. She had crept up behind me to latch onto my other arm.

"I guess I don't really care," I said.

"Why don't you care? It's super important," Veronica said.

"It's really not," I said, "and you two put way too much importance on that kissing stuff." I threw my hands in the air to make my point. "Who even thinks about that stuff all the time?"

Monica and Veronica mirrored each other with folded arms and wrinkled noses.

"Don't start acting weird again. You're popular now," Monica said.

I tried to walk around the twins, but they stood together with their legs stretched apart to block my path. They moved in unison as though they were Josh's defensive teammates on the football field.

"If people like me, fine but I'm not going to force myself to do something I don't wanna do," I said. "And just so you know I don't think he wanted to kiss, either."

"I respect that," Veronica said. "I think about more than boys, by the way. I'm going to be a fashion designer when I grow up." She nodded in agreement but Monica continued with her questions.

"Oh, so having a crush is a waste of time but playing a piccolo all day isn't?" Monica asked. She motioned with her hands like a lawyer in a courtroom.

"Not to me," I said. "Music is what I do. It's who I am, I guess."

"I get it," Veronica said. "She's just really into music."

"Oh," Monica said. She thought for a moment. "Of course! That makes sense! Which singer is your celebrity crush?"

The front door handle whacked against the outside wall of the cabin. Monica and Veronica turned around. When I looked up, I saw Dana staring at us from the porch steps, dressed in a cropped sweater and red pleather pants. "I normally wouldn't hang out with you kids but I heard this party's lit," Dana said. She was standing in front of Zyzzyva on the front porch. Zyzzyva was doing her best to stare Dana down from the front door to keep her from coming in.

"You weren't invited," I heard Zyzzyva tell Dana.

"Yeah, well," Dana replied, "I live in the neighborhood."

"Party?" A loud voice asked. Everyone's head whipped back around to see who had asked the question in a tone of judgment. It was Reema walking toward us but this time she looked like her human self. "What's going on here?" Reema asked.

"Who's that?" Monica asked.

"Who am I? I'm Wilda's babysitter. That's who I am," Reema said, "and this isn't supposed to be happening right now so I suggest you all leave before I find out who your parents are and start making some phone calls." Reema sounded very convincing with her arms crossed, her eyebrows furled and eyes looking wild with false indignation. "You heard me," she said. "This party's over!"

"But it's only just beginning," Dana said. Reema stood face to face with Dana.

"I said the party's over," Reema repeated. "Do you really want to do this now with all of these witnesses?" she whispered to Dana.

"Whatever," Dana said. Then she took a long look at the kids who were gathered around the cabin. She shook her head and walked down the porch steps back onto the driveway. "Next time," she said as she started to walk back up to the road. "See you, Wilda," she said.

I waved back as though everything was normal. Then Reema came down the steps, grabbed me gently by my arm and led me back to the cabin, but not without a secret little wink and an impish smile. "You are in big trouble, Wilda. Wait until I tell your mom!" Reema marched me to the cabin in front of everyone as Charlie followed behind me.

"You wouldn't tell her, would you?" I pled.

"Well, shouldn't I? You're getting a bit out of hand these days. I get that you're cool and your trust fund gives you unlimited resources to do this kind of thing but there have to be boundaries."

Unlimited resources, I thought. *Nice touch.* Reema was trying to make me look cool to everybody.

"I'm sorry. I promise it won't happen again," I said looking down, attempting to look remorseful.

"Well, sooner or later the word will get out and you'll all be in trouble. Won't you kids?" Reema looked at the party guests with a stern face. "I bet Ms. Robertson would be so mad at you all for messing up her house, turning a nice little study session into a big party. She'd want to strangle each and every one of you, and that's after your parents get done with you. And it serves you all right if one of you blabs about the destruction you caused so the rest of you get in trouble along with Wilda," she added.

"No, we won't talk about it," one of them said.

"Please do. I hope you tell them about it," Reema said.

"Sorry," said another.

"Let's go," they said.

Zyzzyva turned off the music. The guests quickly grabbed their coats, purses and backpacks and lined up to leave. They pulled their cell phones out and attempted to text their parents and older siblings for rides home. As if on cue their phones were able to get signals again.

"Nah-uh," Reema said, wagging her finger. "Nobody leaves until each one of you has picked up a piece of trash or a misplaced cup or glass and put it in the right place."

The kids begrudgingly cleaned litter from the rooms of the cabin and filled up the sink and kitchen trash bin. Zyzzyva joined in and blended with everybody else. When it appeared that most of the guests had picked something up and put it away, Reema flitted her hand. "All right. You can go, all of you. Now!" she said.

As soon as she'd said it the kids hurriedly ran out, scurrying away up the driveway as their rides showed up and then scattering in either direction.

Zyzzyva waved her goodbyes. "My work here is done. It was interesting to say the least," she said.

"I owe you," Reema told her.

"See you back home," Zyzzyva said. Then she shrank to the size of a beetle and buzzed away through the front door. Now only Reema and I were left.

The cabin looked like it had been hit by a food tornado. Even with the help of the guests there were still empty pizza boxes piled up on the kitchen floor, half eaten plates of food on the counter and stains on the furniture. "Well," Reema sighed happily, "this worked out very well."

"Yeah, but what am I going to do about all this? Mom will kill me," I said.

"Oh, this? No problem. Just pile the rest of the dishes in the sink," Reema said. She ran some soapy water into the sink full of dishes and as she pulled the plates and bowls out, they seemed to dry themselves spotlessly. She pitched them perfectly into the open cabinets as if they were playing cards. Then Reema took a dish towel and wiped it along the furniture. "As long as I have something to work with, everything gets easier," she said. After she dragged a mop from the hall closet along the floor the whole cabin looked the same as it did that morning. All traces of extra dishes, stains and trash were gone. The refrigerator was as sparsely filled as before and the extra food had disappeared, too.

"Wow," I said. "Is there anything you can't do, Reema?" I asked.

"Well," she said, resigned, "I can't stop time. Of all of us fairies, only Avery can do that. And I can't read minds, either. Only the queen of the Autumn Court can do that."

"The Autumn Court. That's the Unseelies, right?"

"You remember," Reema said.

"So, how do you deal with that?" I asked.

"You have to clear away all your thoughts when she is near. Luckily you can feel her enter in your mind, looking around."

"That's weird. Where did Avery go, anyway?" I asked.

"Back to our homeland," Reema said, and making a sound like a whistle followed by a rolled R she said, "Vreenley."

"To go back to living his old life?" I asked.

"Not yet. He'll have to reintroduce himself first, at the three friendly castles, and he'll start remembering everything. First, he'll go to the castle I took you to, and he will make his return known to them. They should supply him with a personal detail of generals to protect him and carry out his battle commands. Then he will choose his destiny at the castle of the water sprites. Lastly he will travel to the Tower of Alabaster where he must convince the powerful Summer Court fairies and the learned but rather skeptical elves to acknowledge him as king."

"King?" I asked.

"Yes," Reema said emphatically, "the Sky King of Spring Court fairies. It might take him a while, though. One hour in our land is like three in yours."

"He'll be gone all night!" I said.

"Maybe," Reema said. "Worst case scenario is he's reported missing and the cops come here. But you won't get in trouble. There's no way they'll believe some wild party happened. It's spotless."

"The police will be coming here?" I asked.

"In a few hours, but not if he remembers to use his armor to freeze time like a good fairy king is supposed to. He might forget, though. There's a part of him that's still new to all this," Reema said nonchalantly as she sat down on the couch to pet

Charlie. She flipped the TV back on. "A game show," she said. "They're always fun."

"What am I supposed to tell the cops if they come?" I asked.

"Tell them he ran off to fairy land. They're not going to believe you, anyway," she said. "Besides, they won't need to come. I have faith in Grandfather."

"I hope you're right," I said. I opened the refrigerator again, looking for something to eat other than bologna sandwiches.

"Oh, I left you a slice of your favorite thing in the microwave," Reema said. I opened the microwave and there it was, warm and ready to eat. The smell of savory tomato sauce and melted cheese made me excited. I looked back at Reema with surprise. "Did you make it?"

She aimed her fingers at me and smiled with a wink of one of her twinkling hazel eyes. "Sure did. I didn't forget about you," she said.

"Yes, well," I said, sitting down at the table with the plate of pizza, "you'll make a capable mother someday."

Her smile faded to a serious expression. "You really think so?" she asked.

"Yeah, I mean, you're an awesome cook, you're nice, you clean up extremely fast, you protect people and you're cool. You're really pretty, too," I said.

She just sat there on the couch staring at me for a moment, taking it all in. Then she smiled knowingly at me as she breathed a victorious sigh, her hazel eyes twinkling with contentment. "I think you could do well as a child in my country," she said.

I nodded my head. Reema was probably right. With a friend like her I figured I could make it anywhere.

Chapter 9

Thump, thump, thump. I must have been in the middle of a dream when a rattle invaded my sleep. *Thump, thump, thump*, it knocked again. I pried my eyelids open and stared into my dark bedroom, searching for light. A half-moon shone through the curtain, tracing the outline of the window frame onto the edge of the floor. As I roused myself from my drowsiness, I noticed a shadow shift upon the floor. I sat up and stared at my bedroom window. Charlie bolted from the corner of my bed onto the floor, his ears standing up.

"Wilda," a familiar but muffled male voice called loudly. Charlie started barking. "It's okay, boy," he said. Charlie stopped barking but watched intently at the window.

"Avery?" I asked, shocked to hear him outside my window in the middle of the night. "Did you run away?"

"I did," he said, "but I came back."

"You should go home then. Your parents must be worried sick," I whispered loudly, trying not to wake my mother down the hall.

"I was home by dinner. They think I'm in bed now. Nobody's looking for me," he said nonchalantly without even trying to speak quietly.

"What time is it, anyway?" I asked. I threw off the heavy Rapunzel quilt and sat on the edge of my bed.

"It isn't," Avery said.

"What?" I asked, rubbing my eyes.

"There's no time right now. I figured out how to pause it for everybody else," he answered.

"How… Why?" I asked.

"I'll tell you if you let me in. Please?" Avery asked.

"You, a boy, intend to just climb into my room in the middle of the night. You're bold," I said.

"Shouldn't I be? I mean, I *am* king. I set the rules," he said.

"Could your head get any bigger?" I moaned.

He chuckled and shrugged his shoulders. "So, are you gonna let me in?" he asked.

I stood up, tiptoed to the window in my fuzzy socks and unlatched it. Avery helped me pull the window up and crawled inside, angling his way in and landing on his knee onto the floor. He was dressed in thick white socks, Velcro sandals and light blue flannel pajamas with piping around the collar, the kind of clothes one might expect a grandfather to wear. He still wore the armor made of stone around his chest and shoulders, perhaps his saving grace as far as fashion went, the only cool part of his outfit.

"Do you have any idea how much trouble you'd get me into if Mom came in and saw you here in the middle of the night?" I asked.

"She won't. She's incapable of moving at the moment as she's frozen in time."

"That's not a nice thing to do to somebody," I said.

"Why not?" Avery asked. "It doesn't hurt."

"But it takes away her freedom."

"I doubt she'll miss it. It will only feel like a second was lost for her," Avery replied.

"Why did you come here?" I asked, anxiously massaging the back of my neck.

"You see, I've been to some incredible places back home. I know you've been to one of them, too."

"Back home?" I asked, surprised that he was already calling it that.

"Yeah," he said, "the place my spirit comes from. They told me about you," Avery said. "We both know the castle of the vines is real." Avery walked toward Charlie, knelt down and rubbed the back of Charlie's head. "I have to visit the castle of the water sprites, now. The only thing is, they only respond to music, and I don't play anything."

"So, you want me to go and help you?"

"Could you talk to them for me? Through your piccolo?"

"Why are you doing this, Avery?" I asked as I sat back down on the bed. "You barely know these...

people. You had a chance to see 'fairyland.' How many people can honestly say that? Now you can cross it off your list and go back to your parents."

Avery shook his head and let out a heavy sigh. "It's not that simple," he said.

"It is that simple," I said. "You have a different life here, in the regular world. You can make it whatever you want it to be. You don't have to choose your past and all its drama."

"I know now that I was sent to this community as a changeling so that my human parents could keep me hidden away from the Unseelies, but this was always my mission. I was always supposed to go back."

"Who told you that?" I asked.

"Come with me and I'll show you," he said.

Charlie nudged his wet nose against my legs, whimpering to go with us. It was like he understood everything. I reached down and gave him a good scratch behind his ears. "What about Charlie?" I asked.

"We'll be back soon."

I took a deep breath. "All right," I said.

"And bring your mini-flute," he implored me.

"You mean my piccolo," I said.

"Yeah, that," he said.

Avery watched me with his arms folded while I fumbled around in my dark bedroom closet until I could feel my puffy coat and my piccolo tucked into its inside pocket. I didn't bother to put it in its case. I didn't anticipate being gone for too long so I pulled the coat on over my gray night shirt with its purple collar and short purple leggings, nothing I'd usually wear out of the house. Then we slid out of the window and onto the damp ground.

"Come on," he said.

"But Charlie will get out," I reminded him. Charlie was already at the window, looking for the right opportunity to sneak through it. I struggled to slide the window back down.

"Just... move," he said. I was a little annoyed by his impatience but I stepped away, anyway. He nearly slammed the window shut, as though he was in an enormous hurry. "Let's go," he said.

We marched into the darkness of the deep woods, Avery charging ahead like an army general. The only sound was our feet crunching the twigs and leaves that had fallen to the forest floor under the weight of the melted snow. "We'll have to go the way you came the last time. I can't project you there with me because you're not capable," he said.

"What's that supposed to mean?" I asked. He'd been king for less than a day and I was afraid that he was already pulling rank.

"I mean magical," he said, "You're only human." Avery's black eyes looked intent under the light of the moon. He walked with a hunched back, more like an old man than the young, eager hall monitor I knew. I suspected the weight of the stone armor he stubbornly wore was physically weighing him down, perhaps mentally, too. He looked back at me to see if I was able to keep up with his blazing gait, his lips pursed with conflict.

I walked pensively beside him. The old Avery I met on my first day at school was becoming less exuberant and increasingly cranky, so I wasn't sure whether to make small talk or to ask the big questions. Finally, I got up my courage to ask him, "Avery, are you still one person, or are you two people now?"

He turned to look me in the eye but his face was impossible to read. "I am the same person you have always known," he said.

"So, you *are* Avery?" I asked to be clear.

"Of course, I am," he said. "That is the last thing I have doubts about."

"But Reema called you her grandfather," I said.

"Yeah, well, it turns out I'm pretty old, too," Avery insisted.

"But how can you be a grandfather and a boy at the same time?" I asked.

Avery stopped walking along the green footpath with its motionless blades of grass. He turned and faced me, his eyes appearing hollow, almost lost. "I don't know," he said before dropping his gaze to his feet. He took a deep breath and trudged forward. "There are a lot of things I remember," Avery continued, "scary and fantastic things, and I don't know what to make of them. It's like a dream but it's also real. Do you know that feeling?"

"That's how I felt when I woke up after the last time I came here," I said. "Except, when I got back to my room, I was still myself."

"I'm still myself," Avery said.

"You're still a sixth grader who lives with a perfect Mom and Dad?"

"I guess so," he said. "That hasn't changed. But this is something I have to do. It's like my soul demands it and I can't stop now."

I followed behind him and instinctively placed my hand on the armor against his back. "But is that fair?" I asked.

"What do you mean?" Avery asked me, his intent gaze and furrowed brows becoming more relaxed and thoughtful.

"Your old soul has unfinished business, but in order to do it, it has to intrude upon the life that your new soul is living."

"That's just it. I'm not a new soul. Besides, it can't be helped, Wilda. I was born to lead my people. I guess it's my destiny."

"But you have new people now."

"Like who, the kids I monitor at school?" Avery asked. He was incredulous, his voice raising with a sense of humor.

"And your mom and dad," I said.

Avery didn't say anything for a moment. I guess the thought of leaving his parents stunned him into silence. Then he threw his hands up into the night air. "So, what are you trying to say?" he asked defensively.

"Nothing. It's just, are you sure this is the right thing to do?" I asked.

"I am not abandoning my family," he said.

"I didn't mean it like that," I said.

"Then don't ever accuse me of that," he said, sternly.

"I won't bring them up again," I said, now throwing my hands into the still air in surrender.

"I'm not doing that," he said. "I won't do that. I can't." He shook his head as though he were arguing with himself. "No, that's not what this is," he said again.

I tried to keep my mouth shut as we continued to walk along the wooded pathway, wondering if Avery had even taken the time to think through his decision. I decided to go ahead and find out how much he had really thought about his past life. "You know your grandfather soul is married to an old woman, right?" I asked. "You're married to Reema's grandma."

Avery turned to look at me, his stare seeming alarmed and almost fearful. Then he turned and faced ahead without saying anything.

We continued the rest of the way in silence. After a mile long walk, we reached the circle of mushrooms surrounding the crooked oak tree, Reema's sleeping grandmother. "There she is," I said, "your bride."

Avery looked back at me, this time his stare becoming nervous again. "Once I fulfill my mission, it should all make sense," he said.

Avery waved his arms from his sides into the still air and the world came to motion again. I placed my hand against the smooth bark of the oak tree. The tree slowly twisted its canopy of branches to face Avery and me.

"Grandmother," I said. "It is Reema's friend, Wilda. I brought my friend, Avery, but you knew him as the Fairy King. We would like ..."

Before I could finish talking the tree wound itself down from its great height overlooking us and began to speak. "Only one man can rightfully wear the

sacred armor. It will only belong to its true owner.
Who are you?" the tree bellowed.

"I am the one was sent back to reign again as
the Sky King," Avery said. His wings emerged from his
back for a moment and glowed yellow before
retracting into his back.

"Then the magic worked. It is you," the tree said with hope in her husky voice.

It bent towards Avery and embraced him with its branches, suddenly taking on a more feminine form. "You're back! I missed you so much!" the tree roared, holding his face in her branches. She nearly lifted Avery off the ground.

"I'm not exactly as I was in my other life," Avery said.

"It's all right. Perhaps I can be reborn as a child, too. It is Aisosa, your wife. We can start over. You must go to the castle of vines and persuade the regents to transform me," she said.

"Transform you?" Avery asked. "What do you mean?"

The tree stood up straight. She breathed a heavy sigh that felt like a strong wind. "And how could you know about what happened?" she asked herself. "The regents turned me into this tree to punish me."

"So, you are a dryad now? What could you have done to deserve that?"

"I allowed a human to marry our daughter and he betrayed us," she said.

Avery stumbled back upon hearing the tree say that. His eyes widened in disbelief. "This is not what I remember," he said.

"No, Amadi, this is how I was punished after you died. They promised to destroy me if they ever see me there again."

"Why didn't our daughter stop them? Where is she?"

"After Reema was born she was never seen again. The regents took over everything."

"Even Reema? What did they do to our granddaughter?"

"They declared her an orphan. They took her away and raised her to obey them."

"You're telling me that my daughter is gone? Now that I've come back, my little Isoke is gone!" Avery shouted. His eyes welled with tears and confusion. "Why didn't she tell me?" he asked.

I guessed he meant Reema. Perhaps if she'd told him he would have found it too upsetting and he never would have agreed to come back.

"I'm sorry," the grandmother tree said. She released his shoulders and leaned back. "You'll show them all that the prophecy was true. You have returned."

Avery nodded his head and waved goodbye to her. We continued on into the circle of mushrooms.

The air surrounding us opened up and swallowed us into the fairy world where it was early morning, and the air was fragrant and light. I stumbled again to regain my footing in the changing landscape. The lilies in the meadow laughed again at my clumsiness in their world. Avery looked past them, his face etched with urgency. "All right. Let's go," he commanded, ignoring the thick bubble coat that I was trying to shed. I managed to slough it off, pulling my piccolo out of the inside coat pocket as I wondered about the best way to carry it.

Avery shook his head, staring at the castle of vines in the distance. "My own government betrayed my family while the regents sit in my castle, attempting to rule through my granddaughter. I should arrest the regents for treason," he said, seriously. He rubbed his head between his pointed ears and took off jogging into the meadow. I stuffed my piccolo into the back of my waistband of my leggings and I tried to catch up.

"If you do get rid of the regents do you think they try to overthrow you?" I asked.

"They can't if they're in jail," Avery said.

"All right. Supposing you throw them all in jail, what if everybody else thinks you're an imposter? They might say you got rid of the regents because they knew you were lying. Worse yet, what if the military takes their side and rises up against you?"

"Are you saying I need the regents for credibility? So that my people will trust me?"

"Isn't that what our world history teacher would say? Julius Caesar needed the Roman Senate."

"Yes, well, you must not have been in class when Mr. Gumble said that the Roman Senate stabbed him in his back," Avery said.

"You do have a point there but still, if you're really going to be king, you probably shouldn't rule from emotion. That's always gotten kings in trouble," I said.

"So, you actually do pay attention in class," Avery said.

"Sometimes," I answered. Avery chuckled and motioned with his hand to keep jogging.

"To the Blunt Hills," he said.

When we had left the castle of vines behind us Avery began to run faster and faster. We ran until we reached the northern part of the rolling blue hills. Avery leaped over them with boundless energy. He seemed to instinctively know every nook in the path as though he'd traveled it for years. I tried my best to follow him, winded as we hiked.

Once we wound our way to what appeared to be a deep blue river, Avery stopped. He lifted his long eyes toward the sky. I followed his gaze beyond the stream and saw a shimmering waterfall. The waterfall was surrounded by a lagoon connected to a winding river. A branch of the deep river flowed into a large cave.

Although I was already a bit tired and sweaty, I followed Avery as he ran down the green hill into the mouth of the cave, standing before the waterfall. Now that we were close enough to really see the details of the waterfall, I couldn't believe my eyes. "Whoa," I gasped in disbelief. "It's flowing in reverse!" I exclaimed.

Avery looked back at me with an impish smile. "The entrance to the water sprite's castle. Amazing, isn't it? Just as I remember."

He raised his hands to his mouth to shout. "River sprites, show yourselves," he called out, "It is the Fay Sky King from the Spring Court. I have returned with a song." He turned his head toward me and gave an assuring nod. I stood behind him, bent over to catch my breath.

"What?" I asked, totally clueless to his hint.

"Go on," he said. "Play whatever you did to find the last stone."

"You want me to play something now? I can barely breathe with how fast you were going," I said.

Avery came over to me and put his hand on my back in a surprising moment of empathy. "I forgot how out of shape you must be from taking marching band instead of P.E." he said.

"Gosh, how thoughtful," I said, sarcastically. I shook my head at Avery, straightened the mouthpiece onto my piccolo and raised it to my lips. Slowly, I exhaled a winded breath into the hole to tune it. More air came out than music as I squeaked out a tired note.

"That's what orchestra is teaching you?" Avery asked.

"Do you want a song or not?" I asked, still panting.

"Fine," he said, smiling, his arms crossed while he waited for me to catch my breath. I blew slowly into the piccolo again, this time with more energy and focus, and tapped my fingers along the keys in a simple, impromptu melody. I played the tones again and again, adding a little flourish at the end of each sampling of notes. Then the water stirred. I stopped with surprise and we watched it together, Avery dropping his hands to his knees in astonishment. "Play it again!" he demanded. So, I did, adding a few new notes to every line. Out popped six heads from the bubbling water. They had straight black hair, wet and parted down the middle, and bronze skin that glowed green under the blue flickers of light reflecting from the amber cave walls.

"Keep going," Avery whispered. Although my heart was racing I continued to play, adding flourishes and running scales, landing upon high notes for every trill. To my delight the emerging water sprites leaped out of the water, doing back flips in the air before landing below the surface. Splashes of water landed on us before we could step back to escape them. I nearly dropped my piccolo when they did this. I caught a glimpse of their beaded gowns with glassy ribbons streaming down their chests. Their black braids formed crowns upon their heads, tied up into elaborate shapes, with the rest of their hair flowing freely down their backs.

"Should I keep going?" I asked Avery.

"Yeah. Keep it up," he said.

I wiped the piccolo on my night shirt and lifted it up to my lips again, trying to play a similar melody to the one I played before. The six water sprites' heads bobbed up from the water again. This time I could see their full torsos, and I had never seen such stunning women before. They appeared to be native to the forests around Belfair. Their eyes were filled with starlight and their lips were as red as roses. One by one they emerged from the water in their long ropey dresses until they surrounded Avery and me.

"We accept your song," they said, almost in unison. "Come with us." The six water sprites walked together back into the water. Avery followed, stepping across stones along the water's edge. I stuffed my piccolo into the back of my waistband again.

"Where are we going?" I asked them.

"To see the queen," Avery said, "Right?"

"She will see you," the water sprites answered. "Do not be afraid," one of the water sprites said. Then they spoke nearly at the same time, laughing as they advised us. "You are protected."

"We will protect you."

"You will not be harmed."

"There is no need to hold your breath."

"You won't even get wet."

Avery looked back at me and smiled before walking into the water behind them. "You trust them?" I asked from the bank.

"I have my armor to protect me," he said.

"What about me? What do I have?" I asked.

"You're with me," he said.

I took a deep breath and followed him into the water until I was waist deep. I shuddered in panic at that point, not sure whether I could go on, feeling stuck in a cold lagoon. I turned to look back from where we had come. To my surprise, one of the water sprites emerged from behind me, placing her cold hand on my shoulder and laughing as she splashed water in front of me. The water landed on my chest but it didn't soak through my shirt. I stared at it, confused. "See?" the water sprite asked, laughing. She nudged me closer to the others. I reluctantly trudged my feet forward from the weight of her push and watched the current part around me. "You know, I never learned to swim," I said.

She laughed and guided me further into the middle of the lagoon. Soon I lost sight of Avery as his head dipped below the water's surface. I looked back again at the water sprite behind me for reassurance but just then my feet dropped down onto what appeared to be a staircase.

Then I saw Avery and the other river water sprites again. We were all descending the stone staircase leading to a hall in an underwater longhouse. The hollow, round windows in the walls revealed fish swimming beyond them, but the inside of the hall itself was completely dry. It was as though we were in a giant bubble. Avery looked back at me with a smile on his face. He knew he'd taken a gamble that paid off. We weren't harmed. In fact, we were being escorted like royalty to the queen of the water sprites herself.

We stepped onto a long carpet made of reeds that stretched nearly half a mile across the wooden chamber, passing ornately carved alcoves imprinted with the images of sea animals, the kinds of carvings I'd seen in Mr. Gumble's history class when he told us about the Salish people who roamed this forest long before Washington was a state, tribes like the Quinault, the Puyallup, and the Tlingit. As we walked past the alcoves the designs turned and shifted, their thick black and red lines transforming from one animal into two, then three, morphing from two dimensional designs into three dimensional versions of themselves that grew larger and seemed to watch us as we walked past them. The designs of fish also contained the designs of frogs, eagles and salamanders within them, with parts of the designs disappearing and reemerging from my view. The designs seemed to watch us, too. They must have been living beings imbued with spirits that made the water sprites' dwelling possible, I thought.

The nooks within the hall glowed with pale green light. Avery and I noticed globes of shining mushrooms attached to the walls.

"What kind of lights are those?" I asked Avery.

"They must be bioluminescence," Avery said.

"It makes the mushrooms glow?" I asked.

"I think so," he said.

Avery and I looked up at the same time to see a stunningly beautiful, raven-haired woman seated high above us at the end of the hall, but before we could come any closer we were halted by a sea of jumping frogs. There must have been over a hundred of them, all bouncing toward us and around us. Once we were surrounded by the water sprites and the multitude of frogs, brown and green, the frogs stood on their hind legs and began to grow before our eyes into a tribe of people. They were male and female, young and old, and all of them wore long gowns or shirts and pants with glowing glass beads and shimmering ribbons upon their chests. Likewise, fish jumped through windows, turning themselves into guards armed with spears, bows and arrows. They assembled themselves in front of their queen.

The royal water sprite was seated on a stool made from a tree trunk, steps above us. Her long black hair, braided at her sides and left loose behind her, flowed down to her ankles. Her long, shimmering dress, iridescent like a rainbow trout's scales and filled from head to toe with gleaming beads, had wide sleeves dripping with beaded metallic ribbons. It was a marvel to behold. Her boots were also beaded and glistened with white shells. A beaded crown rested upon her head, and large eagle feathers were tied into her silky hair. With dark, shining eyes, red lips and copper skin, her striking looks were almost paralyzing.

"Your Excellent Grace," Avery said, quickly averting his eyes away from her as though her great beauty endangered his life and trembling as he dropped to a bended knee before her. She smiled at him, content with this display of humility, before her long eyes drifted toward me. I wasn't sure what to do so I dropped to bended knee faster than I could even think. She giggled when she saw this.

"I am Avery... known as Amadi, the Sky King from the Spring Court, and this is my human friend, Wilda."

The water sprite queen nodded at him and rested her hands peacefully at her sides, her head tilted as she observed us.

"I have come to ask for your insight into my past," Avery continued.

"As you know, we are spirits of the water. We could have easily drowned you. What is it that ails a king, that he should risk his life to see me, River Singer?" the queen asked with a voice of mesmerizing calmness. I imagined she embodied every quality that had ever been said about a siren.

Avery spoke with his head bowed. "I hope that I may become free from self-doubt, so that I may serve as king to my people without any mental reservations."

"You appear to be quite young for a king," the River Queen said. "Please come closer so that I may see you clearly."

Avery stood to his feet and took a few tentative steps forward, his head still bowed, and motioned to with me with his hand to stand up. I clumsily stood, nervously tugging at the hem of my shirt. The river queen stepped down from her throne and stood before Avery, lifting his face toward her with open palm. "You *are* a boy!" she exclaimed.

"I am," Avery admitted, "but my soul belonged to an old king who died bravely in battle."

"So, your spirit was allowed to return, but now you live two lives, caught between two different destinies. Such a situation cannot sustain itself. One life's plan must be let go so that the other may be lived fully," she said. "Go to the reflecting pools. The water speaks truth to those who seek it, showing them what they do not know, and what they know but do not accept. The pools will help you see, so that you may make your choice. Then you must drink from it to clarify your heart. May the truth be born in your spirit, and the false path be drained away."

The river queen spoke to the water sprites who surrounded us in what sounded like loud whispers. I looked at Avery, confused. "Can you hear what she's saying?" I said softly in Avery's direction.

"I don't know. I think she's speaking a local language, maybe Squamish or Twana, or Lushootseed?" he asked.

"That's not Spanish, or French, even," I said.

I guess I said that a little loud. Avery gave me a wide-eyed stare as if to suggest we better stop talking before the queen turned around.

When she did turn to us, she gestured with her gleaming, outstretched arm. "See for yourselves," she said. Several water sprites gathered around Avery and led him behind the throne to the pools of reflecting mineral springs. There were four pools, each with four corners, and each one shown like a mirror. I followed

Avery to the pools as he wandered about, his chin resting on his balled fist as he thought to himself. We first came upon a shimmering blue pool. Avery stood over it while I waited behind him, not sure of what we were about to witness. Avery watched with curious eyes as he leaned over it, letting his fingertips wade across the surface. His parents, Mr. and Mrs. Johnson, rippled into a living portrait on the water. The pool revealed them to be at an airport. Mr. Johnson was assisting Mrs. Johnson in lifting a brown baby boy wrapped in a colorful West African printed blanket out of a basket that was carried by perhaps an aid worker. Mrs. Johnson was laughing through happy tears, and Mr. Johnson's eyes were wide with excitement and hope.

The waters rippled again and Mr. Johnson was now pushing a young Avery, maybe no more than six years old, on a bicycle. Mrs. Johnson was standing in the kitchen window wearing an apron, stirring chocolate chips into a batter as she watched them in the driveway and waved from the window. A woman whose face resembled our babysitter, Dana, slinked into view at the corner of the street. She seemed to a little younger, maybe thirteen years old. Her eyes and hair were brown, and she was carrying a large duffle bag. Her eyes projected a focus that almost looked desperate. She turned and glared at Avery from the reflecting pool with a gleaming intensity in her eyes that nearly knocked Avery back on his heels.

"Are you all right?" I asked.

Avery shook his head, then nodded. "Yeah, I'm fine," he said.

He looked away from the image of the strange woman toward a different pool. This time he -saw a young Dahomey woman tucking the blanketed boy into the arms of a white nun at a hospital. Then she turned to walk away. The waters shifted and the young woman's actions played in reverse. Now she was walking backwards with the baby in her arms until she was alone and the city skyline receded into the distance. Then her feet lifted off of the ground. She flew backwards from the power of large, dragonfly wings and floated through the doorway of a large, hut shaped building made of white coral. When she reached a young Dahomey man from the village of similarly floating people, her feet touched the ground again. The young couple held hands and stared into each other's sad eyes. They spoke a language I couldn't understand but somehow I felt I knew what they must have been saying, that is was something that had to be done for the good of all fairy people.

Avery moved closer to the rippling waters, rubbing his eyes in amazement. He saw a different African woman, now. It was Reema's grandmother as a younger woman, her hair in long, tiny braids filled with golden ornaments. She was holding onto the shoulders of an elegant little girl who must have been Reema's mother. Avery himself was a tall, commanding African warrior draped in fabrics full of some sort of fairy glyphs, with large square gold medallions in a necklace draped around his torso. He wore the armor, too and it beamed with wings of amber light. He wore a tall gold helmet on his head. He watched his past self embrace Reema's grandmother passionately. She seemed to delight in his arms beneath the yellow glow of Avery's impressive armor.

Then Avery lifted his arms above a battlefield without so much as a second thought, and shockwaves of energy were emitted from his outstretched arms. The encroaching Unseelie fairies and their hideous Fomorian giants stopped in their tracks while his family looked on, confidently standing behind him. He waved his right arm, tracing the horizon. It turned from day to night. With his other arm he waved across the horizon again and it turned from night to day. He did this several more times to his daughter's amusement. Then he raised his palms together and the sun rose to the middle of the sky. When he clenched his trembling fists, the sun burned hotter. When he released his hands and rested them at his sides it was as though hours had passed during the battle as his enemies seared in the sun. In a moment in time he was able to freeze, Avery had harnessed the power of the sun and unleashed it like fire upon his enemies. The Unseelies retreated from the battlefield, conceding defeat.

Avery the warrior easily lifted his little girl into the air. The surface of the pool rippled and her image had morphed into a woman with a human husband by her side. Another ripple revealed baby Reema was in her arms as she flew fearfully through the woods. It seemed like she was being chased by someone but I couldn't see who was chasing her.

In a different pool Avery saw a reflection of himself slumped over in a chair while his terrified son-in-law ran out of the cabin carrying the armor in his arms. Avery moved toward it and saw himself kneeling on the ground on the African savannah, clutching a lance that had pierced his heart as ghoulish giants closed in on him. Turning away from the reflecting pool, Avery pulled open his collar to stare at the long birth mark that ran down the center of his breastplate. His eyes widened with astonishment. "This is how I died," he said to himself.

For a moment I heard the faintest sound of a woman singing, soft and cooing, echoing through the chambers and their reflecting pools. It must have been the River Singer because I felt my shoulders soften and my hands drop calmly to my sides. That's when I noticed my own reflection in one of the pools we walked past. The green waters rippled at first, then smoothed into a glossy surface. I stared at my face as though I had never seen it before. It had contorted itself so that my mouth grew hideously large and my red hair appeared frizzled and messy. As

I walked my image followed me, daring me to stop and pay attention.

I stopped walking and watched the pool. It showed me an image of myself as a toddler sitting in a highchair at the kitchen table in my old apartment in San Francisco, looking at my mother. She was sitting on the couch, wiping tears from her cheeks as she pulled a bottle of scotch out of a box labeled "Michael Robertson Estate, For Valerie." My image disappeared into the water, and all I could see now were Belfair neighbors and sheriff's department officers traipsing through the woods in the middle of the day, calling out my name and Avery's name. Monica and Veronica were there with Charlie too, along with Avery's parents, and several volunteers from school. They marched through the thick woods with sticks and flashlights. A ripple in the water revealed a sheriff in my bedroom. He was flipping through my notebook. He carried it outside the front door of our cabin and showed it to Mr. Gumble, asking him if I ever drew troubling pictures in class or talked about running away.

Shocked, I stepped back, unsure what to make of what I'd seen. When I turned around a different scene awaited me in the reflecting pool that had been behind me. The rippling waters revealed my mother, rubbing her matted head with worry. "She's never run away before," I heard my mother say. "I can't believe she's been gone for twelve hours. And I noticed one of my bottles I had in the kitchen the other day is missing. I hate to think she stole it."

"Which bottle was it?" I heard a familiar voice ask. I watched as Dana walked up to my mother and put her hand on my mother's back. They stood next to our Dodge Avenger on the side of the road, somewhere near Highway 300.

"The strawberry vodka I use for mixes at work," Mom said.

"You mean this one?" Dana asked, pulling a bottle of rum from her backpack. She seemed to manifest the bottle, as though it were not really in her empty backpack all along, but it became a reality as soon as my mother mentioned it.

"Where did you..." Mom started to ask.

"I caught Wilda trying to sneak it into school in her backpack. She probably wanted to try it herself, maybe in the bathroom," Dana said. I couldn't believe the lie she was telling my mother.

"I knew it," Mom said.

"You just need to relax," Dana said. She unscrewed the cap on the bottle and handed it to my mother. "A little taste of that will do you good," she said, setting the cap on the hood of the car.

My mother took the bottle from her and stared at it. "Yeah," she said. She took a swig from it, screwed the top back on and set the bottle on the ground by the car. She exhaled a long sigh and peered back at Dana.

"Thanks," Mom said.

"Don't worry, Ms. Robertson. She'll show up," Dana said.

"She's had it hard but I never thought she would just run away," Mom said.

"What do you mean?" Dana asked.

"It's really my fault. Everything she's had to deal with, it all comes back to what people think of me. All the whispers about us ..."

"Like what?" Dana asked.

"You're too young to understand," Mom said.

"Try me. I'm not as young as you think," she said.

Mom took a deep breath. "Life wasn't supposed to be this hard. I've been trying to make it work. But not being able to tell anyone the truth about her father ... It's just hard. People assume things."

"Why can't you tell the truth?" Dana asked.

Mom shook her head. "Because it would hurt Wilda if she fully understood," she said.

"You can tell me. I don't judge, and I don't talk," Dana said as Mom sighed. "So, what happened?" Dana asked.

Mom stared at Dana, beginning to relax. "Yeah. Who would you tell?"

"Right," Dana said. "How'd you meet her dad?"

Mom shook her head. "In a class he was teaching. I was eighteen. He was forty-five."

Dana nodded as Mom looked at her. "He was a tenured linguistics professor. There was basically no way he could get fired for anything he did," Mom explained. Dana nodded her head again as she sat on the hood of Mom's car. Mom sat down next to her. "He invited me to help him with his research for a textbook. I was so excited," Mom continued. "It was an unheard-of honor for a freshman, really. Maybe he picked me because of how naïve I must have been. I was … mesmerized by his brilliance. Pretty soon we started dating. I thought we were a real couple."

"What happened?" Dana asked.

"I found out I was going to have a baby, so I told him. And then he dropped me. He wouldn't return my calls. He wouldn't respond to messages. He even stopped going to his office on campus." Mom stared at the rocky ground. "It didn't take long for my parents to find out. They said I had to come home. They weren't going to waste any more money on me."

"So, you dropped out of college?"

"To raise the baby," Mom said. "It was terrible at home. I needed a break, so I went to visit my friend, Lisa, who was living in Pleasanton back then. She had offered to get me a stroller, and it just so happened that we were at the mall when I ran into the professor, and his wife and their three children! I couldn't believe it. He never even wore a ring on campus. I confronted him right then and there, in front of his family. And... I'm not too proud to say, I lost my shoes that day."

"How'd you lose your shoes?" Dana asked.

"We got into an argument and his wife was calling me names, so I took them off... and I threw them at both of them."

"Wow."

"But one of my shoes hit a store clerk and she called the cops. They took me to jail. I was handcuffed to the hospital bed when I had Wilda." Mom grabbed the bottle off the ground and took a drink before she set it down.

"Did he bother to show up for that?" Dana said.

"Of course not. I wasn't going to get a penny out of him unless I sued him so that's what I did. He agreed to pay a lump sum of money to get me to go away. You know, it's pretty hard to have a real career with no degree and a criminal record."

"God. People are awful. At least you found a job."

"Well, I already knew how to mix drinks. I have my dad to thank for that." Mom shook her head. "You know, I mailed Wilda's dad a picture of her once. Can you believe he mailed it back to me? He didn't want anything to do with her."

"No help from Professor Silva," Dana said, shaking her head.

"That's not his name," Mom said. "There was no way I'd put a deadbeat like that on my girl's ID.

Absolutely no way. I picked Silva. It means forest, you know. I want her to be able to stand tall, on her own."

"Makes sense. I prefer her to be independent," Dana said.

"You know, Wilda's already asking why her father never calls. That kind of thing is hard on a kid."

"Yeah," Dana said. She stared back at Mom. "You might as well go ahead and finish that bottle."

Mom picked up the bottle from the ground and stared at it in her hand. "You must want me to get drunk," she said, smiling at Dana.

"Oh, come on. You're a big girl. You can handle your liquor. It's just to make this a little easier. You know, take the edge off," Dana told her, placing her hand on my mother's shoulder. "You know you need to relax."

Mom nodded and took a sip from the bottle as though in a trance. Then she took another sip, and then a longer drink until the bottle was almost empty.

"Atta girl," Dana chuckled, rubbing my mother's back. "Just let all of that stuff go."

My mother took another long drink from the bottle until it was empty. She sat down on the ground. Then my mother lay down on the ground, there by the side of the road, and closed her eyes. It appeared that some time had passed as I watched their shadows move quickly along the ground.

"You know you can't stay here. You have to find her," Dana finally said.

"Of course, I will. She's my child," my mother slurred.

"Get up and go find her," Dana said.

"Where are my keys?" my mother asked, biting her trembling bottom lip.

"They're in your purse," Dana answered. "Hurry, there's not much time left."

"I don't think I can... I mean, I ..." my mother stuttered. "Blah! I can't even talk!"

"Get in. I'll drive," Dana said. She helped my stumbling mother get into the passenger's seat of her car, and when my mother dropped the key on the driver side floor, Dana picked it up from between her feet and put the key in the ignition. Then she got into the driver's seat and closed the door. Dana drove until she and my mother were deep into the woods, taking a path off of the paved Belfair-Tahuya Road to an isolated dirt and gravel road that ran along a sheer drop over the rugged cliffs. The road overlooked the Hood Canal. Dana turned the engine off and dropped the car keys in my mom's hand.

"Mrs. Robertson, can I call you Valerie?" Dana asked.

Mom scoffed. "I was wondering when you were going to stop being so formal. I practically told you my life story."

Dana placed her hand on Mom's hand and wrapped Mom's fingers around the keys. "You did the best you could, Valerie, but let's face it. Your life's a mess. You can end all the pain pretty easily, though. What if Wilda's dad was forced to step up and raise her?"

"That's not gonna happen," Mom said, closing her eyes leaning her head against the headrest.

"I'm serious," Dana said. "The answer is right in front of you."

Mom opened her eyes and stared out at the lapping waves of the Hood Canal below.

"Look at me," Dana said. "You could be done with all this. You know what to do. And if it's your destiny to walk away, you'll be fine. But if not, you'll be free." She pulled the vaping pen out of her purse and offered it to Mom. "One last hit for old time's sake?" she asked.

Mom struggled to look her in the eyes, squinting through the sleepiness of the alcohol she'd consumed. She stared at Dana for a moment. Finally, she managed to smile. "You're so fired," she said.

"You know what? It's getting late. I need to get back home. You can make it from here," Dana said. She got out of the car, angrily slammed the door shut and walked away into the woods. I watched the reflection of my mother in the pool. She was stumbling out of the passenger side of the car, holding the keys in her hand.

I turned away and ran to Avery, nearly colliding with him. "What is it?" he asked, surprised.

"We gotta go home now!"

"I am home," Avery said.

"No, I mean back to Belfair. My mom's about to have an accident!" I shouted.

"What are you talking about? How do you know that?" Avery asked.

"I saw it in the reflecting pool. It's an oracle," I said.

"But how do you know that's happening now and not in the future?" Avery asked.

"I don't. I just know that people have been combing the woods looking for us for hours now. Did you remember to watch the time?" I asked.

"I always do," Avery said. "I stopped it when I came to get you."

"And then you released it when you met Grandmother," I said.

"Yes, and then I..." Avery paused, realizing his mistake.

"We've got to go now!" I pleaded.

"But I haven't finished what I came to do," Avery protested.

"You can always come back here. They welcome you now, but I may only have right now to save my mother!" I said.

Avery let out a heavy sigh. "All right," he said. "Let's go."

Avery hurried back to face the river queen. "I apologize, Your Majesty. There is an emergency. We have to go," he said as he leaped down to his knee and bowed his head. Noticing this, I mimicked his gesture before the queen. She nodded back toward us and we turned to go. This time he walked behind me, trying to remain dignified before the court as I jogged ahead of him.

When we passed the guards with their long staffs, we both ran up the long flight of stairs back to the surface of the water. "What's happening to your mom?" Avery asked.

"I saw her in her car back there. She's drunk," I said.

"How do you know? Has she ever done that before?" Avery asked.

"You know that time when you all picked me up by the road?" I asked.

"Yeah?" Avery asked.

"She left me there because she was drunk," I said.

Avery didn't speak for a moment. I think he was taking it in.

We waded to shore, and before I could climb the hill Avery tapped me on my shoulder. "I think I remember a shortcut. It's flat ground," he said finally.

"Okay. Lead the way," I panted.

"I really wish you had said something sooner about … things at home," Avery said.

"Mom made me promise not to say anything. Besides, what was I supposed to say?" I asked as we started up the hill.

"Help, maybe," Avery suggested.

I followed Avery in a different direction from the way we came. We ran across a rocky field, stumbling along the way, leaving the range of blue hills in the distance. "How did you find out about this shortcut?" I asked.

Avery shrugged. "Instinct I guess."

"Instinct?" I asked, nervously.

"It's strange but I still remember a few things from when I used to live here," Avery said. "Come on."

We ran across the coarse ground into a grassy knoll surrounded by evergreens. "Through the trees,"

Avery said, grabbing my hand. We pushed through the long branches of tree saplings and Scotch broom, fanning ferns out of our way as we hiked across the loamy earth.

"Where is this portal?" I asked.

"It's here somewhere," Avery said. We continued to press against the elastic nature of the brush, trying to search out any sign of a fairy circle of mushrooms or a winding old oak.

A female voice rang out from the misty clearing behind us. "Avery! Thank goodness I found you. We've been searching all over." Jolted by the unexpected voice, we quickly turned around. My eyes widened when I recognized the teenage girl in a black hoodie, denim jacket and jeans standing in the clearing. It was Dana, seeming to appear from nowhere.

"How did you get here?" Avery asked.

"I don't know. I just followed your tracks," Dana said, shrugging her shoulders.

"That's not possible. You have to be allowed to enter this world. Either someone let you in, or you're a ..." Avery wondered.

"Fairy," I said flatly. "An Unseelie fairy! There's no point pretending, Dana. I saw what you are, back at the cabin when you had that fight with Reema."

"My, you have a big imagination," Dana said.

"I believe her," Avery said. "I know enough about this place to realize that a human can't just walk in."

"Then you should know that you won't find a portal there, anymore. Developers paved it over," Dana continued, smiling. "The more subdivisions the humans build over fairy circles, the fewer ways there are to enter this world."

"What is she talking about? Why can't we leave?" I asked Avery.

"Tell her, Avery," Dana said. "Do you remember that, too?"

Avery took a frustrated breath. "The fairy world is a part of nature. Every tree that's cut down, every wall that's built in the wilderness, just further separate the human and fairy worlds. And once a portal gets paved over..."

"It's gone forever," Dana said. "Very good, Avery. It looks like all of your old knowledge is coming back to you, for better or worse."

"What are you doing here, Dana?" Avery asked.

"Looking for you, like everybody else."

"But why did you conceal your true nature?" he asked.

Dana shrugged her shoulders and lowered her head. "I didn't want to scare you, or your friend. These things are hard to explain to an outsider."

"What did you do to my mother?" I asked, angrily.

"What are you talking about?" Dana asked.

"I saw you and my Mom in the reflecting pool at the water sprites' castle."

"So, you went to the reflecting pools? What did you see there, Avery?" Dana asked.

"Did you try to hurt her?" I asked, ignoring her question.

"Why would I do a thing like that?" Dana asked. "Prophesies only reflect your fears."

"I need to see my Mom," I said. "Let's go."

Avery stepped forward. "Go home, Dana. Let my mom and dad know I'm safe. I'll be home soon."

Dana scoffed, "But we have to make up for so much lost time."

"What are you talking about?" Avery asked.

"Don't you remember who I am?" Dana asked.

"You're a nosy babysitter," Avery said.

Dana tossed her head back with laughter. "Sure," she said when she regained her composure. "You can call me that. But I've been looking for you since before you were born, so that you could be my friend." A set of green veined black dragonfly wings unfurled from Dana's back and she lifted several feet off the ground. "My friends spent years working at medical clinics and schools in Benin, changing diapers, checking for scars, searching for you, hoping your bright eyes might come through the schoolhouse doors. They searched airports in Nigeria and France and scoured this country from Boston to Chicago. Then I joined the search, babysitting in house after house looking for you, waiting for your soul to come back, tracking your spirit. We were so close to finding you for so long. But I had a hunch that you were really King Amadi. And now that you know who you really are, join me, my friend! We will rule over all these lands unopposed!" It was at this moment that I first noticed that Dana was carrying a large wooden staff in her left hand, her eyes shining wildly in the morning light.

"I have always ruled alone," Avery said.

Dana shook her head. "That was a different time. I can guide you in this place, now," she said. "Take my hand, my dear king. Accept my offer."

"I can lead my country on my own," Avery said. "Wait, did I just say that? I can't believe I just said that."

Dana looked confused. "So, you *do* accept my offer to help you," she said.

"No, I didn't say that," Avery responded. This made Dana look even more confused. Avery continued, "If you have searched for me in all those places then you can't be who you say you are. If you want me to trust you, reveal your true self."

"We've known each other for years now. Have I ever tried to hurt you before?" Dana asked.

"Then it should be no problem to remove the mask you have created to hide your real identity," Avery said.

Dana paused for a moment. "Of course," she said. "Come, my dear friend. I will teach you everything you need to know. Stick with me and you we will rule this land and the whole human world!"

Avery unfurled amber wings and lifted himself into the sky to meet Dana face to face. I stared at them from below, amazed that Avery could fly, too. At first, he seemed a little surprised as well even though he floated effortlessly, as though he had been able to fly all his life.

"Take my hand. Join me," Dana said, stretching her right hand toward Avery. Avery reached out and grabbed her hand. She smiled at Avery, confident that she had won his support. Avery smiled too, clasping her hand tightly as he pulled it close to his chest.

"It's too bad that there is no word for thank you in our language," he said, "because I would tell you... no, thank you." He dropped her hand and floated back to earth. "Let's go," he told me. As soon as he said that two fairy men, dressed in roughhewn black and green leather emerged from the trees. They were accompanied by several hideous green ghouls, tall and lumpy with boils over their skin. They were also dressed in animal hides and they carried heavy wooden clubs. "Fomorians," Avery whispered to me, positioning himself between me and the monsters. He waved at me to back away. We tried to walk cautiously through Dana's group of men, back toward the way we came.

"He's had his chance," one of the male fairies said, angrily. A blue, hunched-over Fomorian with a club in his hand emerged from behind the trees. "Let's finish him," he said.

Avery and I stopped walking when we realized they weren't going to allow us to walk any further. We turned around to find Dana and her two male fairy followers floating above us and the Fomorians gathered around us. We looked at each other with wide eyes and bated breath as we stood back to back.

"Call Reema," he whispered.

"I don't have my phone," I said. He looked at me incredulously. "It wouldn't fit in my waistband and I don't have any pockets," I explained.

"How do you not have pockets? All of my pants have pockets," he said.

"Well, not all girl pants do," I said.

"But that's ridiculous!" he declared.

We nervously stepped closer to each other as the Unseelies and Fomorians closed in on us. Avery motioned with his eyes toward the piccolo. I realized what he wanted to say, hurriedly pulled it out of my waistband and blew the highest notes I could, hoping the message of fear would cut through the misty air and reach anyone who might be able to help us. Then I instinctively stuffed the piccolo back into my waistband as though continuing to hold it might get me in trouble with them.

"Run!" Avery yelled, pushing me away from him. Then he spun around and threw his hands out at his sides. A field of energy expanded from his armor, creating a thin layer of protection around his body like a cocoon. At least he was able to defend himself from the horde. I wasn't sure at that moment whether Avery remembered how to fight. I started to run, hoping that he would follow me.

"The girl!" Dana yelled. "Seize her!"

I stumbled and fell to the rocky ground as I tried to run away. Before I could get onto my feet one of the male fairies grabbed me from behind and locked my arms together.

"Let her go! She's helpless!" Avery yelled.

"She's a smart girl with her own mind," Dana said. She drifted toward me, smiling through her anger. "She knows I'll be her friend if she'll be mine, don't you, Wilda?"

I was too stunned to speak. Dana sighed and continued, her smiling face hiding the contempt she must have felt for Avery. "If you only knew the oppression my people have suffered under this king and his Seelie kind, you would understand," she said. She squatted down in front of me, her wings drifting behind her. "My people are good. We merely see the human world as it is. We only want the freedom to correct it, for the good of everyone." Dana held my hands in hers. They were hot. I felt the energy in her hands fill me with electricity. "You understand freedom, don't you, Wilda?" she asked.

I nodded nervously, trying hard not to show fear.

"You should join us, Wilda," she said. "We could use an enchanted child for the cause... of freedom." She folded my fingers into the palms of her clasped hands. "I was always there when you needed me.

Who do you think got even with the twins on their birthday, huh?" she smiled, letting out a light laugh.

"That was you?" I asked, briefly looking up at the swirling light in her eyes.

"That was me, and I can make you powerful, too. How would you like to fly, Wilda? How would you like to do magic?" she asked.

"And the piccolo in the cafeteria, was that you, too?" I asked.

"The piccolo?" she asked, looking confused. "I don't know about that but ... I can get you any instrument you want. Would you like a giant flute made of gold?" She asked.

"A bigger flute wouldn't sound the same," I said.

"Oh, Wilda." Dana laughed. "You could have whatever you want! ... I can even give you wings like mine. We're friends, you and me," she said, pointing at me and back at herself.

"But I saw you in the reflecting pool. You *did* hurt my mother. It *was* you," I said.

Dana's expression changed from one of kindness to impatience as she looked away. She took a deep breath and looked back at me, trying to smile, but her eyes remained cold. "Well," she said, "if you really think I did something to hurt your mother then you should cooperate, shouldn't you? I mean, I would have to know where she is and how to help her. So, you need me, don't you? So, tell your buddy over there to hand over that armor to help you out."

I felt a sense of unease welling up from my chest. The things she was offering me - that I could be, do and have anything I ever wanted felt too good to be true. It all seemed too easy. Besides, if she was really my friend, why was she so mean?

The more I thought about her offer, the more her eyes glistened and swirled with hypnotizing light. I couldn't look at her. I closed my eyes, took a deep breath and dared myself to give her my honest answer. "You don't know the first thing about friendship," I said. "It's not about buying people, or blackmailing. It's about helping them."

"You really believe that?" Dana asked.

"Yeah, and I mean it. I don't want you anywhere near my Mom because you're ... you're evil." I said, this time looking into her face in a moment of courage.

Her eyes narrowed with contempt. She laughed, tossing my hands aside. "Do you believe this?" she asked the group of frightening people she'd brought with her. "My, what a stupid girl! I wondered what Reema saw in you. I'd hoped you were more cunning but now I see you're just common trash!" Dana stood up and turned to Avery again. "You know what you have to do, Amadi," she told him, yanking me forward by the collar of my shirt with her clenched fist, "Take off your armored vest and give it to me, or Wilda dies."

Avery watched with a look of horror on his face. "Dana, why are you doing this? This isn't like you," he said.

"You know why I'm doing this," Dana said, coldly.

"But the Dana I know would never hurt someone," Avery said. "You've been like a sister to me."

Dana seemed unaffected by his words. "It was always a job."

"Can't we talk it over?" Avery asked. Dana let go of my collar, and I felt relieved. I gasped for air as Dana nodded to one of her men.

"The time for talk is over," she said.

One of the male fairies held me down on the rugged ground as Dana coolly floated above me and held her staff horizontally in front of her body. The staff glowed hot with bright white light that formed the shape of a double-bladed sword. Dana held the staff close to my neck and turned casually to look at Avery. "There is nothing you can do, Amadi. So be a good king. Sacrifice yourself for your friend."

Avery stood motionless, shocked by Dana's sudden ultimatum. "By your silence you have chosen," Dana said, pulling the staff back to prepare to strike. I watched in terror as the blinding light of the blade came down toward me, sure that I would die then and there.

"Wait!" Avery said, "I'll do what you ask. No one has to get hurt."

"Good," Dana smiled.

"At least show me who you are before I surrender," Avery said.

Dana removed the blade from my neck. "I guess you're entitled to know that before dying," she said, as one of her fairy guards stepped into her place and held his sword of light against my neck instead. As Dana stood up straight her hair grew long and white, reaching her waistline. Her eyes became etched with wrinkles, her mouth drawing up into a scowl. Her buttoned sweater transformed into a worn black cape, long, black tunic and dark green tights. Her black skater shoes morphed into long and pointy black boots. She looked like the Unseelie I saw fighting Reema back at the shed in my backyard, the one whose name Reema dared not say out loud.

"Gwaelwyn!" Avery called her. When Avery called her name, she soared even higher into the morning sun until she appeared almost as a shadow against it.

"Do you dare defy me now?" she shouted down to us.

Avery looked at me with a hopeless gaze. He slowly slid the armor from his shoulders.

"No!" I shouted. "You can't! Don't do it, Avery!"

"You don't understand," Avery said, his voice tinged with regret. "I don't have a choice." He removed the stone armor and laid it on the rocky ground in front of him. The force field he created around himself dissipated like mist. Then he stepped back, took a deep breath and touched the scar on his chest, preparing himself for his fate.

"Take it!" Dana yelled.

The Unseelie fairy who had been clutching a sword to my neck pushed me to the ground, rushed past me and landed on his knees before the armor. He scooped it up in his arms and hastily slung it over himself. Then he raised his arms from his sides, hoping to experience the power of the armor for himself, but the armor did not respond. It remained

dull upon his chest. "How does it work?" he asked
Avery.

"Fool!" Dana shouted. "You are not the chosen
owner. Give it to me!"

"Why only you?" the fairy asked, angrily.

Dana drew back her staff and slung it at him.
The staff landed like a spear, piercing the ground
before the Unseelie fairy's feet. The spear then split
into three wooden pieces that in turn writhed and
morphed into two glowing snakes. They twisted and
hissed and climbed up his torso. "Get them off of
me!" he screamed.

Dana smiled. "Bring it here, then," she said.

Once the fairy jetted into the sky the snakes
recoiled into Dana's staff. Realizing his mistake, the
fairy met Dana halfway in the air. He bowed before
her, removing the armor and handing it to her. Dana
looked down her nose at him and yanked his head up

by his chin. He stared into her eyes, terrified. "You were bold enough to challenge me. I suppose now you would like me to forgive you," she said.

The fairy nodded his head as he trembled. Then the two snake heads reemerged from Dana's staff, drew back and launched forward, biting his neck. The fairy went limp instantly, his wings no longer fluttering. Dana grabbed the snakes by their rattles and with a whip of her arm, wound them together again into her staff. The male fairy fell to the earth with a loud thud. Streams of light flowed from his body and dissipated in the sky. Then the fairy's body fell limp, his limbs seeping into the gray stones on the ground. Blades of grass grew up from between the rocks, slithering in and out of what remained of his clothes. Dana's venom was so powerful that nothing remained of him but gravel and dust.

Dana held her staff near her side, ready to fight, as she lifted the armor into the air. She exhaled a breath of triumph. "Is there anyone else who will challenge me for this?" Dana roared. She tossed her gaze wildly among her remaining crew of fairy warriors and Fomorian monsters. They bowed to her on bended knees. "I hold the fabled armor of time! I alone shall lead the nations! And you," Dana scowled at Avery, floating down to face him as she slung the armor onto her body, "you shall bow down to me."

"I'll do whatever you say. Please, just let Wilda go home," Avery said.

"Hmpf." Dana sighed. She dropped down to the rocky ground and strolled toward me as her fairy guards held me down. I stared at Dana's black boots up to her dismissive gaze as she loomed over me. "You could have had everything you ever wanted, Wilda."

"Leave her alone, Gwaelwyn," Avery said. "She has nothing to do with any of this."

"You're right. She doesn't belong here," Dana said, smiling. "Maybe we should use her for target practice." Dana laughed as she pierced the ground next to my head with her staff. Her companions laughed with her and began to move toward me from their positions in the woods. Dana pretended to pout. "Awe, poor girl. We'll let you go. Why don't you run back home, Wilda?" she said, smiling with widened eyes. "Run, run, run."

I was focused on watching whether the armor lit up instead of Dana's taunts. It didn't seem to be working for her. On Avery the armor shown brilliantly but on Dana it looked like dull, unpolished stone. I looked at Avery. He nodded quickly at me to go. I hurried to my feet. "Give her a head start," I heard Dana say. I ran as fast as I could, ducking around maples and stumbling over rocks as the first two arrows whirled past me, crashing into clouds of energy against the trees. When I looked back I could see Dana and her henchmen in the distance, aiming arrows of light at me.

I could only hope they would not chase after me. The arrows kept coming, covering a greater distance than I could run. I knew I wouldn't make it out alive unless I got some help. As I reached for the piccolo under my shirt my big toe hit a rock. I fell flat on my face. It was a good thing it happened, though. As soon as I fell to the ground another arrow passed over my head. If I had been standing up, I'm sure it would have gotten me right in the back of my knee. I blew a few high-pitched notes again, like a distress call, and crawled behind a giant oak. I saw that its roots formed a crawl space so I crouched down into its partially hollow trunk for safety, hoping Dana and her horde wouldn't find me there.

Suddenly the ground began to rumble. Dana's henchmen stumbled back as they looked in all directions with surprise. "What did you do?" Dana shouted at Avery.

Avery's army was fast approaching from the west on horseback, on foot and in the air carrying clubs, bows, arrows and swords. They appeared to be from many nations in their appearances and clothes, with some of them having great dragonfly wings or butterfly wings on their backs. There were perhaps a dozen male African fairies with butterfly wings. They carried spears and shields, and there were Viking elves on horseback, carrying spiked balls on chains. They raced past me as I ducked inside the tree. Their black horses had twisted white horns on their heads, like the unicorns I had read about in fairytales when I was little.

After the small army had passed me by, I took the opportunity to run across the rocky meadow toward the dense woods ahead. I thought if I was careful and I ran quickly perhaps I could figure out the way back home, and I would be able to help my mom. I hadn't gotten very far when I felt myself being lifted up from the ground and laid across the back of a unicorn. "What are you doing here? You're gonna get yourself killed," a gruff voice said. I looked up to see a strange man's aged face looking back at me as we rode together on the unicorn. The old elf's shoulders were full of ribbon stripes. I assumed he must have been one of Avery's generals. We galloped around the trees in a half circle and he slung me back into the hollow of that same old tree where I hid before. "Stay put," he ordered before racing off into the battle.

I crouched down in the hollow and watched Dana's crew of Unseelies and Fomorians exchange arrows with Avery's army. The Seelies and Unseelies were flying into the sky with their swords swinging at each other. Several Seelie fairies wrestled with Dana's Unseelie fairies through the air and on the ground.

An elf charged with his unicorn at top speed and leaped over a fallen tree. As his unicorn leaped, the elf jumped through the air and landed on an Unseelie fairy's back. He held tight to the Unseelie's long hair, tussling the Unseelie to the rocky ground where they exchanged punches. They continued to tussle back and forth until the tough old elf got the better of the Unseelie. The elf grabbed one of the rocks below and hit the fairy in the head, knocking him out. Then the elf leaped to his feet and back onto his unicorn, racing to find more enemy Unseelie fairies to tackle.

A pair of Seelie fairies with long black hair emerged from the trees carrying Tinikling poles. They spun in unison, striking a Fomorian with the bamboo poles with such force that the Fomorian fell to the ground. Then the pair of Seelie fairies smashed the Fomorian's legs between the two poles, causing magical sparks to fly from the impact.

One of Dana's right-hand fairies, a soldier with a long brown braid and a young-looking face, spun around in the air, his bow and arrow drawn. He landed the lit arrow into the neck of a unicorn. The unicorn stumbled and threw off the elf who was riding it. But the elf quickly got to his feet. When the Unseelie fairy fired his second arrow the elf was able to draw his sword and slice the arrow in half before it could reach him and pierce his body. The arrow shattered into flashes of light against the elf's iron sword.

Another elf who had been riding a unicorn nearby was not so lucky. A stray arrow struck him in the back. He fell from his unicorn onto the ground.

A line of Seelie fairy marksmen in ancient Mongolian armor had scaled the trees. They drew back their bows and shot light beams at the Fomorians below. The Fomorians cowered and ran for cover, swatting wildly with their clubs.

As Dana floated in the sky, she appeared to give a military signal by throwing her hand forward. When she did that a score of new fighters, perhaps forty or more, emerged from the northern woods to join the fight. Then she took her staff and held it in front of her. Her staff emitted three snakes this time, glowing red with fire. She slung the snakes at a trio of Seelie fairies who were flying towards her. A snake landed on one of the Seelie fairies, biting into his arm. He fell instantly from the sky. The Seelie fairy who had been flying next to him batted away the second snake with his shield while the other Seelie fairy cut the third snake in half. The two halves of the glowing red snake dissipated into small balls of red light and faded away, but Dana's defense had discouraged them. They retreated from her and hurriedly flitted about as they tried to regroup.

A group of tiny pixies emerged from the clouds and floated toward the battle. They appeared to be on Avery's side. They clustered together like a ball of

468

light before spreading across the sky, creating a blinding mist around a group of Unseelie fairies. Unable to see clearly, the group of Unseelies who were caught up in the pixie dust swung their swords wildly. The Mongolian Seelie marksmen who had scaled the trees took advantage of the Unseelies fairies' confusion to shoot light arrows at them. The marksmen were able to hit several of the Unseelie soldiers, dropping them from the sky back down to the earth. Their bodies hit the ground like heavy stones.

At least one Unseelie soldier managed to escape the blinding mist and floated back to the ground. He quickly loaded an arrow into his bow, drew the arrow back and landed it into the heart of a Seelie fairy marksman, dropping him to the ground, too.

Terrified at the sight of seeing one of Avery's powerful marksmen fall to the ground, I ducked into the hollow of the tree. As I scooted further into my hiding place, I hoped I had not been noticed. But my hope was in vain. A pair of giant, rotten smelling blue feet, wrapped in worn sandals, stepped slowly in front of the hollow where I'd been hiding and an impossibly large hand grabbed my shoulder with its fingers, squeezing my shoulder blade into my collar bone. The crusty hand yanked me from the hollowed tree trunk. Before I could react to being caught, I was already dangling in the air as I stared at the blue Fomorian's ugly face. His heaving chest was partially uncovered in tattered clothes. His back was hunched over and he had large, pulsating boils all over his face and body. He held me so tightly that there was no way I could escape his grasp.

He grinned as he raised a giant club over my head. Still, I struggled to get free, kicking and punching at his thick arm. This only made him laugh as he raised his spiked wooden club into the air. All I could do was watch helplessly as the club loomed over my head, sure that I was about to die. Then, from the corner of my eyes I saw a familiar white deer galloping toward me at a furious pace, leaping through the forest.

"Reema!" I cried.

Before the Fomorian's club could drop on my head Reema had transformed herself from the white deer into a fairy shape in a single bound. Huge, white butterfly wings unfurled from her back as she kicked a rock hard at the Fomorian. The rock landed on the back of the Fomorian's bald head. That got his attention. When the Fomorian turned around, still clutching me in his rough hand, Reema slung a ball of light at him that crashed into his temple. The monster fell forward, dropping the club before landing on it. Since I was still in his hand, I fell forward, too. Luckily his grip loosened and I was able to squeeze out of his grasp. I gratefully stood to my feet. "Reema," I yelled. "I sure am glad to see *you*."

"Didn't I tell you never to come here without me?" Reema angrily shouted back as she landed in front of me. Then she hurried past me, manifesting from the air a glowing orb in one hand and a hook sling made of pure light in her other hand. Reema flew into the air as her giant white veined wings propelled her. Her sling morphed and expanded to lash two Unseelie fairies in the air like a whip made of light. With a flick of Reema's wrist the whip snapped back into a sling.

473

Reema stepped on a couple of Fomorians' heads as she flew over them. She snatched one of Avery's elves out of the way of a coming arrow. Then she broke the arrow apart by slinging her glowing orb at it. Reema spun in the air with another orb in her sling and released the orb in front of several of Dana's Unseelie fighters. The orb exploded into an ever-growing ball of light, knocking the Unseelie fairies onto the ground with a blast.

That's when I heard a strange rumbling sound coming from the ground. I looked back to see two halves of the same oak tree rushing towards me. They looked like a single tree that had been split evenly down the middle. Their roots powered forward through the ground, leaving a trail of churned earth behind them. They slung their top branches from side to side through the air, accidentally catching two Seelie fairies that had been flying in the sky. The two halves of the tree moved independently from each other, winding the Seelies fairies up in their separate branches. "Hey, put us down," one of the Seelie fairies yelled. "I'm on your side."

"Sorry. We didn't know," one half of the tree moaned.

"We're kind of new here," creaked the other as they unwound their branches and let the two Seelie warrior fairies fly off.

I crawled out of the hole in the tree where I'd been hiding and stared in amazement. Their voices were familiar but I couldn't imagine that they were who they sounded like.

"Hey Wilda, it's me," one of them bellowed as though they'd read my thoughts. "Veronica."

"And Monica," the other one said, loudly. "We're dryads now."

"What? How?" I asked.

"Long story," Veronica said as she and her sister rumbled toward me.

"I'll listen," I gasped.

"Another time," Monica said. I was amazed by how loud their voices were. They continued to rampage through the meadow, snatching a Fomorian between them and winding him into Veronica's branches.

"Ow," Veronica said. "You're getting it tangled in my hair."

"It's not like I meant to, Vi," Monica said.

A lit arrow landed in Monica's trunk and quickly went out. She moved the knots on the sides of her trunk as though she was shrugging her shoulders and kept going.

"I'm surprised their arrows don't hurt me," Veronica said.

"Maybe light arrows don't hurt bark as much as they hurt skin," Monica said.

"Oh. Like a rock, paper scissors thing?" Veronica asked. "Arrow beats skin. Bark beats arrow."

Just then a light arrow landed in a couple of Monica's branches. They quickly caught fire. "Oh my gosh, Moni! You're on fire!" Veronica exclaimed.

"Ack! Put it out," Monica screamed.

"Stop, drop and roll," Veronica said.

"How am I supposed to do that?" Monica asked.

"Just rub your head in the dirt," Veronica said. Then with her branches Veronica tipped Monica over so that Monica's canopy of branches ended up in the grass and dirt. It worked. The flames went out. "There," Veronica said. "Now we're even."

Monica straightened up her trunk. "I can't believe you still think I pushed your head in that cake!" she exclaimed.

As I watched Monica and Veronica roam the battlefield, I noticed a dog leap from behind the trees. It was Charlie! He was running toward me because he had seen an Unseelie fairy sneaking up on me as I crouched in my hiding place. The Unseelie fairy seemed to land out nowhere and he carried a sword of light in his hand. Charlie soared through the air, landing behind the Unseelie fairy. He bit the Unseelie's arm so hard the fairy dropped his sword and flew away. Then Charlie stood on his back legs and barked ferociously at anyone who could hear him. "If you try to hurt Wilda, I will rip you to shreds," he growled.

"What are you doing here, Charlie?" I asked.

"Looking for you. You should have taken me with you," he whined. Charlie stood in front of me to shield me from the battle. He continued to bark and growl at anyone who came near us.

Monica and Veronica continued to trudge forward, slinging the Unseelies and Fomorians into each other and dropping them on top of each other before snatching up others. With the twins' help Reema's pathway to Dana was now clear. Reema lifted herself up in the sky to face Dana as the fighting continued around them.

"Do you always have to butt in?" Dana asked.

"So, it was you all along," Reema said.

Dana held her staff in front of her chest with both hands. Reema held the orb in the crux of her sling. Dana swung the staff across her body and a slice of flaming red light cut across the sky. Reema swung her orb at it above their heads. The orb crashed into the fiery red ray, bending it into a bow above them that broke and rained down as harmless embers. Dana huffed angrily. She then slung her staff in the opposite direction. This time several flames flew across the sky at Reema, so Reema pushed the orb forward in her hand, allowing it to swell until it enveloped her and protected her from the flames. Then the orb grew larger until both Reema and Dana were inside of it. Dana pushed her staff with both hands in front of her chest again. This time a large snake emerged from its side, partially connected to the staff but growing ever larger as it snapped at Reema. Then Reema swerved back from Dana. It seemed like she was trying to avoid being bitten by the snake's growing fangs. They seemed to be dripping with sparkling poison.

Reema drew up the orb back into a ball in her hand. Dana laughed as she saw this but Reema stayed focused, slinging the orb into the snake's mouth. The snake's head burst into red rays that shattered like glass.

Dana gasped and fell back. At this time, three more Seelie fairies saw an opportunity to surround Dana. One of them swung at her staff with his iron sword while the other two wrestled Avery's armor off of her. As they wrestled the armor off of Dana, she released another snake from her staff. The snake crawled up a sword one of the Seelies was carrying and bit into his hand, but the other two fairies were able to fly away with the armor. Dana pointed her staff at them. Two more snakes made of red light emerged from her staff. The snakes chased the two fairies, caught one of them and bit him on his heel. That fairy fell to the ground, but the remaining fairy caught up to Avery.

Avery was busy using the thin force field around his body as a shield to fend off several Unseelies who were attacking him with swords and arrows at the same time. Avery's energy force field developed a small crack with every hit he took, and it looked like he might suffer a death by a thousand blows. When Avery saw the Seelie carrying his armor, he leaped into the sky to meet it. The Seelie fairy slid the armor over Avery's head.

Avery shot forward into the sky, his enormous amber wings growing so large they seemed to eclipse the sun. Many of the fighters momentarily paused to see why the land suddenly became dark. "Stop this right now, Gwaelwyn," Avery yelled.

"You fools," she yelled at her fighters. "How did you let him get the armor back?" Dana flew higher into the sky. She held her staff behind her back and when she brought it forward, it produced a rain of fire. Avery swung his arm across his head, unleashing a wind that blew out the fire and flattened everything in its path below. "Whoa," he said, looking at his hands. "Cool."

Dana placed her staff under her arm and clapped condescendingly. "Not bad, little man," she yelled, smiling. "You are the king again. The more power you assume as King Amadi, the sooner the young Avery dies."

"What?" Avery yelled over the noise of the battle.

"You heard me," Dana said. "I guess turning your back on your parents isn't so hard after all. Such a sweet old-fashioned couple. Or have you forgotten about your parents already? I hope it's worth it."

Avery sank back down to earth, shaking his head as he tried to shake her words off, but Dana continued. "Look at their son now. All grown up! And a killer, too."

"Shut up, Dana!" he shouted.

"I'm done taking orders from you. I'm Gwaelwyn here, remember?" Dana continued. "Once you take on your full power you can never go back to your old life. You'll always have to deal with me."

One of Avery's generals, the grizzled and burly elf who'd rescued me, fought his way through Dana's guards to reach Avery's side. He stood next to Avery and placed his hand on Avery's shoulder. "We are behind you. Unleash the time weapon," he told Avery.

Avery assumed a warrior stance. He held his breath and clenched his fists. Then he lifted his arms in the air as he had in the memory we watched in the reflecting pool. His plain pajamas morphed into the clothes of a West African warrior with a chainmail shirt and what looked like a leather kilt. I held my breath with anticipation, expecting time to freeze. As Avery stood with his arms extended and I continued to watch, nothing happened.

"Go ahead. We're ready," his general prodded him.

Avery took a heavy breath. He seemed to be contemplating something. "I don't know if I can still do it," he said.

"Of course, you can," the general said. "Come on. Let's finish this."

Dana seemed to stare across the field. I turned and looked in the same direction and saw in the distance, far away, two faint figures moving closer. Dana tipped her head to one of her men and motioned to him to go in the direction of two figures that were coming over the distant hills. The Unseelie nodded his head and flew away, low to the ground, in the direction of the approaching figures. Then Dana turned her attention to the fight, unleashing balls of fire and energy at an approaching group of elves.

"Amadi," two voices called out from across the field. I turned to look again. Avery looked, too. We both seemed to notice two girls who looked like Monica and Veronica running towards the battle. "Where are you going?" they called at the same time towards a third person in the distance. "Come see me! I have become young like you!" Their voices, in unison, spoke with a familiar lilt that I had heard a couple of times before.

Could it be...? I wondered. No, it couldn't be Reema's grandmother, Aisosa, who had been transformed into the old oak tree at the edge of the fairy world. That would mean that Aisosa had transformed herself into the bodies of the twins, Monica and Veronica. But Monica and Veronica were already here, as two sides of an oak tree that had been split in half.

Since Monica and Veronica were dryads, then some other spirit must have been inhabiting their old, human bodies. Otherwise, their human bodies would not have been able to speak. *Did they trade bodies with Aisosa, the Grandmother Tree? If so, why? Because they felt sorry for her?* Monica didn't seem like the type of person who would do that, and although Veronica was nicer than her sister, she wasn't *that* nice.

Monica and Veronica's human bodies were so far away that I couldn't tell who they were talking to at first. As they continued to call out in unison, I assumed that some trick had been played and that Aisosa was somehow masquerading as the twins.

Soon I recognized a boy coming towards us. It looked like another Avery, except it couldn't be him. Avery was fighting with his generals and soldiers. Therefore, the other Avery had to be an imposter, some Unseelie fairy who had shifted to look like Avery. It must have been the same fairy Dana sent off on an investigation. He was leading Aisosa, whose spirit now inhabited the two human bodies of Monica and Veronica, closer to the battle. The imposter fairy raised his hand into the air. When Dana turned his way, he signaled to her by dropping his hand to his side. Then he flew off, out of the line of fire. Avery soon realized what was happening.

"Wait, Aisosa! Don't come any further!" Avery shouted. Upon hearing Avery's cry, Reema turned around from the battle. She soon realized what was happening, too.

"Why do you fly away?" the two girl voices of Monica and Veronica's human bodies called out to the imposter Unseelie fairy.

Dana was watching them, too. I saw her lift her staff, hold it straight in front of her eye and pull a strand of red light back to her cheek. Then she released it and two red snakes, straight as arrows, flew forward with amazing speed all the way across the rocky plain, piercing the body of Monica in her chest and the body of Veronica in her neck. The snake arrows undoubtedly released a venom from the fangs of the two snakes.

"Grandmother!" Reema yelled. She dropped down to the earth and flitted over the rocks to the two girls' sides, tucking her wings as she fell beside them. Monica and Veronica halted their slow trek through the battlefield to watch what was happening.

"Hey! That's our bodies!" Veronica yelled.

Dana coolly lowered her staff to her side and looked at Avery, smiling. "Go home, Avery. There is nothing here for you now," she said.

Avery stood motionless. "Why?" he asked.

"You're in our way," Dana said. "You always were."

"You used to be my friend," Avery said.

"Give up. You're in over your head," Dana said.

Charlie leaped out of the hollow of the tree to get a better look at the twins' fallen bodies. He sniffed the air and straightened his ears. "What is it, Charlie?" I asked, but Charlie didn't answer me. Instead, he took off galloping over the rocky plain toward the twins' bodies.

"Charlie!" I yelled. I wanted to go after him but it was too dangerous. The battle was raging all around the tree where Charlie and I were hiding. I frantically looked around, hoping someone in Avery's army would notice and stop Charlie from running into trouble.

"Help!" I yelled. My worried cry got Dana's attention, instead. She turned quickly and spotted Charlie. Then I saw her look back at Avery with a devious smile on her face as she lifted her staff in front of her chest again. She pulled a glowing red string from her staff toward her cheek. Flickers developed in the air that began to take the shape of an arrow pointed in Charlie's direction. I didn't know what to do. I just knew I needed the help of someone who could get to Charlie and protect him before Dana's arrow got to him first.

I ducked back into the hollow of the tree. In a panic I reached into my waistband, pulled my piccolo out and fumbled to get it to my mouth. I blew into it, moving the stream of air across the tone hole to produce the highest notes I could play. Each note formed a spark of color in the air. I closed my eyes so I could focus as I continued to play, not really thinking about the melody. All I saw were the many colors of the notes. I played as loud as I could for as long as my breath would carry the notes. I ran out of breath just before the wind picked up. It started to swirl around me. I felt it sweep past my bare arms, brushing against my face, fluttering near my cheeks and whipping through my hair. The wind sounded like whispers in Reema's language as it moved beyond the tree where I had been hiding. I caught my breath and played another line of notes.

I opened my eyes and looked back at Dana as she floated in the sky. She appeared to be stunned. Then I peered around the other side of the tree at Avery. He seemed to be energized and his armor shined like the sun. He clenched his fists and yelled, "Stop!" When he did this everything within a hundred feet halted immediately. The air vibrated, caught up in time, and it was released violently as waves of energy pulsed through everything in Avery's path. It looked like everything and everyone was tied up in the air. When Avery finally released the world around us it felt like I had been suspended without breath for hours.

Dana and her army remained frozen in air. Then Avery threw his arms to his sides and dropped them down. When he did that, the energy from his arms blew them back as though a bomb had been released. Dana was knocked back by the blast as well, and when the effect of the time freeze wore off, she signaled with her staff for her fighters to retreat. Avery's army took the opportunity to chase any Unseelie stragglers who'd fallen behind, striking them with arrows and clubs until the last of them had either fallen or fled the field.

Avery scrambled to the twins' human shells as they lay on the ground, trembling in shock. I stumbled over the gnarly roots of the oak tree and to catch up with them. Charlie was already by their sides.

"Why, Aisosa," Avery asked. "Why did you risk your life like this?"

Veronica's throat had been slit by the snake's searing fangs and she could not speak. She mouthed the words as Monica spoke as Aisosa. "I thought I could help you," Aisosa said through Monica's voice. "I didn't know about the battle."

Monica and Veronica dropped the remains of a vanquished Fomorian from their branches and slid their roots across the meadow until they reached us.

"Help me understand," Avery said to them.

"It's my fault," Reema said. "I should have come sooner. Maybe Grandmother wouldn't have done this."

"What happened?" Avery asked.

Reema answered, "When I came to the portal I saw that Grandmother had transferred her spirit from the oak into the twins' bodies and forced the twins' souls into the tree in order to join you."

"But why did she switch into both of their bodies?" I asked.

"The ancient belief," Reema said, "that twins are really one soul split into two bodies. I don't think she meant it to be permanent."

"When Reema recognized us in the tree she split it in half. She said if we helped her stop Dana from finding you first, we might also find her grandmother and get our bodies back sooner," the true Veronica said from her half of the oak tree.

"Why did you tell me to follow you?" Aisosa said from Monica's human body.

"It wasn't me," Avery said, tucking his wings in frustration.

Aisosa touched the bite wound in her chest. "I've never been a human before. I guess I forgot how fragile they are."

I looked at Veronica's human body. It seemed to squirm for a moment before giving out completely. "My body!" the real Veronica called out from the half of the tree she inhabited. The loss of Veronica's human body gave Monica's body a jolt. It seemed now that Aisosa's soul was no longer split between the two bodies. The life force in Monica's body grew stronger, if only for a moment. "I'm sorry, Amadi. I always hoped we would have more time together," Aisosa said.

Avery knelt down next to Aisosa, stroking her head as she looked at him with pained eyes. "Please don't leave," he begged. "You're the only one who can help me make sense of all of this."

"Maybe I will get to come back, like you," Aisosa said. "Just please do one more thing for me?"

"Anything you ask," Avery said.

"Don't let them win," Aisosa said.

"Of course not," Reema interrupted. "Everything will be fine if you're here," she pleaded. Reema knelt down to grab her hand.

"Reema, my darling granddaughter," Aisosa said. "I need to tell you. No matter what you may have been taught about us, you come from good people. Every secret will be known someday." She reached to touch Reema's face with the side of her weakened hand. She touched Avery's cheek. "Amadi, my king," she said. Then she closed her eyes. Her head drifted softly to the grassy field as she breathed her last breath.

Charlie milled around the two bodies, frantically wagging his tail and sniffing for signs of life. He howled and sat next to me, realizing that she was gone. Avery stood up in disbelief. When I looked up from the twins' human bodies, I saw that we were now surrounded by Avery's army. Avery held his head in his hands as tears streamed through the cracks in his fingers. All was quiet for a moment. Reema sobbing on the ground was the only sound. She wiped her face on her sweater and breathed a heavy sigh.

By instinct I reached for Reema's cold hand. The gesture caught her off guard as she looked at me, stunned by what had happened. She squeezed my hand in hers. I realized then that she was vulnerable, too. "I'm sorry," I whispered. Reema covered her mouth with her fingertips. She seemed unable to speak. Monica and Veronica leaned upon each other. I assumed they were crying too. Their trunks were wet with sap.

No one felt like saying anything for a long time. It felt terrible to break the silence but I felt I had to remind Avery that I still needed to get home. "I'm sorry, Avery," I said, "but my mom ..."

"It's okay," Reema said, staring at the twins' human bodies. "Don't worry. It's okay."

Finally, Avery stood up to address his army. "You came as soon as you heard the call. You fought valiantly and we are victorious because of your efforts. I stand before you now, a boy king having just returned after an absence of years, and you have welcomed me with unquestioning loyalty. I feel like I don't deserve it, but I appreciate each of you for everything you've done. Not just for me, but for our peoples, and for the sake of the humans. When you go back home, tell them... tell them..." Avery paused and lowered his head for a moment. "Tell them we lost my dear queen, but we honored her spirit by winning the battle."

The tired warriors raised their weapons in the air and celebrated with subdued cheers. They seemed reluctant to go, conflicted about whether to give their grieving king space to mourn his loss.

"Your Majesty," a deep voice spoke. Another one of the generals stepped forward. He was a gray-haired elf, short and portly, with a chest full of armor and a large saber attached to his side. "It is with great humility that I request that our soldiers be allowed to follow fairy tradition, following in procession with you as you journey home, to honor our queen."

Avery hung his head with resignation. "All right," he said plainly. "Monica, Veronica, could you carry your bodies back with us? We must go to the Tower of Vines to see if anything can be done to help you get back into them."

Monica and Veronica bent their trunks down and slid their branches underneath the twin bodies, holding them as though they were resting in woven baskets. Then Monica and Veronica, Reema and I, with Charlie at my side, and a fleet of fairy soldiers several paces back, followed Avery back towards the sixth tower.

Chapter 10

Aisosa was a queen, so custom required her people to walk her body back to the tower. Releasing Aisosa's essence there would give it the best chance to regrow from the castle's branches someday. I gathered that information from the solemn fairies around me. Most fairies like Aisosa grew like fruit on the tower's vines and emerged as adults, just like the water sprites that bubbled up from the waves of the river. But fairies like Avery and Reema were born. That's what made them royal: they shared a bloodline.

As we walked toward the tower Reema's sweater and jeans morphed into regal clothes. Then she looked at me and my clothes changed, too, from a sleep shirt and leggings to a fancy dress. When I asked her why she changed our clothes, she said it was for her grandmother's homecoming.

We eventually reached the winding vines of the sixth tower. Under the waning afternoon light, we found a large crowd of fairies waiting for us. There must have been hundreds of them surrounding the tower, spreading into the fields of now-quiet lilies. Then I realized why Reema changed our clothes. She had to be on duty now no matter how terrible she felt on the inside. She was a royal, after all, and the queen had died. She had a responsibility to reassure her people of their royal family's power.

There were no flower petals hurtling down upon Reema, Charlie and me this time. It appeared that the tower had been emptied of all its inhabitants as they stood in the field, waiting for us. It was as though the occupants there already knew what happened. A few small pixies with round wings circled the spires of the tower high in the air like little sparrows, taking turns diving to the crowd below as though they were delivering messages on what they were seeing. Zyzzyva was there, too, buzzing above us like a loud beetle. She floated down from the sky to kiss Reema on her cheeks before flitting back to her sentinel position in the sky.

The tower was open and surrounded with a crowd of soft speaking winged people numbering in the hundreds. The last of the inhabitants, the four mysterious regents I had met there before, emerged from the tower doorway. The crowd parted and the pixies who had been darting back and forth from the sky settled down to wait. When the four regents reached the front of the crowd they fixed their eyes on Avery, knelt down and bowed their heads as Avery approached them. He was followed by Monica and

Veronica who carried their pale human bodies in their branches. Then rest of the people who were there lowered their heads, but Reema unfurled her wings with pride. Avery also untucked his glowing wings as if by instinct as he approached the castle. They were generated by his armor since he had not yet grown his own wings like an adult fairy.

Monica and Veronica dragged their root systems to a stop and the ground grew quiet. Reema walked just ahead of them, and Charlie and I followed behind Avery as his soldiers stood at attention with the crowd behind us.

Then a slender fairy male dressed in a long blue robe with a chain of ornaments across his chest came forward and yelled out to all who could hear, "The queen is dead, but our miraculous king, the gracious and brave Amadi of the Spring Court of Fay, has returned from his exile in the afterlife. He was reborn in the earthly realm and has now come to reclaim his kingdom's throne! All Hail the King!" Then he spoke in a language I could not understand. The fairies and elves around Avery repeated it dutifully in whistles and chords. Then Avery beckoned his subjects to stand, and his people surged forward, showering him with wreaths of white roses. The mood quickly took a festive turn. Bands of fairies broke out in song, tossing flowers and playing hand instruments, but Avery remained serious. He never took his eyes off of the four regents. "My daughter was lost in the land of shadows," he said.

"We did everything we could to save her," Princess Yipuna said.

"And then," Avery continued, "you transformed Aisosa into a tree. First my family was betrayed by a trusted human. Then, they were betrayed by their own people. You must have thought I would never come back."

The four regent fairies lowered their heads with shame.

"We apologize, Your Majesty. May I speak?" Shöniin Luu asked.

"What can you possibly say to defend yourselves?" Avery asked.

"What we did was wrong, but we did conceal them from their enemies, the Unseelies and the Fomorians, by cloaking your wife in a tree and your daughter in darkness. They surely would have been hunted and killed sooner if we had not done so."

Avery shook his head and walked past the regents, placing his hands at his waist. He looked back at his soldiers and then at the regents. Upon being reminded of their king's power, the regents bowed down to him again. Then Avery motioned with his hand for them to stand up. "Show me my throne," he said.

The four regents led us into the castle and flew with Avery up to the nest at the top of the tower, though the guilt over their treatment of his family in his absence still weighed heavily like a cloud in the air.

Reema, Charlie and I stood at the bottom of the steep ladder that led to the nest above our heads. Reema looked down at me. "I'll carry you," she offered.

Charlie said gruffly, turning to Monica and Veronica, "How are you two going to get up there?"

"I don't think they can, but they can stretch themselves," Reema said.

"You mean grow taller?" Veronica asked.

"Right here?" Monica asked.

"Is there any other way?" Reema asked with a shrug.

"Don't worry, Monica," Veronica said. "We're supposed to get our bodies back anyway. Who cares what happens to this tree?"

"But what if it doesn't work? Then we'll be stuck in this castle," Monica said.

"If you don't want to stretch I could order Avery's men to cut you both down to size," Reema said, "or you could take my advice since I might know a thing or two about magic."

Charlie paced between Monica and Veronica's tree trunks, paused and lifted his leg next to Monica's trunk. "Your dog better not use it on me, Wilda!" Monica yelled.

Charlie gave her a fanged grin. "Then make a decision. The longer I have to wait, the more likely I will," he said.

"Wilda!" Veronica demanded, "Tell your dog to get out of here!"

"I have my own mind." Charlie laughed.

"He's his own boss around here," I told them.

"Okay! Okay!" Veronica whined. Monica dropped some of her branches to the middle of her trunk as though she were putting her hands on her hips in disgust as Veronica reached with her branches and held her human body as high up as she could lift it. When she still could not reach the platform at the top of the ladder, she dug her roots into the ground. Then, miraculously, her trunk slowly stretched longer, vibrating from her top branches to the ground. She lost a few leaves as she grew taller and wider. Monica followed her sister's lead, stretching and rumbling in the ground as she pushed her own human body toward the tower's highest platform.

Reema then transformed herself into the white deer with its black and brown striped nose. I climbed onto her, hugging her around her neck as she and Charlie made their way up the ladder.

When we joined the four regents of the sixth tower again, they were standing at attention. Avery was seated in the once empty middle chair of the throne, waiting for us. He sat at the edge of his seat. His clasped hands covered his mouth. Monica and Veronica laid their twin bodies on the floor with their branches. Then Reema, Charlie and I knelt before Avery.

"Your Majesty, we welcome your visitors to the Sacral Palace, the sixth tower of the known realm," Dalkkas said. "But if they intend to use these human shells, they are too late."

"Can't you do something?" Avery said with his head bowed. "If you can't these dryads their human bodies back, they won't be able to go back home."

"Even if we could transfer their souls completely into these human shells," Cētanā spoke, "with the injuries these bodies have sustained, they would not survive."

Monica and Veronica groaned with despair. Their roots rumbled with anxiety at the terrible news. Sap ran down their long trunks as they cried.

"That's not fair!" Veronica roared.

Monica stomped one of her heavy roots on the ground. "You promised us our bodies back!"

"The regents didn't make that promise," Shöniin Luu said.

"But it doesn't seem fair," Avery said. "They came here to protect me and Wilda. Then they volunteered to fight for our people against our Unseelie enemies. Because of that they will now be trapped as dryads here."

"Besides, right now Grandmother's spirit is in these human bodies," Reema said. "Whatever happens to Monica and Veronica, the queen's spirit must still be freed to make her spiritual journey to the first tower."

Monica let out a frustrated, pollen-filled sigh. "Whatever happens to her, we need our bodies back, now!"

"Yeah," Veronica said, angrily. "We deserve them! We can't go home like this!"

Princess Yipuna stood between the two bodies on the wooden floor. "Maybe there is something that we can do. We cannot repair these old bodies to take on their original souls, but we may be able to graft their human qualities onto their tree bodies, so that the dryads appear to be their old selves as much as possible. That way they will be able to blend into the human world. This won't change them from being dryads. They will have to learn to control their nature, only revealing it when necessary. As for the queen, we will do all we can to release her from the bondage of these human shells."

"Dryads, what are your names?" the Shöniin Luu asked.

Monica leaned forward and spoke her name. Then Veronica answered with her own.

"Lay the bodies upon the Sacral Altar," Shöniin Luu said. "You come from the seventh tower, the Root plane which you call "the world." It is the place where your earthly existence was lived out as human beings, learning to trust yourselves and others. You may find your new physical expressions to be challenging to that end."

"It may be easier to stay in here in Vreenley where you would be accepted as you are, rather than to return to your home as hybrid dryads," Cētanā said. "Do you still wish to proceed?"

"Yes, please," Monica and Veronica bellowed from her trunks below the platform on which the rest of us stood. "We have to get home," Veronica cried.

"Very well. Lay down your branches over your human forms," the elf, Princess Yipuna said. The three fairy regents, Cētanā, Dalkkas and Shöniin Luu gathered around with Princess Yipuna around the human bodies, joining hands and chanting in the secret language of Vreenley. Reema transformed herself back into her fairy form and stood behind them. I crouched in a corner of the elevated rotunda, holding Charlie at my side, as a stream of shimmering, golden light floated down from the sky upon Monica and Veronica's oak branches. A band of white light emanated from the girls' human forms and spilled into the branches themselves until they were illuminated from within. The trees shrank, their branches retracting, until they were no longer visible from the platform. Then the light faded from the human bodies on the floor. The regents bowed their heads in silence, their magic complete.

Avery hurried to the edge of the platform. Then I saw a hopeful smile stretch across his face. Reema nodded toward me. I bounded across the floor to the edge of the ladder, next to Avery, and there I saw them: two girls, slightly taller than before, standing barefoot in plain white dresses. Their skin seemed slightly marbled and their black hair was full of leaves. Despite this their faces hadn't changed. Most importantly, they looked passably human.

They stared at each other with their mouths agape, touching each other's hair in amazement. "You don't look like a tree anymore, Moni," Veronica said.

"Neither do you, Vi," Monica said.

Then after a moment of complimenting each other on how great they looked they remembered their fairy guardians' help. "Thank you," Veronica said.

"Oh… my gosh! Thank you, thank you!" Monica gushed.

"You're like, the best … people … ever!" Veronica added.

"Totally," Monica agreed. Shöniin Luu and Dalkkas chuckled at their exuberance.

"Just remember to return the favor someday," Shöniin Luu said.

"We will," Veronica declared. Then she remembered their bodies were still on the platform high above them. She grabbed her sister's hands. "What happens to our old bodies now?"

Before anyone could answer, Monica and Veronica could sense something fluttering above them. They looked up to see their human forms disintegrating into hundreds of white moths streaming out of the opening in the tower dome. The crowd beyond the tower gasped as they knelt again, seeming to understand that their queen was leaving them now. Upon reaching the sky the moths dissipated into the air. "Goodbye for now, Grandmother," Reema said softly as the last moths emerged from the tower.

The regents then turned their gaze toward Avery again. Princess Yipuna opened a chamber within the wall and returned carrying a golden crown in the shape of a helmet, resting on a red pillow. The crown was decorated with a long oval disk at the center of the crown, engraved with scenes of lands under the Spring Court's control. Princess Yipuna carried a pallium with an orb made of light in her left hand. She approached Avery, raising the crown and pallium toward him, but Avery turned away from her. "Now it's over," he said. "I have no reason to stay here anymore."

"What do you mean?" Dalkkas asked, surprised.

"I mean I am going home now," Avery said.

"This is your home," Shöniin Luu said.

Cētanā smiled to himself and stepped back from Avery. "If his majesty wishes to leave, it is an entirely reasonable choice," he said.

"But you must now be crowned again," Reema protested. "It is your duty and your right. It's what I've worked for all these years."

Avery walked away from Princess Yipuna who stood in shock as she continued to hold the crown and pallium. Dalkkas tried to calm Reema, smiling as she pat her on her shoulder. Then she turned toward Avery. "Your Majesty, we have awaited your return for many years. We are here to assist you now. You won't be alone," Dalkkas said.

Avery paused for a moment before taking off his armor and laying it in the center of the floor.

"I cannot be your king," Avery said, resolutely. "Not now." Then Avery walked to the edge of the platform.

"Grandfather, please just think about it," Reema said, holding desperately to Avery's arm.

"I left another life when I came here. I can't just leave it," Avery answered.

"But you're leaving us?" Princess Yipuna asked.

"Just for a while, to finish a few things. This land will be in your hands for now," Avery said. "Besides, there is so much I don't know or can't remember. I'm sorry."

"Your Majesty," Cētanā said, "the Sky King Armor is a great weapon. Perhaps if you will choose to give it to one of us, the kingdom will be protected from its enemies. Perhaps, Reema …"

"Me?" Reema asked. "I've tried. It isn't mine to wear."

"Your Majesty, please reconsider," Princess Yipuna pleaded.

"Then the armor will be safe with me," Cētanā said, stepping forward to retrieve it, but Dalkkas snatched it up from the floor and foisted it into

Avery's chest. "The armor has already chosen. Guard it until you return," she said. "I have faith that you will return when that time in your life is ripe."

"Dalkkas is right," Princess Yipuna said. "As Princess and Ambassador of the Autumn Court, I can assure you that my government will stand beside Princess Reema until that time comes."

Avery reluctantly nodded and allowed Dalkkas to put the armor back over his head. Then he floated from the platform down the floor and met Monica and Veronica near the doorway. "Let's go," he said. The branches of the doorway opened up and they walked out together.

Reema transformed herself back into a deer and beckoned with her head for me to climb on. Charlie reluctantly led the way down the ladder. Once we were at the bottom of the ladder Reema transformed back into her fairy self. "I should stay here for now," she said. "You should go with them."

"Please, come with me? My mother needs you," I begged.

"She is safe," Reema said, holding my face in her cold fingers.

"How do you know?" I asked.

"You asked me to watch over her, so I did. When I saw that she was able to drive drunk, I charged at her so she'd drop her keys on the ground," Reema said, pulling the two keys for the Dodge Avenger's ignition and trunk out of her front jeans pocket and dangling them by the key ring along her index finger. "She's probably a little cold right now and a lot frustrated, maybe even a little afraid of deer, but she's not going anywhere. That's why I was so late getting here in the first place. I had to clean up Gwaelwyn's mess."

I instantly flung myself around her. "Oh, Reema!" I said. "You're amazing!"

"I just returned a favor, that's all. Oh, and I hope you don't mind but I notified the Sheriff's Department when you first told me about things with your mom. That way they'd be on the lookout," Reema said. She smiled as she hugged me back.

"You're a hero! And you're fearless. You're not afraid of anything. Not even dying," I said.

"Dying? What do you think I am?" Reema asked.

"A warrior princess with magical powers," I said.

"If you say so," she laughed.

"Being royal makes you immortal," I supposed.

"No, Wilda. We are all mortal," she said. "I've just trained my mind to accept my fate. Whatever happens to me, I will be at peace because I've done my best to do good things in the world. Besides, death is a myth anyway."

"How is that possible?" I asked.

"Well," she shrugged, "It's an idea that supposes that life has an end. It doesn't. It gets interrupted and has to transform. Sometimes a soul returns, but nothing in the universe ever really ends."

"But aren't Fay special?" I asked.

"So are you," Reema replied.

"Not me, I'm common," I said. "Dana was saying..."

Reema interrupted me. "The only thing that matters is the value you put on yourself. We're all ordinary and being ordinary is actually kind of special. It's the reason why I fight, you know, for the rights of all beings to live their ordinary lives," she said.

"Yeah, well, she also called me trash," I sighed.

"You're taking her word for that? You saw the side she's on," Reema said.

I shrugged.

"You really don't know what you are, do you?" Reema continued.

"What do you mean?" I asked.

Reema swept my red hair out of my eyes. "Where's your piccolo?" she asked.

I pulled it from my waistband to show her. "Play me something, like you really mean it," she said, so I played a few flecks of notes from the top of my head and giggled with shyness.

"Look," Reema said, pointing at the blossoms clinging to the castle walls. It was then that I heard the vines of the tower creak and I saw the petals of the blossoms loosen. I looked back at Reema, trying to read in her face the meaning of what was happening. "You're a regular pied piper. Didn't you know that?" she laughed, tapping her finger on my nose, "Music is magic, Wilda, and you're really good at it."

"Because the air from a piccolo blows things around?" I asked.

Reema laughed. "More than that happens when you play. Didn't you see those fay spirits come when you called them to the battlefield? That helped Amadi regain his strength. They flew right past you. You didn't notice them at all?"

I shook my head, surprised to hear about it. I'd been playing with my eyes closed. I didn't see anything.

"You can reach anyone," she said. "That's what your music can do." Then Reema gave me a squeeze and a wink. "I'll see you later," she said.

I waved at her as she floated back up to the platform above my head.

I met up with Charlie, Avery and the twins outside of the Castle of Vines. They had made their way to the middle of a crowd of festive people. The happy fairies were still celebrating their king's arrival, strumming harps, beating tambourines and pouring a sweet-smelling dewy drink into raised cups. A few of the revelers had only just begun to wonder what their king was doing outside with them instead of going about his long-neglected business inside the tower. I could tell they must have been curious. I could see the confusion creep across their faces.

"You might want to freeze things before they figure out …" I started to say.

"Right," Avery said. "Stop!" he commanded.

The twins, Charlie and I looked at each other and back at Avery. We were still able to move, but the crowd around us was perfectly still. Even the flowing liquid dew fairy wine that one of the fairy women had been pouring had frozen in air.

"That is so cool," Veronica said.

"Yeah, I can't believe you got your hands on something like that. You're so lucky." Monica said. "And to think you almost left it behind."

"Yeah, Avery. Why did you almost do that?" Veronica asked.

Avery shook his head silently and started walking through the frozen crowd, allowing his large wings to fade into the back of his armor. When we realized he wasn't going to turn around, we followed him. Once we caught up to him, he answered Veronica.

"I don't speak the language. I can't even defend myself," he said. "And the worst part about it is having to forget my parents. They want too much. They just should have found me sooner."

"You don't think Reema was looking for you?" I asked. "Because she was."

"I know that," Avery said. "But nobody else from the Spring Court was looking for me. Maybe they weren't too serious about finding me. How could I trust people like that?"

"Why didn't they look for you?" Monica asked.

"Maybe it was easier to just start over with a new royal and raise her the way they wanted her to be," Avery said.

"That sounds like all the more reason to go back," Veronica said. "You know, set them straight."

Charlie growled, "The best alphas don't get scared."

"I wasn't scared," Avery protested. He twisted his mouth. "All right," he admitted, "maybe I was a little bit but weren't you all scared?"

"I wasn't," said Charlie.

"I was scared when I caught on fire," Monica said.

"You were so scared, Moni! It looked worse than it was, though," Veronica said.

"What about you, Wilda? Were you scared?" Monica asked.

"I was when a giant monster grabbed me out of my hiding place," I said, "but Reema rescued me just in time. I thought he was going to eat me or something!"

"I didn't even see that," Avery said. "I guess I was too busy fighting my own battle. I would have helped you if I had known that was happening."

"That's wild," Veronica said.

"I know you would have helped, Avery. You already tried to help me get away," I said.

We continued past the crowd, toward the fairy circle beyond the meadow. The air remained warm and still, and the sun cast shadows in front of us.

I looked at Monica and Veronica. "Avery gave the Unseelies his armor so they would let me go."

"That's nice," Veronica said. "You always were kind of a hero."

Avery smiled. "I try," he said.

"Is it okay to tell you thanks?" I asked Avery.

He smiled. "You're welcome, and thanks for coming with me," he said.

"Sure," I said.

"How'd you end up meeting Reema, anyway?" Monica asked.

"Fairies have been stalking Wilda," Avery said. "That's how they found me, through her."

"Yeah," I said. "I think they wanted me here."

"It's because of your talent, isn't it?" Veronica asked. "You should have seen those fairy spirits flying to fight alongside Avery when you started playing your piccolo. Then they merged into his armor. It was amazing!"

"Yeah," Avery said. "It was."

"Did you know you could do that?" Monica asked.

"No," I said.

Charlie yawned. "I always knew you could do something like that," he said, grinning. "The fairies knew it, too."

"How did you know that?" I asked Charlie.

"Instinct," he said.

We continued to walk until we reached the fairy circle at the edge of the meadow. The coat that I shed earlier was still on the ground in front of the circle. I picked my coat up and folded it over my arms as we gathered inside the circle of mushrooms. Monica and Veronica looked at the hollow ground where Aisosa, the Grandmother Oak had been standing.

"What should we tell everybody who's been searching for you?" Veronica asked.

I thought for a moment. *Should we tell them the whole story, that Avery was a fairy king and I left with him to help him regain his throne? Should we lie, instead?* I wasn't sure what kind of lie could explain the amount of time we were gone. Then I sighed, realizing that it would be easier on everyone if I took the blame.

I turned to Avery. "Just say I walked off again. Say I was planning to hitch a ride to Seattle this time, and I told you I was going to do it first thing in the morning. Then you got worried and came looking for me to protect me, but you didn't want to wake your parents." I said.

"Are you sure you want to do that?" Avery asked. "We'll probably both get grounded, but you'll never come out of it if we say that."

"I might as well take the blame," I said. "Everybody already thinks I'm weird, anyway."

"Gosh, I'm really sorry about that," Monica said. I nodded to let her know I accepted her apology.

"All right, Wilda. If you say so," Avery said. Then he raised his arms over his head and lowered them to his sides as though he were opening the air. "Back to motion," he said.

We found ourselves shifted forward. I noticed that Avery's clothes had morphed back into the plain pajamas and slippers he had been wearing the night before. The air picked up again and the sky was black. We were back in Belfair in the middle of the night and the moon lit the path back to my cabin.

"Now what?" Veronica asked, rubbing her bare arms in the damp air.

"We walk," Avery said.

Charlie barked at us to get started as he stood in front of me. Veronica looked at him quizzically. "I thought Charlie could talk," she said.

"He can," I answered. It's just harder to really hear animals here."

"Bummer," Veronica said, rubbing her arms.

"Do you want my coat?" I asked her.

"You're the one from California," she said, smiling. She waved it away. Monica looked unconcerned so I went ahead and put it on. I was pretty cold.

We treaded around the hollow ground where the oak once stood and felt our way through the woods until we came to the clearing behind my backyard shed. There was a small command station set up by the kitchen door of the cabin.

We crouched down so no one at the cabin would see us as Avery slipped into the shed to hide his armor in the shed floor. Charlie knew to be quiet, too. When Avery snuck out of the shed, we all got up and walked toward the cabin. A couple of sheriffs spotted us and started running towards us. I could also see Monica and Veronica's worried parents running after them. The twins took off running into their arms. They embraced for a moment. Then Mrs. Chaichana said, "Your clothes!"

"They got messed up when we were looking for her, but we brought these spare dresses just in case," Veronica said, casually.

"Veronica made them in sewing class," Monica fibbed.

Then I saw Avery's mom. She started running towards him, and she seemed to be on her cell phone, telling his dad to stop searching. They found Avery.

A tall sheriff bent down and held my shoulders. "Are you all right?" he asked me. I nodded my head 'yes.' "Did anybody follow you?" he asked. I shook my head 'no.'

"Where's my mom?" I asked.

"She's all right," he said. "We just have a few questions for you."

"I want to see my mom," I demanded while clutching Charlie to my side.

"You'll get to see her," he said. "Did anybody make you leave with them?"

"Where is she?" I asked.

"Unfortunately, you can't be out here by yourself. Do you have any other relatives in the area?" the sheriff asked.

Veronica turned to face the sheriff. She straightened her shoulders and held her head high with all of the confidence that came with being class president. Then she told the sheriff, "She has us, sir."

"That's not what I mean," the sheriff said. "She needs somewhere else to sleep. We can take her down to the sheriff's office tonight and arrange for protective services to pick her up in the morning if there's nowhere else she can go."

I looked at the twins and Avery. Monica and Veronica looked at their mom and dad. Mrs. Chaichana sighed and looked at Mr. Chaichana. He looked at the twins' pleading faces as he rubbed his neck.

"We have the space," he said.

Then Mrs. Chaichana put her hand on my back and asked, "Would you like to stay with us tonight?"

"What about Charlie?" I asked.

"My folks are cool. He can come with me," Avery said, "right, Charlie?"

Charlie barked and jumped onto Avery's legs. "Good boy," Avery said, rubbing Charlie's head.

I turned back to Mrs. Chaichana and nodded. "Thank you," I said. "I know it's just words, but I really mean it."

Mr. Chaichana smiled. "Come on," he said.

Chapter 11

The Chaichana family's house was one of the nicest in Belfair. Monica and Veronica each had their own room. Their parents were kind enough to let me stay in their guest room. Actually, it was pretty sick. I had a private bathroom with a jetted tub all to myself. Monica and Veronica didn't even have their own private bathrooms. I had my own smart TV that I could watch apps on. And best of all, the kitchen was right outside my room. If I wanted a midnight snack I could go ahead and get some cookies and ice cream or leftovers from the fridge.

Mrs. Chaichana could seriously cook, too. I never tasted Thai food before I lived with them. It was actually the best food I'd ever tasted other than pizza. Who knew that coconut milk and spices could go together so well? Monica and Veronica knew!

I'd been staying with the Chaichanas since the sheriff's deputy found Mom locked out of our car, sitting on a dirt road near the sea cliff. The car was angled between two trees like it was ready to be driven off the cliff and dropped three stories into the ocean. If Reema hadn't forced Mom to drop her keys when she did, who knows what would have happened. Mom's cell phone had no service in that area so she couldn't call for help, and I'm pretty sure she would have tried to drive home in the state she was in. The sheriff said she was over the limit for alcohol when they got there. Since she never found her keys, Mom avoided a charge of driving under the influence. Instead, the sheriff took her into protective custody so she wouldn't be able to hurt herself.

I felt a little sorry for her that she got stuck out in the cold but at the same time she kind of deserved it. Now she knew what it felt like to be stranded by the roadside.

The sheriff told Mom she could either be arrested eventually for attempting to drive drunk because they were watching her, or she could let them take her to rehab. I'm glad she chose rehab. Even though Monica and Veronica promised not to tell anyone that Mom went to rehab, I was still afraid people might find out. You can't keep a secret like that for long in a small town like Belfair. The official story at school was that Mom went to visit my grandmother in California for a while.

Family Services was going to put me in a stranger's home the night we came back but Monica and Veronica's parents said they would take me in. That way I could stay in my old school. It was their daughters' idea. The twins threatened to go on a hunger strike to get their parents to keep me for more than just that weekend. It turned out the twins don't really get hungry anymore as a side effect of becoming dryads but of course their parents didn't know anything about that. I never knew the twins cared about me that much until then but I guess we've gone through a lot together. Avery's folks took Charlie, so I'd get to walk him every day after school. It felt good to have real friends.

Dana turned out to be a fake friend but she helped us in a way. If she hadn't set Mom up to have an accident that day, Mom never would have gotten detained, and then she never would have gotten the opportunity to get sober.

Mom called me every day she was at the women's alcohol and drug rehab center. It was always a really long drive to Kirkland for Friends and Family Days, but Mrs. Chaichana never minded driving me. Monica and Veronica were nice enough to come along, too so I wouldn't get too bored on the way there and back.

It used to be really hard for Mom to admit that she's an alcoholic. When she first got to rehab the staff immediately sent her to the hospital. She stayed in intensive care for a week. The doctors said they had to monitor her body to make sure that she didn't get too sick from not drinking anymore. It's weird. I guess alcohol made her sick whether she drank it or not. The doctors said she was lucky. If she didn't drink for a long time, she wouldn't feel sick anymore.

Since Mom started staying at the rehab center, she started taking different classes. She said she wasn't going to do bartending anymore. She planned to do hair, instead. The family therapist kept saying how we all needed to be supportive of her new goals, so I let her practice on my hair during our previous visit. She actually didn't do a bad job. She let me keep my bangs but she insisted on cutting me a bob in the back. It had a sort of 1920s flapper look. I kind of liked it.

Mom came to the visitors' area as soon as the friends and family support class ended at the center and she gave us all a hug. Then Mrs. Chaichana, Monica and Veronica left to go to the mall. They said they'd be back later. It was cool that they didn't mind driving all the way out to the eastern side of the Puget Sound just to give me and Mom time together.

"So, how's school?" Mom asked. She always asks that.

"It's good," I said.

"Do you have a boyfriend yet?" she asked.

"Mom!" I said.

"How about that Avery? You two still hanging out together?" she asked.

"Oh my God, Mom. We're just friends," I said.

"Sometimes a boy and a girl become more than friends," Mom said, smiling.

"Not him!" I said.

"He's a nice boy," Mom said.

"And complicated. Really complicated," I said.

"How can someone your age be complicated?" Mom asked.

"I guess you could say he's wise beyond his years," I said. "It's better to just stay as friends."

"Well, good," Mom said. "I don't want you chasing after boys just yet. Concentrate on school." Mom fidgeted a little with her hands. I could tell she was nervous and she was fighting the desire to pour herself a drink. I tried not to let it show that I realized that.

"The Chaichanas have been really nice," I said.

"Withdrawal's a real ..." Mom gasped, catching herself and nervously tucking her hair behind her ear. "Never mind. It's just ..." she said, shaking her head and biting her lip. I could tell she was a little scared. She closed her eyes and took a deep breath to calm down. "I'm glad to hear things are working out over there. How is Mr. Chaichana's business doing?"

"Thunderstorm Wireless? Sales are slowing down a little. Mrs. Chaichana spends more time at home these days, but she says the demand for Wi-Fi always picks up at the beginning of a new school year," I said.

"Makes sense."

"We should look into getting it," I said.

"Their house looks nice in the picture you texted. Do you like it there?" Mom asked.

"It's okay," I said, "but I miss our house."

"When I get out of here, we'll have a barbecue at our own house and you can invite your friends. How about that?" Mom asked.

"Cool," I said.

"Good kid," she said, softly. "You're a good kid." She leaned into me a little when she said it that time.

"I know," I said, happy to see her relax a little. "Um, I need to tell you something," Mom said as she held my hands. Her hands were not clammy this time but warm and dry. "I don't remember everything I've done ... as your mother, and that bothers me, but I know you didn't deserve my bad behavior ... and I'm sorry."

For a moment I didn't know what to say. "Okay," I said, finally. We sat for a moment. I think neither one of us knew what to say next. Then Mom sat up straight and folded her hands.

"My counselor says it's okay to sit in the awkward silence," she said.

"I forgive you," I said, "but please do better."

Mom buried her face in her hands. "Okay," she said. I wasn't quite sure whether the time was right to go through with what I had planned but when I looked up, I saw a white deer outside of the window. It was Reema encouraging me to go through with it. "Music is magic," I said to myself.

"Mom," I said, "There's something I was hoping I could play for you."

I reached into my oversized purse that the twins picked out for me the last time they were at the mall. As I pulled out my flute case, Mom got distracted for a moment as she glimpsed the white deer trotting back into the wooded hills beyond the window. "Another white deer," she said. "What are the odds?"

"It's a good sign. It means we're both well taken care of. You know, like a guardian angel of sorts," I said as I fitted the three pieces of my flute together.

I lifted the flute to my lips, but Mom was giving me a quizzical smile. "Look at you," she said.

"Don't make me laugh," I said, giggling. "I'll lose my mouth shape."

"Sorry," Mom said. She sat back, trying hard to stay serious as I lifted the flute again. I puffed a couple of notes to check for tuning.

"Okay," I said, trying not to smile. Then I started to play a song. This time notes flowed out smoothly into a golden pattern I had created just for our time together. I played the chorus first, then a verse, then the chorus again while I closed my eyes and tried to feel the golden notes. When I opened my eyes, the notes soared like encouraging words and clouds of warm colors and sank down with resolve. I played a song about how proud I was of my mother, that she was seeing this through as hard as it was for her to be so far away in such a sparse place with all of its curfews and rules. When I finished the last refrain, Mom was smiling from ear to ear. She clapped for me as though no one else was around. "I don't think I've ever heard you play something like that before," she said. "That was beautiful. Where did you learn it?"

"I made it up for you," I said, smiling.

"What's it called?" she asked.

"Victorious," I said.

"Victorious?" Mom asked.

I nodded yes.

"You think I'm going to be victorious?" She asked.

"I do," I said. "I still believe in you."

Mom grabbed me and squeezed me tight. "I am not worthy of you, Wilda," she said, "but I promise I'll stay out of trouble if it takes all the energy I have in me!" Then we just held each other for a while, and I couldn't control my tears. But they were happy tears. For the first time I felt like life was going to get better in our little old cabin in the deep woods. After all, what could possibly hurt us, now? I closed my eyes, allowing myself to feel safe in Mom's arms.

About the Author

A. A. Jeffery is an attorney and educator who splits time between Northern California and Mason County, Washington. Her background includes teaching students at all levels from Kindergarten to college. She wrote for several years as a columnist in the Sunday Morning News in her hometown. An Oakland, California native, Jeffery began to write illustrated stories while she was a student at U.C. Berkeley. She continued to develop her writing abilities as a student at Vanderbilt University Law School. Jeffery enjoys learning foreign languages, playing piano and spending time with family, friends, and a Chihuahua-pug.

You can find more of her writing at www.aajeffery.com

About the Illustrator

Nassima Amir grew up on the small island of New Caledonia. She has harbored a love for all things fantasy and sci-fi for as long as she can remember, which prompted her to move to France where she achieved her degree in applied arts at the Ecole Emile Cohl. She has since never stopped travelling, moving between continents to find that perfect inspiration for her paintings. You might catch Nassima wandering in nature, her head in the clouds and her nose pointed at the trees, seeking that special branch or leaf to capture. Or you could find her more often in her cozy apartment, enjoying a cup of green tea while working on her paintings or playing a game of Go.

You can see more of her work at:
https://www.artstation.com/nassimaamir

Wilda Silva's story continues with the next book in this series!

Visit www.wildasilva.com today and sign up to receive for the latest news!

Made in the USA
Middletown, DE
15 March 2021